The Legend of the Dwarf

The Beginning

To my darling Tracy, I hope you enjoy reading this as much as I enjoyed writing it!

Warmest wishes,

Kate Bloom

Copyright © 2016 Kate Bloom

All rights reserved.

ISBN: 1540574172
ISBN-13: 978-1540574176

DEDICATION

This is dedicated to my entire support system. I may not always believe in myself, but it means the world to me that I have people standing behind me that believe for me.

Kate Bloom

CONTENTS

Acknowledgments	i
Preface	1
I	4
II	44
III	83
IV	113
V	141
VI	180
VII	205
VIII	215
IX	226

ACKNOWLEDGMENTS

This story would not have been possible without three of my favorite people. My dad, Shaun, who has always given me crazy ideas for my stories. My mom, Suzzanne, who always leads me through the big jumps in life and helped so much with the editing. And one of my dearest friends, Alex, who was also my first reader. She helped me fix the holes in the story and listened to me talk for hours. And, finally, Getrude, my mentor in all this, and one of the most amazing women I know. Thank you for all the work you guys have put into this story for me! Alex, let's make our dreams come true!

PREFACE

Zundrdat Trollkiller stood on top of the gate, pacing back and forth. The sun had set long ago, and he was watching the wooded area past the gate that stood in front of the dwarven kingdom of Isola. What was he watching for? The greatest enemy in history. Terrisino's armies had attacked nearly every night for some time. After the sun set, the armies would march in, thousands at a time, and plunder the kingdom. The strong dwarves had pushed them back, forced them into a retreat every time they came, but not without paying a hefty price. Many of the warriors had lost their lives, as did many other innocent citizens who did not pay heed to the warning bell. The dwarves were hurting, and they needed time to recover. Time was not given to them. Zundrdat had assumed that Terrisino was after the dwarven treasure. The myths about the abundancy of gold and jewels were true enough. The dwarven ancestors had spent so much of their time mining, it was a wonder they did not find more. But now Zundrdat wondered if Terrisino was simply out to wipe the race of the dwarves right off the map and out of existence. After all, the armies never wandered far into the kingdom at all. Their only goal seemed to be death.

Zundrdat choked on a slimy wet cough, making the cold of the night even less bearable. He had fallen victim to the mysterious illness that had claimed the lives of so many of his kin already. No one knew exactly where it had come from or when it started. It seemed as though one day the dwarves just started dying off. It started as nothing more than a sniffle, but it always escalated. The fevers would rise to rival the heat of the furnace in which the bodies were being cremated, a measure taken in an attempt to stop the ultimately inevitable spread of the epidemic. His prognosis was grim, he knew. He had but a few more battles to fight before the illness would take him, if the orcs didn't get to him first in his weakened state. That was half of the reason that the orcs were doing as well as they were. Terrisino seemed to be able to simply make more orcs on a whim while the dwarves were finite in number. Most of the dwarves were not even able-bodied.

Just then, he spotted the hoards that he knew would come that night. Even with the weakness, he had the best eye sight among the dwarven warriors. He saw hundreds of thousands, still leagues away, but headed quickly to the gate. His axes clinked together as he suddenly jumped from his post and ran down to sound the alarm – a bell so massive that the sound would surely wake anyone who still had the luxury of sleep in the night.

After sounding the alarm, he ran down to seek out the General, Valddal Sheilddelver. The moment he set foot on the ground, he could hear the clanging of metal weaponry and armor. The armies had already woken and begun to prepare for battle.

Zundrdat ran through the armies, shoving aside those of his kin that did not move immediately. He was greeted by a few grumpy grunts and moans, but more often than that was he greeted by a sneeze or a cough. He knew that this battle was going to be the end of the dwarves. He knew not only by the size of the hoards coming in, but by the condition of the dwarves going out. If he did not do something, then his race would cease to exist. He could not bear that fact, especially when he thought of his family.

"How many did you see?" Valddal asked him, having sought out the watchman as furiously as he had sought out the General.

"Too many. Terrisino must have sent out every orc at his disposal this time. The end is here, and we have but one option left." He coughed, spitting out the phlegm and blood that came with it.

"What are you saying?"

"I'm saying that it is time we send out to the cave. We need to hide those of us that are able to carry on the race. Any man, woman, or child who is able to leave should flee to the mountains now. Leave those that are too sick or too wounded from the last battles, as they will only slow down the chances of getting anyone to the harbor safely. Be selective in who you choose to leave us, for they will be the ones who keep the dwarven race alive. Let no one, and I mean no one, who coughs even once flee with them."

Valddal didn't take more than a second to think the matter through, knowing he was speaking to his most trustworthy and dedicated warrior.

"Will you lead them?"

"Alas, no," he coughed again. "Let me and any others that have fallen ill die here, with our kingdom. But General," he hedged, "if I may ask a favor... My wife is with child."

A brief nod was the only answer that he received, but it was enough to know that his child would be born in peace. Valddal went off, in search of anyone that could lead away the few dwarves that were still safe from disease. Zundrdat prepared for his final battle.

I.

      Not far from the Mountains of Inunia was a dense forest called Fardocain. The forest was populated with various animals, some big and some small, on which many people from the surrounding cities and villages chose to dine. Sometimes the hunters would catch only a rabbit or two, and sometimes they were able to find elk or even wild goats roaming the area. The trees bore fruit abundantly, and the bushes were full of berries. The weather and general climate was most ideal for keeping food plentiful all year long. Rarely did one go hungry if one chose to gather a meal from Fardocain.

      A young dwarf by the name of Ever Trollkiller was out in the woods, crouched low in the lush foliage. She gripped the dirt in her hands, catching moist grains under her nails. She was supposed to be hunting, but she was distracted at the moment. She was watching the beautiful elf hunt instead. He had spotted the same elk that she had. Really, it should have been her kill. It was pretty big, too. Her clan would have been well-fed and pleased. But she would let the elf have it, partly because she liked watching the rays of sunshine that peeked through the trees as they danced off the soft brown of his muscles when he pulled back the string of his bow, and partly because protecting her secrecy was more important than feeding the clan.

That part she didn't understand completely. She knew very little of her dwarven history, something that her elders seemed to always make sure of. She knew that, twenty-three years ago, a small group of dwarves fled their kingdom to hide in the very cave that she lived in now. There were only eighteen dwarves originally, including her mother, who had been carrying her still. Elda Trollkiller. She had died giving birth to her only daughter, leaving Ever orphaned and in the care of the surviving eleven dwarven men and one woman. There used to be children, but they did not survive, either, making Ever the youngest by far. The elders refused to tell Ever anything, save for that the dwarves were nearly wiped out of existence. Had the order for them to leave come a second later, the race would have been annihilated completely. And thus, until they rebuilt the race and took back their kingdom from the Great Terrisino, the sorcerer responsible for the attack that destroyed the dwarves, they were forced to remain a myth to the rest of the world. So Ever patiently sat behind a bush as she watched the pretty pointy-ear take her kill back to his own clan.

The elf shot down the elk with precision, needing only a single arrow. As he went over to examine his winnings, Ever's eye caught on the sparkling gold beads that were woven throughout his braided dreadlocks. They were covering his ears, as they always were when she saw him hunting, but she desperately wanted to sweep them back to see the perfect point of his ears. She had never laid eyes on elven ears. She had really only assumed he was an elf at all rather than a mere human because of his grace and beauty. His tall, toned body seemed to be carved out of marble while her four foot eight dwarven body seemed to be carved from gruff stone. It didn't help that her hair had nearly formed black dreadlocks of her own, but far dirtier, nor that the dirt covering her pale white skin could make her pass for a girl of dark skin like his. She was somehow a mirror of his beauty, but matching in the exact opposite way. Where he had grace, she fumbled about on heavy feet, not unlike an infant learning to walk. Where he sparkled and glistened under natural sunlight, she looked best hidden in the darkness of her cave.

She sighed and returned home after watching him leave. She was returning empty handed, an unfortunate circumstance that she knew she would be made to regret. But all the same, that was how the hunt went – sometimes you won and sometimes you starved.

She quickly welcomed the coolness of the cave as she walked through the large opening. Except for in the dead of the night, the main area of the cave was always well lit by the natural sunlight. It gave the space a welcoming feel before in broke off into smaller tunnels. Dwarves were never supposed to feel claustrophobic, but somehow Ever was uncomfortable at night when they all retreated to those spaces. Perhaps that was simply because she was never allowed to experience anything else. She always felt more at home in the woods than she did in the dwarven cave.

"Empty handed again," Marra Pickshadow complained upon Ever's return, speaking exactly what Ever predicted. She was very pregnant with her third child. The first two didn't survive, one dying before he was born and the other living only a few hours. Marra liked to blame the deaths on Ever's frequent empty-handedness, but Ever knew that the reason was more likely the elder dwarf's age. She was two hundred and seventeen years old. She could not support life anymore. It was a duty that she felt like she had to carry out for the sake of the race as one of the only two surviving females, and it was a duty that was constantly pressed on Ever as soon as she came of age.

"My kill was taken from me by a man," she explained, leaving out, as she always did, her suspicion of his true identity. "I felt secrecy was more important than the elk."

"You could have killed the man and brought back twice the kill," Marra argued indignantly.

"And then there would be myths of a monster in the

mountains," Vek Rockheart came to her aid. "Not to mention that we do not eat man. She did what was right and we will have to portion what we have for now."

Vek was gentle. Ever liked him very much. He was older than she – nearly twice her age – but she felt close to him, like a sister to a brother. His black beard was braided nicely into three parts, as was his long black hair. He had been responsible for raising her, training her to hunt, and now for convincing her to fulfill her other duties to the race. She supposed that if she was going to be forced to procreate with any of the dwarves, she'd prefer it to be him, but she would hold out as long as possible. She made every excuse she could think of.

"You will be fed, Marra," Otak Hammerheart, the eldest of the dwarves at two hundred and eighty nine years, and by far the most frail, told her. Ever had a soft spot for him, and would always take care of him even before herself. The hair on his head used to match the color of his beard before it began to fall out. Now his long and thin gray beard only made her melancholy, reminding her that he hadn't much time left.

"I'll go out tomorrow," Faron Ironmaker put forth. "I'll make sure everyone gets fed."

He had never even looked Ever in the eye, yet insisted that he would be the one to impregnate her. That's how he had always said it too, as if she were no more than a means to fill the world with dwarves once more. He told the other dwarves how he was the strongest and brightest, and how his lineage was always the best of the warriors. He insisted that his genetics were the best to be passed on. But Ever would never allow someone who has slept with Marra the Crank to sleep with her, even if she had no say in the matter. She would sooner die than let him touch her.

"And I'll go with him," Donif Ironmaker, his brother by blood, put in, "to make sure he doesn't screw up."

And now she knew that the twelve others would begin to argue. Why did she have to be born into such a disagreeable folk, she wondered? She left them and went down into the tunnels of the cave.

The tunnels were where she felt the safest, even if she was cramped. There was cover at all points, and despite the darkness, she could see quite clearly. The woods were okay, as there was still thick wooded cover, but not so secluded as the tunnels. There was something about them that felt almost magically protected, whereas the tales that the others told of the world beyond certainly did frighten her. They had made the land out to be such a wide expanse. There would be no hiding in a place like that. She quaked at the very thought. For instance, she could hear Vek now, his distinct footsteps echoing on the walls, and could pinpoint his exact location. She would be more susceptible to a sneak attack if she was out in the open expanses of the world.

"Thanks for having my back out there," she began in a somewhat curt manner, "but I'd like to be alone right now." It was easiest to be alone. No one had ever pestered her to make baby dwarves when she was alone.

"You should eat," Vek told her, ignoring her request completely. He slid her a plate of robin eggs, scrambled and seasoned to her liking. Immediately, she softened to the dwarf, regretful of her tone. He cared about her in a way that the other dwarves wouldn't understand. She made room for him beside her as she began to wolf down the eggs. She hadn't realized she was so hungry. He waited patiently for her to finish.

She set down the plate at her feet, all but licked clean. Vek reached for it, intending to leave her after seeing her eat a proper portion, but she reached out a hand to catch his wrist and stop him. He obeyed the unspoken command, freezing mid motion. Ever withdrew her hand.

"Tell me," she began, "what do you miss most about the kingdom before it fell?"

He looked at her, perplexed for a moment, but answered anyway. He was always willing to answer her questions – most of them – about the world.

"The ale," he answered with confidence. "And the food was a thousand times better. What brings this to your mind?"

"It's just… It's nothing, I suppose. I've just been thinking a lot."

"About what?" he implored.

"About a lot of things. About what it would have been like to grow up where I belong. Perhaps with other dwarven children in real dwarven schools. About being a myth instead, for my entire life, missing out on everything that you and the others experienced. There's no documentation of my life, no records of my name anywhere. I get to hear what you will tell me of what you have seen and learned, of the battles you have fought in, and I treasure each story I hear, but… but I want my own."

Vek understood, but he also knew the importance of the dwarves' secrecy. He reached his hand out to tuck a loose strand of hair behind her ear.

"You have the greatest story of us all," he told her. "You survived the coldest and hungriest winters, and you were only an infant."

"And thanks to that, I don't even look like a dwarf," she answered. It was true, too. Whereas her dwarven clan was short and stout like any dwarf should be, she was slimmer, which gave the impression of added hieght. She could almost pass for a short human. She wasn't the thinnest, by any means. Otak, as the eldest, felt it far more important to feed the younger and stronger, and thus went many days without eating when food was scarce. He was no more than a withering dwarven skeleton now. At least Ever's bones were still covered by a healthy layer of skin.

Not knowing what else to do or say, Vek simply pulled Ever close and held her in a comforting embrace. Even if she didn't want to admit it, she liked Vek very much. He had a kinder disposition than most.

"Tell me about the ruins," she asked him as she snuggled

her head into his shoulder.

"The Kingdom of Isola," he began, "home of the Dwarven Kingdom, the best warriors of any kingdom."

"And friends of no one," Ever added jokingly. Vek chuckled in delight.

"We didn't need friends, no one else could make ale like ours."

"That's not all that friends are good for."

"That's true. Perhaps someone would have come to our aid if we had bothered to make friends. But we were surrounded by no more than weak human settlements and hoity toity elves," he joked.

"Elves?" she asked, her interest spiking. "No one has told me about elves before."

"That's because they weren't our friends," Vek dismissed her interjection. But Ever's sarcastic look prompted him to expand on the subject anyway. "The elves of Brisdale. They governed most of the east side of the river. Most of the surrounding villages were mixed with humans and the elves that preferred to live more humble lives. Never human-elf mixed breeds, though. The elves wouldn't dare taint their own blood."

"Unlike the friendly dwarves, right?" Ever challenged his judgmental tone.

"At least we never hid our exclusivity behind a veil of friendship. But anyway," he continued, "the elves aren't as pure as they think they are. On the west side of the river, the elves of Sedona and the surrounding elven cities are much more exclusive amongst their kind, and have stayed out of trouble completely simply because they refuse to dirty their hands with the circumstances of other races. The elves of Brisdale are the ones who bred the evil Terrisino, and were thus responsible for the destruction – and, nearly, the extinction – of our race. He was an elf who fell to the ways of sorcery. He was trained by the elves of his kingdom, and stole their secrets before he fled across the river.

So he created the race of the orcs and unleashed them on us."

"Surely it wasn't personal on the elves part," Ever said. "The dwarves didn't do anything to them, right?"

"Other than existing? No. But that was enough for the elves to seek out our destruction."

"But it wasn't the elves," Ever defended, thinking of her gentle elven hunter. "It was the sorcerer."

"That's true enough," Vek conceded. "He even cut the tips of his ears to renounce his race."

Ever couldn't imagine hating one's own race enough to mutilate their own body in such a way. And especially when that race was such a beautiful one to begin with.

"He is truly the very definition of evil," Vek continued. "When we are able to build back even just a fraction of our race, I will personally seek him out and dig my axe into his flesh for what he did to my family. I will avenge my race and bring back the Isola Kingdom." His mood had darkened quite a bit. Ever sensed that it was time she changed the subject, lest she discover that vengeful side.

"I'm going hunting tomorrow," she announced, "regardless of Donif and Faron. I need to make up for my loss today."

"You don't need to do anything," he argued. "I'd much rather you stay with me, safe and sound." He held her close to his side, as if to demonstrate the safety she had with him.

"Nevertheless," she argued back, "I will not let Marra further degrade my hunting. I'll bring back the most food she's ever seen. You'll see."

Vek couldn't help but laugh.

"Your spirit is one of the most ferocious and stubborn that I have ever seen. A true dwarf if I ever saw one. Just like your father."

He was beginning to reminisce about the darker times again, and so Ever decided to drop all conversation completely. She was tired anyway. She snuggled deeper into him and gave in to sleep.

* * *

She woke late the next day. Vek had evidently left some time during the night to retrieve blankets for a makeshift bed for the two of them. She chuckled to herself. It was the first time the two of them had slept in the same bed together. Surely the others hoped that Vek would tell them that something more had happened. She slipped out of the covers as silently as she could and donned her armor and weapons. Then she left the mountain without seeing the other dwarves. It always pleased her when she was able to leave before anyone else had woken.

Unfortunately for Ever, she did not have to do much wandering in the woods until she came upon her fellow hunter. It was disappointing, especially since he was once again stalking the same elk that she had found. Why was he hunting again anyway, she wondered? Surely his clan was not so big to have finished yesterday's kill so quickly.

She sighed, but she was determined not to go back empty handed again. She decided to wait and watch him. Surely there were more elk around the woods anyway. Perhaps even bigger. She would best the elf at his own game and prove her worth to Donif and Faron, and even Marra.

But she was just as hungry as the others, and as the elf released his arrow, so did her stomach release a growl. She felt as though it was the sound of a great beast in the quiet forest, but at least the elf seemed to take no notice. He was too busy watching his kill as it fell to the ground. He pulled out a rope from his bag and went to collect his single arrow, perfectly shot, from the animals heart. As he began to tie up the legs of the animal, her stomach growled again, louder this time as if it wanted him to notice.

And notice he did.

"You know," he said without looking up from his work, "if

you are so hungry, you should stop letting me take the elk."

Ever was frozen, her feet rooted to the ground. He made it sound as if he had seen her before. Maybe as many times as she had seen him. Suddenly, she no longer cared to prove her worth – she only wanted to retreat to the mountains. Her feet remained unmoving, though.

And then the elf turned to look her directly in the eye, seeing through her cover in the thick leaves and branches.

"Are you going to introduce yourself? You can have the elk if you'd like," he offered. "I can find another. I won't bite," he added when she made no move.

He had ceased all pretenses of roping his kill, choosing instead to stare into Ever's eyes. She stared back into those beautiful golden orbs. He seemed genuine. But then, Vek had told her before that the elves were a tricky race. Could this be a trick of his?

Something told her to ignore Vek and trust the elf anyway.

"Who are you?" she asked in an embarrassingly shaky voice. She cleared her throat.

"Why don't you come out here and we'll talk?" he asked.

Ever's legs made no motion to comply. A moment passed until the elf sighed and spoke again.

"I am Jesper of Brisdale, and I truly mean you no harm. Please come out. You really can have the elk," his hand motioned to the animal as an offering.

Jesper. She finally had a name – and a honey golden voice – to go along with the face that she so loved to admire. She took a few hesitant and wobbly steps out of her cover. She showed herself completely, but didn't dare step very close to him at all.

"You know," he said thoughtfully, "I thought you were much taller. It's nice to finally see you in full."

"How long have you watched me?" she asked, ignoring his banter and pleasantries.

"As long, if not longer, as you've watched me. You don't

think that you could really hide from an elf, do you?" he chuckled a bit to himself. "Don't worry, I've been fair with the food. I make sure you get your share, too."

"Have you seen any more?"

"Any more?" he asked, confused. "Elk? I can find them."

"Of my clan. Have you seen the other hunters?"

"No," he said, bewildered. He thought for a moment. "I've heard them, perhaps. A few males, usually in pairs but never alone. And never quiet, either. I stay clear of them as they don't interest me and only scare off the prey. How many are there? Perhaps I am not entirely fair with the portions if you are responsible for feeding a whole clan."

She chose not to answer the question.

"If we don't interest you, why do you watch me?"

"I said they don't interest me. You do. A female hunter wielding an axe of all things. You took me by surprise the first time I saw you. Nearly mistook you for dinner. Wouldn't have been much of a feast – you're the smallest human I've ever seen. So I watched you hunt instead. I was amazed by your strength and agility, but then I saw, too, your kind heart. You thank each animal for its life before you haul it off."

A trait that her dwarven clan would have disowned her for, as it made her seem like a weak hunter. But it would help her, surely, as it made her appear even less dwarven. He thought her to be human, and hadn't seen the others. Even if he had told anyone else about her, they wouldn't know that she was a dwarf. The myth was safe.

"Are you from Thaedal, then?" he asked.

"What?" she asked in utter confusion. She had never heard of such a place.

"Perhaps not. The Sandy Brooks, then? They are a gentle folk, too."

He was trying to figure out who she was. She didn't know how to respond. It would be too easy to catch her in a lie. So she chose instead to keep her silence.

"Surely you and your entire clan cannot live in the forest?" he asked in bewilderment. She answered with more silence. "I see," he said, turning back to the elk and giving up on her. "Well, I'll leave this for you. It's the least I can do." He rose to leave.

"Wait!" Her legs finally found strength again as she walked forward, an arm stretched out to stop him. This was her first connection to the world outside of the mountains. She couldn't resist the temptation. "They call me Ever, and you should keep the elk. I could never explain an arrow wound to my clan."

"It's nice to finally meet you, Ever," he said sitting back down and patting the dirt beside him. Reluctantly, Ever walked forward and sat across from him, far enough that she could defend herself if he decided to spring an attack. He seemed amused by her strategical seating.

"Can you tell me of these places?" she asked. He looked at her, taken aback by her question.

"You mean, you've never heard the names? Seen them on a map?"

"I've heard stories of Brisdale and Sedona. I've heard of Isola before it was lost. Is that close to here?"

He was bewildered by her ignorance.

"Brisdale is a couple nights ride south of here, and the ruins are some nights further. Where are you from?" he inquired.

But Ever would not answer that question.

"You have to be fair," he complained. "How about we play a game? Question for question. We both answer honestly." She pondered this offer. "We'll start out easy, since we're just getting to know one another. What's your age?"

"Twenty-three years," she answered. Surely that did not need to be a secret.

"Hmm... Twenty-three years ago, Isola fell and Terrisino rose." Ever panicked. Perhaps she should have lied. "The dragon hatchlings hatched and the goblins fled. It was a dark time. Pray thanks that you were a small babe and had no understanding of it all."

"And what was your age, then? More than a wee child?" she challenged.

"I am thirty-one years old today," he said, holding his hands in surrender at her feisty tone. "So, a mere eight years then. A… *wee* child myself." He said it with emphasis on her word choice. Was it odd? Could it have been specific to dwarven drawl? She panicked again and jumped to change the subject.

"What of these other places?" she asked. "The brooks and the, uh…" she had already forgotten the strange names.

"Tut – tut, you had your question. You copied mine, but it was a question, nonetheless. And I answered truthfully. It's my turn now."

Ever gulped, wishing she had not let her feisty temper take control and challenge him. She was going to have to be very careful in how she answered the questions. But she didn't want to walk away, either. This was an adventure that she couldn't turn away.

"Where were you born?" he asked.

"In a mountain," she answered quickly, honestly, and, yes, more than a little vaguely.

"What mountain?" he further questioned.

"Tut – tut," she mimicked him, wagging a finger at him. "It's my turn. What happened to those who lived in Isola after the kingdom fell?" On a sudden bout of inspiration, she decided she wanted an outsider's rendition of the past twenty-three years. Jesper thought for a moment.

"Truthfully, I could not say. I could tell you the rumors."

"That'll do," she allowed, desperate for anything, really.

"Some say that the orcs never completely vanquished the dwarves of the Isola Ruins, and that they live there still. However, that cannot be true, as even their crusty selves needed to come out of their kingdom to trade and no one has left those gates since the orcs came. Some say that a few survived but are stricken still by the illness that plagued them before the orcs came. Now they wander, hallow and frail, shaking the ruins with their moans. But that can't be true, either, as the disease was killing the strongest dwarf before. How could it suddenly have changed to keep them walking for so many years without so much as seeking medicine in the trade? No, I do not believe either of those rumors. I believe that the moans that have been heard are nothing more than the wind passing through the hallowed stones of the empty kingdom."

So, there were some that believed the dwarves survived, if only barely. Could it be true? Ever wouldn't get her hopes up, though.

"Now, my turn. What mountain?"

"I don't know," Ever answered truthfully and quickly, knowing that she was tricking the elf into supplying more information than he'd receive. But it was his game, and it was not her problem that she was simply better at it. "What do you know of Terrisino?"

"Terrisino is an evil man – I mean you no offense when I call him 'man,' as he is no man at all. He is his own breed, but has denounced his own elvish heritage, if one can do such a thing. We were happy enough, though, to disown him. He spends his time in the castle of his land, twisting magic and spells to create his kingdom. Every orc and man and creature that follows him has been affected by his magic in some way. Perhaps they are not even in their right minds, or perhaps they have grown greedy with what he has offered them. I am quite surprised that he never did use the dwarves in any way. He never captured them or changed them, simply killed them off. It isn't his style, really. He likes to use them in his evil to take over the entire land. I think that's quite a bit of information. Now it's my turn again." Jesper pondered his next question, determined to get a better answer from her this time. "Why don't you know where you're from? And by that," he clarified, "I mean the entire land, and not simply this mysterious mountain."

"Because I have been kept a secret," she answered. "I have seen the mountain where I live and this forest. It is important that my existence remains a secret." Hopefully he would understand that and keep this meeting to himself. "My turn. Who are you always feeding so much?"

"I am royalty in Brisdale. Adopted royalty, that is – I was orphaned at a young age. The queen took pity on me and raised me as her eldest son – mind you, I do not inherit the throne as the blood heirs have claim before me. But the subjects in the kingdom are still my subjects, and I will keep them fed and protected."

"How valiant," she offered.

"The same question to you," he said, eyeing her.

Ever took a moment to contemplate her answer. Something inside her told her that she could trust this elf – and besides that, he thought she was a human. A human girl living in the mountains should hardly be worth investigating, as long as she led him to believe such a thing.

"I live with a dozen members in my clan, one of them is a pregnant woman and another is a very elderly man. I am the best hunter, as the others are too loud, thus I must be out quite often to supply food."

"Why do thirteen people live secretly in the mountain?" he asked with genuine curiosity. Although he had broken the rules of his own game, Ever allowed it, partially because she had begun to forget that it was a game at all.

"I really don't understand the matter too well – the others don't tell me enough. But, I suppose, it comes down to the fact that we're hiding from Terrisino."

"That seems like reason enough. Come," he said, suddenly standing. "We must find you another elk to bring them. I won't be the reason a woman who is with child goes unfed. It shouldn't be too much trouble – these woods are full of them."

Jesper finished tying his own kill and slung it over his back.

Ever was surprised that it did not slow him down as they tracked down another elk – and a bigger one – for her to slay with the blade of her axe. She thanked him properly, truly grateful for his help. She struggled a bit in trying to figure out how to carry the animal back, but denied Jesper's offer to carry it back for her. On top of keeping her home and clan a secret, there was also the matter of her own dwarvish pride. He had not been slowed down with a kill slung on his back, and she was determined not to be slowed either.

By nightfall, she had returned – alone. Donif and Faron had given up sometime before her, returning with two small squirrels. She took pride in her kill when she looked at the faces of eleven shocked dwarves and one proud Vek. Of course he had believed in her. And she wasn't surprised, either, that he was the only one.

All of the dwarves had their fill that night. Marra scarfed down at least two sizes a normal portion. Otak ate very little, simply because he could not eat much in his fragile state. Donif and Faron, pouting in their pride, ate only the squirrel that they had fetched.

Ever took her time dining on the meal that Vek had prepared. Although they never had many cooking supplies, he had always done a delightful job with what they did have. Ever was always in awe of the magic he seemed to perform with their food. That night was elk with a berry sauce that he had somehow managed to throw together.

When she was done, she quietly retreated to her own part of the cave to be alone. Really, she wanted to ponder all that Jesper had told her of the world outside the forest. What he had said of the dwarves stuck with her. He was sure that the race was dead – or endangered, she supposed. But rumors had to come from somewhere. He called the Isola Kingdom the ruins. She wanted to see the ruins with her own eyes. But more than that, she wanted to live amongst other people. She wanted to see the world as Jesper was free to do. She wanted to meet these gentle folk of the places he mentioned – Sandy Brooks, was it? She loved her clan, make no mistake, and felt a great sense of loyalty to them. But perhaps they were simply too stubborn in their dwarvish ways to admit that their cause was a lost one. Surely two females – one very old, no less – could not rebuild an entire race. It was foolish to think. After twenty-three years of hiding away, why were they not the least bit eager to see the world as it was now? Jesper had painted such a nice picture – at least of some of the world. Surely they could find a place amongst the people out there. And if they didn't want to, Ever thought, surely she could find her own place. After all, she could trick even an elf into believing that she was a human. And she already had a friend who would surely help her. Besides, he now knew of her clan, and surely he would get curious and decide to find the rest of them and they couldn't pass for as human as she could. Their secret would certainly be uncovered then. Even he could not resist telling his people that he had seen people of a dead race. Perhaps that was what she wanted, anyway – to be led off on an adventure around this world that was bigger than she had imagined. Without much trying, she had begun to convince herself of her next move. She would embark on a journey and, since he knew no one would approve, she would do it in secret.

But first, her dwarven loyalty did beg of her to do one thing for them.

She rejoined the clan in the common place of the cave, stopping to admire the carvings that they had done along the walls. They were carved with daggers, each carving detailed in the finest way and telling a story that, for the most part, she did not know. They were beautiful, and that was the last time she would admire them.

She stopped at the entrance to the common place to look on her dwarven family. Marra had passed out, pleased by her meal. Donif and Faron were begrudgingly picking at the left-over elk, their pride surely suffering, while Otak watched with an approving smile. Bazak and Dwan were passed out by Marra. Dogir, Kilyr, and Sandkas were still enjoying full plates – a dwarf's appetite never satisfied – while Thiflar and Yurin were conversing in low tones by the small fire. Vek was with them, and had locked eye contact with her when she stepped in the room. No one else had seen her, to her relief. She beckoned him to follow her. Without question or alert to the others, he followed.

"You did good today," he told her when they were alone.

"Thank you," she said, taking credit for something she knew she could not have done alone. She led him to the bed that she had prepared for them. "You're a good cook," she offered. She felt awkward, not knowing exactly how to initiate her plan.

"Are we going to play fifty questions about dwarven history again tonight?" he asked her, knowing that she was usually curious about something.

"Not tonight," she said. She was not making eye contact at all, which Vek picked up on quickly.

"Then what?" he asked. "Something must be on your mind."

He lifted her chin so that she was forced to look into his eyes – which only made her blush a deep, embarrassing color of red.

"Ever?"

"I've been thinking about… certain things," she admitted.

"What things?" he asked, perplexed by her behavior. In answer, she only blushed more. "Oh… Oh, Ever," he said, looking at the bed in realization. "Ever, whatever they say, this is not your responsibility."

"I know that Marra has very little chance of success," she said in a frank tone, trying to look anywhere but at him. "Besides, I want to do this for my race."

"But you aren't ready, I know that. Besides, I thought Faron wanted y – this," he changed his mind mid-sentence, liking the idea of Faron 'having Ever' less than she did.

"You really want to bring him up right now?" She was

finally able to look at him, her fiery spirit overtaking her embarrassment for a moment.

"No, no, of course not. I just mean to say… Ever, there is plenty of time for this when you are more ready."

"Vek," she said, scooting closer to him. "Please don't talk me out of this." She knew he was right, and appreciated that he never tried to pressure her into beginning the new race like most of the others did, but she also knew that if she were to leave that they might never have another chance. She wanted him to always remember her, and remember her as someone who did try to fulfill her duty to the race. She leaned in to kiss him hesitantly, and hesitantly, he accepted her.

* * *

When she woke, she felt a sort of sadness about her. She was about to leave everything she knew, and for what? She didn't even know. She only knew that she needed to do this for herself. She got up from the bed, carefully, so as not to wake Vek, and dressed her naked body in her plain clothing, then she fitted her armor on top. She didn't know if she would need it, but it was better to be safe. She took her axe, as well as a few daggers that she rarely used. She was trying to be prepared for anything that she might possibly need.

She looked at herself in the glass. Everything she owned was forged by a dwarf, and she was worried that it might give her identity away. If she was lucky, no one would even remember the dwarves, but she didn't know how far her luck might stretch. She was skinnier than a dwarf should be, but what else did she have to help her hide? She feared that she would still be found out. She unsheathed her dagger. There was still another thing that made her seem exceptionally dwarven. She raised the dagger to her head and cut off her long braid. She let it fall to the ground and ran her hands through what remained. Basically nothing. The hair that used to fall to her thighs now hung at her chin. She hated the way it seemed to enhance the look of her hollowed cheeks. But it helped serve its purpose - surely no dwarf would be seen with such short hair – no one ever seemed to do more than trim anything that grew from their heads or faces. She turned away from the glass and re-sheathed her dagger. She was through looking at her reflection.

Besides that, it was time for Ever Trollkiller to start living her life.

She did not get too far, though. That morning, strangely enough, was the very morning that someone chose to wake up before her. And, to her utter disappointment, it was Otak, sitting by the entrance of the cave with his pipe, seeming to have been waiting for her. Her heart sank to the core of the earth.

"My eyes must be very old," he told her, "because I cannot even see your braid from this short distance."

There was a deep silence then. She wasn't sure how to respond, wasn't sure what his next move would be. She wasn't even really sure why he was up so early. At his age, he slept for most of the morning.

"Something told me this day would come," he said, breaking the silence between them. "I didn't want to believe that we would ever lose you." There was a deep sadness in his tone, reflected in his eyes.

"You're not losing me," she assured him, not knowing if that would be true or not. "Besides, I have fulfilled my duty to the dwarven race now." She wasn't sure why she decided to add that, except that she needed to add something to make her seem less like someone who was running away from responsibility.

"That was never your duty, my dear."

"So, what, then, the plan was to hide out here for three hundred years till we were all dead? And what when you all die before me? What was I to do then? Live in a lonely, haunted cave?" She was getting defensive. Her tone was heating up, along with her face, as she tried to reason her freedom.

"I'm not here to stop you," he said calmly, taking another

breath from his pipe. "I'm only here to smoke." His tone matched its calmness to her heatedness.

"Then let me go." She was stunned, but also unsure that he really meant what he was saying.

"I was never stopping you." He motioned to the cave opening, assuring her that she was free to go.

Hesitantly, Ever walked to the opening, eyeing him all the while. Surely this was a trick, was it not? But it wasn't. In just a few steps, she was outside and free.

"The world is a dark place," Otak warned her. "It's full of magic and evil that are often the same thing. It's full of ugly monsters and horrid beings. The world could use a heroic girl like you, but it doesn't want you. You are different, even among the dwarves. Be careful."

Gravely, she nodded to him.

"I will see you again, Otak."

"Don't make promises that you cannot keep," he rebuked her, taking another breath from his pipe. "Be wise, be brave, and do not forget who you really are, no matter what you learn."

She nodded again to him before disappearing into the forest, her goodbye unspoken but not unfelt. Otak sighed with a great sadness. He knew that she was wholly unprepared for the journey that was set before her, but he also knew that she was about to be faced with her destiny. Perhaps the world was about to be set straight once again. Perhaps she could restore the light in the darkness.

Ever had not even considered doing something so great. She had thought only to see the world and be free for the time being. She knew very well that she couldn't do it alone, either, so her fate depended on Jesper's willingness to take her – and her ability to find him again.

She crept deep into the woods, searching for elk. Her hope was that, as it usually was when she happened to see him, he would be in the middle of her hunting grounds, shooting down the biggest one.

As fate would have it, luck was not on her side. She crouched under the bushes, the only sound escaping her was the calmness of her breath. The elk soon began to crowd her, unaware of her presence. Hours passed by without event. She began to wonder if this was a good idea or not. By now, the dwarves would have learned of her absence and were probably going to come after her. Unless Otak convinced them that she was simply out hunting. Ever hoped that that was the case.

Until she remembered the braid, lying on the ground between Vek and the glass. He would begin a search for her, regardless of what Otak said, or any argument that he gave for him to let her go. Ever had to leave the forest, else she be made prisoner with her friends. Vek would surely never let her out of his sight.

So she set off, without the aid of her elven friend. He said that the land he was from – Brisdale – was south. Perhaps, then, that was the direction in which she should travel. She would find him at his own home. What a surprise that would be for him!

She ventured further into the forest than she had ever been before. The elk avoided her, as she by no means tried to keep quiet. She was desperate to be gone before anyone else found her. The sun was getting lower and lower in the sky and she was not even close to the end of the foliage.

After miles and miles of running, Ever began to wonder why Jesper had been out so far in the forest at all. She hoped dearly that she was not traveling in the wrong direction. Before the sun had completely set, she came across a path that looked as though it had been frequently traveled. The dirt was covered with tracks of various kinds, some of which she did not even recognize. In front of this path was the place that she came to a complete halt. If she continued, would she be met with strangers? Or would she be met with her fatal end?

But if she turned back now, what would be waiting at home

could be far worse. To face the wrath of Vek would be the hardest thing she had to do. Surely harder than seeing where this path might take her.

She decided to follow it, keeping off the actual road and opting to instead remain hidden by the cover of the trees.

At that hour, the path was completely abandoned. She saw a few small frogs hopping across, feeling secure enough in the emptiness not to be trampled. Even a few elk were crossing the road. She crept along, now going as quietly as she could. Her stomach growled, her armor softly clanked, and her tired feet scuffed along the dirt road, but even that was quieter than her run through the forest.

Ever had walked for seemingly endless amounts of time, until the sun had nearly set. Her eyes were trained on the ground in front of her. She was so hungry, she began to feel faint. Perhaps packing food would have been a good idea, but it was too late to regret her decisions now – like the one to run out on her own. She was so weary that she didn't even realize when the trees had become thinner and thinner until they were gone altogether and she was walking on the side of the road without any cover or protection. She just kept forging forward, keeping one foot in front of the other, and wondering if it might perhaps be time to set up a sort of camp for herself. Then, realizing she had no bedroll, wondering how she could dig herself a make shift bed.

"Excuse me, miss?" a small voice startled her back into reality.

It came from a small child, almost as tall as Ever was herself. She suddenly realized how far she must have gone, suddenly realized that there were no trees and no sun at all. Upon looking around, she discovered that she saw no home for this child, either. Perhaps she was imagining her? Then surely it would be okay to talk to her, would it not?

"Are you lost, miss?" the child asked.

"I'm afraid so," Ever answered, and quite honestly. "I don't suppose you could point me in the right direction?"

"Where are you going?"

Would it be okay to confide in her, Ever wondered? Even if this were a real child, she supposed that she could not do too much evil with that information.

"I'm making my way to Brisdale," she confessed.

"Brisdale? Of the elven kingdom? That's far off. In that direction." She pointed in a direction just a bit off from where Ever was already headed. "But surely you do not intend to make it there tonight. Why, that's a few more nights away! Come, we must get you fed and rested. Perhaps father can offer you a map or directions better than the ones you've come this far with."

Maybe it was poor judgment, maybe she was simply too hungry to protest, but when the girl grabbed her hand, she let her lead her away from the main road. It forked off into several smaller, less traveled roads. They hadn't walked long till the girl stopped at a small, quaint cottage, with a garden off to the side and a giant pile of firewood stacked on the other. Smoke was gently rising from the chimney, the homey smell wafting up to Ever's nose.

"What's wrong?" the girl asked when Ever stopped suddenly.

"I shouldn't be intruding. I should go now. I'm sorry."

Surprisingly strong for such a small girl, she held her grip on Ever's wrist and quite firmly as Ever began to struggle away.

"But miss, I can't let you die. Mum always says to take care of kin and that means *all* the kin."

Surely she thought of Ever as a human, then. Would it be right to take advantage of this child's innocence for a meal and a map? What would they think when they learned that they had fed a dwarf?

But Ever knew it wouldn't matter in the larger scheme of things. She needed to eat, and this child seemed willing to offer. So she hoped and silently prayed that the family she was about to meet was as kind as this child seemed to be.

The inside of the cottage was warm and smelled of something delicious that she could not even recognize. But that was what registered second. What registered first was the seven different faces that stared at her – two faces of grown people older than she, and five of other children of varying ages.

"Tamari," the older woman spoke, "who is your friend here?" She seemed calm about the matter, and definitely friendly. Although she was a bit surprised by Ever's entrance, she seemed to have been expecting it in some way as well.

"Miss, who are you?" the little girl – Tamari – said, turning back to Ever. Amusement flashed across the older man's face.

"I am Ever," she announced.

"She is Ever," Tamari told her family, in case they didn't hear Ever in the first place. Then she turned back to Ever. "What kind of a name is that?"

But instead of answering, Ever turned to address the woman.

"Forgive me, I did not mean to intrude on your lovely home. I was lost, you see, and, uh, Tamari here said you might offer me directions."

"Oh, to be sure," the woman said, "you are of no intrusion to us. Tamari brings travelers quite often – in fact, so often that we've taken to cooking extra portions of dinner each night on the chance that she finds someone whilst she is out playing. She's never brought in one quite so skinny as you, though. Come, we shall eat, and then we shall talk."

Tamari grabbed Ever by the hand once more and led her to the dining area of the cottage. She pulled out a chair for Ever, which she reluctantly sat upon. Then the family and Ever were served by one of the older girls before she, too, took her spot at the table. There were potatoes cut into cubes and seasoned with flavors that Ever had never even dreamed of. There was meat, which tasted like elk but it was prepared in an entirely different way from what Vek had ever done with it. There was a lovely pear dish that balanced out the savory meal with a sweet ending. It was so delicious that Ever wolfed it down in just a few minutes. The children stared at her in wonder, never having seen a dwarven appetite, and began offering her their own portions. She had to decline several times until their father finally told them to settle down. He cleared his throat to address her.

"Now, then, Ever, I believe introductions are to be made. This is my wife, Lia, my daughters Tamari, Tsisia, and Tekla, my sons Ioane, Ramaz, and Kote, and I am Akim Pavalandish. Tell me, what brings you to our quiet village?"

Now Ever knew that she had to guard her words. The amusement had vanished from Akim's eyes and a serious hush fell on the entire table.

"To be honest," she began, clearing her throat, "I don't even know where I am. I am terribly lost. I was supposed to have a guide, but he was nowhere that I could see. When he did not meet me where I expected him to be, I tried to find my way to his home to meet him there."

"This is Ioka," Tamari offered in an excited tone. Ever lifted her hands apologetically.

"I've never heard of it."

Shock went around the table.

"Do you *own* a map?" one of the boys, Ramaz, said with sarcasm.

"Actually, no, I don't." Ever could see that Lia and Akim were growing more and more confused by her.

"Are you running from your parents?" Lia asked. "Is your mother worried? Akim, perhaps we should send word. Surely her mother misses her dearly."

"I have no mother," said Ever. Sad sniffs from the children offered consolation to her. "And no father, either. My father died in battle before I was born, and my mother wasn't strong enough to survive the harsh conditions after I was born. I never met either of them. I'm trying to reach old friends."

"In Brisdale, she told me!" Tamari squealed, excitement back in her voice. "Brisdale, mother! Elves of all things!"

"Are you an elf?" Tekla asked. "Ever is a strange name for any other race."

In answer, Ever simply tucked her hair behind her ears and shrugged. Though they did have an odd shape to them, pointing out just a little at the top, they were clearly not elven ears.

"What business do you have with the company of elves?" Ramaz asked with condescension.

"Ramaz, clear the table," Akim told him. Begrudgingly, Ramaz complied. "It's true, then," he turned back to Ever, "you are going to Brisdale?"

"Yes," Ever stated firmly, hoping that he would not ask the same question as his nosy son. "If you could just point me in the right direction, I will be on my way."

"Of course," he said with a smile. "But there is no way I can let you go tonight with a clear conscious. Just look at you! No, tomorrow I will give you a map and some direction, but tonight you will sleep here. Girls, please go prepare a bed roll for our guest."

Tamari, Tekla, and Tsisia walked off, excitement in their steps as they prepared to host her for the night.

"Ever," Lia began softly when all of the children had left, "what is your business in Brisdale?"

"I'm looking for a friend," she answered. That was true enough.

"Have you news from the outside?"

"The outside?" she questioned, dumbfounded. "Er, I suppose not."

"Terrisino… He has been quiet, then?"

"I… suppose so. The last I heard was when he killed the dwarves of Isola." She could tell by their expressions that something else was going on. "What is it?"

"It appears that, for once, we will be giving the traveler the news," Lia said with a satirical chuckle.

"The orcs have been raiding the villages of Ranton," Akim said with worry. "It might be on the other side of the river, but it is only a matter of time before they cross over. And then not much more time till they find Ioka."

"Is no one doing anything to stop them?"

"To what end?" Lia said dismally. "The only thing we can do is stall them by sending out an army to die. Terrisino is the greatest sorcerer in the land. There is no stopping him."

"Surely he has a weakness?"

"None that is known to humans," Lia sighed. "Don't trouble yourself too much now. Perhaps your elven friends can see to it that your life is spared."

Ever went to bed that night with her first taste of empathy and uncertainty. This family had fed and housed her, all the while fearing that the orcs – strange creatures that Ever knew nothing of – were going to raid their village at any time. They probably feared for their children's lives, all the while assuming they would be sending Ever off to safety. She felt selfish, even though she did not know that she would be welcomed at Brisdale at all. She felt guilty, even though there was nothing that she could do. And she felt overwhelmingly stupid for leaving the safety of the mountains without even making a plan with Jesper first. She had followed a whimsical urge and it could possibly cost her life.

* * *

That morning, Ever was again treated like a guest at an inn. She was served fresh fruits and warm porridge, but Lia had also prepared her a knapsack full of provisions, like bread and cheese, for her journey. Akim had supplied her with a marked map and very clear directions.

"It's a two-day journey if you take the main road. I suggest you take a less used road, this one here," he pointed to the map, "which will take you an extra night, but you will be far less likely to run into trouble."

"What kind of trouble? Orcs?"

"Goblins," he answered. "Minor nuisances, really. Sometimes they come over from the goblin island to cause trouble."

"Goblin island?" Ever asked, wide eyed. The dwarves had never mentioned such a place.

Akim looked her directly in the eye, studying her with concern.

"Marzur, where they live freely. In the main land, they are frequently caught and sold as slaves. Mostly by the dragon clans."

"Dragon clans?" Ever knew that she was giving away her ignorance too easily, that she should pretend to know more about the world and show some confidence, but panic was all that could come out.

"Ever, where did you say it is that you are from?" he asked, ignoring her question and preparing to voice his concern.

"I didn't," she offered as her only response.

"You don't know anything about the world that you are walking into. Terrisino is in control of most of it, then the elves and the dragon clans. And, although the elves aren't evil, none of those forces are to be trusted. To see you running off to an elven friend, I thought you might have been the enemy. But you truly haven't any idea of what you've begun to tangle yourself into." He looked at her with a grave expression on his face, the worry of a father in his eyes. "You get yourself there safely, at any cost, and stay out of trouble. Mind your own business, and the elves will mind theirs. Got it?"

"Yes sir," Ever answered very seriously. This man meant business. He handed the map to Ever after carefully folding it. "Thank you for your kindness."

Akim nodded, then Ever turned and left his home. She would remember him and his family and all that they had done for her, and she would find a way to repay them.

Ever decided to take the safer road rather than the quicker one, mostly because of Akim's concern. It made the most sense, anyway, since she clearly had no idea what to expect in this new world she was discovering. But it was boring. There was nothing but dirt and brush to look at. She trekked on all morning with no companion, not a single person nor a simple bird in sight. It seemed eerie to her, and she didn't feel as completely alone as she should have. To distract herself, she had begun to sing a dwarven lullaby.

>Light the candle, friend,
>The sun is all but gone.
>The birds have sung their last,
>The trees have gone to sleep.
>
>Sit closer here, friend,
>For a story I must tell
>Of a fire forged by thee,
>And all it's done to me.
>
>Gone, gone, gone is my lover,
>Swallowed by your flaming tongue
>Gone, gone, gone is my home now,
>You've taken all the gold.

It was a sad history woven into the melody, and suddenly Ever felt even less alone. She stopped singing, now certain that someone was listening. *This is the safe road,* she told herself. *You're imagining things. Akim's warning must have gotten inside your mind. That's all.*

She stopped anyway and scanned her surroundings. There was still no one in sight. With a deep breath, she set her resolve forward and marched on. To distract herself, she began to think of Jesper. Of his beauty that far surpassed even the humans that she met last night, and definitely surpassed her own or the rest of her clans. Surely there was little doubt as to why the Iokan family was so stunned that she was to have an audience with an elf. They were two pieces of a puzzle that did not go together. Perhaps from two different puzzles entirely. She wondered if she was ever going to see him again. It seemed unlikely now. So much evil could happen before she even arrived. And even if she did arrive safely, perhaps he wouldn't even want to see her. What would she say, anyway? A human-looking dwarf come to speak with an elf, and for what? Would he turn her away, force her to make the long journey back to the mountains alone? Would he demand answers that she had refused to give before? Perhaps he would think her a loon. She was certainly beginning to suspect a hint of lunacy in her brain.

Snap.

She jumped, turning around in a circle at the sound. She was not alone; she was now certain. What could be lurking, and where was it? Perhaps one of those goblin creatures was out. Possibly an orc. But she was sure that they had to be big and monstrous to make the raids that Lia had spoken of, and the snapping was small. Perhaps just an animal, then.

"Hello?" she called out. Nothing answered her. "Hello? I don't want trouble," she told the – what? The bushes? "Please, go away," she said as she turned away and began her walk once more. Faster. She heard a shuffling noise behind her. Faster still. She had nearly broken into a sprint now. Was it still following her?

After her breath began to fail her, she stopped. She crouched over, hands on her knees, and panted, trying to catch her breath. Once it had quieted, she scanned her surroundings. Nothing was in sight. Nothing was creating any more noise. Ever pulled out the map then, to make sure that she was still on the right path. Satisfied, if a little uneasy, she kept walking forward.

The sun began to smolder, high in the sky. Ever had been walking for hours, and now the cool breeze of the morning had disappeared completely. The heat was becoming unbearable, and she had nothing to protect her skin, save for the sweat that was pooling at her feet with every step. She was quickly becoming miserable.

Several times over the next few hours, she pulled out the map. She studied it intently to see how long it would take her to get to the main road. She could see that she had already cost herself some time. If she stayed on the safer road, she should be at Brisdale's gates in three days, as Akim had said. However, if she changed course, instead of two days, the main road would still be three days of journeying, as she had already walked a ways away from it. But surely she'd feel safer amongst other beings than on an abandoned road, and perhaps she would be able to trade for something to shade herself.

But she never strayed from the path. She kept walking, determined to make Akim as happy as she could, on the road that he had deemed safe to travel. She kept walking until the sun had set, and then kept on still until she was ready to drop from exhaustion. At that point, the moon was high in the sky and she decided to make camp right where she was. She dropped to the ground and pulled out the provisions from Lia. She broke off a third of the bread and a third of the cheese. Although she was starved and wanted it all, she knew that she had to put the rest back for the remainder of her journey. Once she had packed it back up, she stuffed that night's provisions in her mouth.

Snap.

"Stop!" she yelled with a mouth full of cheese, startled with the returning noise. "Show yourself!" She quickly swallowed her food and tried to sound more threatening than threatened. "I have an axe, and I know how to use it! I've killed before!"

"Shush!" a voice called out to her, approaching from the bushes. "It's me." It was a small female voice, but Ever didn't put down her axe. "I thought I was going to lose you – you run fast for a skinny thing. And then I thought you'd be dumb enough to make the whole walk at once – you wouldn't stop!"

"Tekla?" Ever asked, baffled.

"Uh-huh, it's me, how do you do, and all that," she said, standing up straight and brushing dirt from her clothes. Her long blonde hair was tied back, exposing high cheek bones and freckles on tanned skin.

"What are you doing here?"

"Can you put down the axe, please?" she said, lifting an eye brow impatiently. Ever complied. "I want to see the elves."

"No." Ever turned back to her dinner.

"Excuse me?" Tekla asked in shock.

"No," Ever repeated herself. "I would not have you disappoint Akim and Lia. They were kind to me, and I won't thank them by stealing their daughter. Go back home."

"Hardly! I am sixteen years old this summer. I am practically grown, and surely old enough to marry. That means I'm old enough to leave my parents."

"Go home, Tekla."

"Not on your life. It's late now. I think I'll eat."

She sat away from Ever, pulled out her own rations, and ate in silence. Ever had to admit, she'd be less paranoid in her first night on the journey with another soul to keep her company. After a moment of annoyed thought, she decided to allow it.

"You may stay the night," she said, "but in the morning, you will return home and leave me alone."

"I will do no such thing, and you have no say in the matter anyway. I know the way to Brisdale, even if you left me behind. Besides, if I am to go with or without you, isn't it wise to make sure I arrive safe? You can repay my parents that way."

"I haven't got time for you. I should repay your parents by swiftly kicking you in the rump and sending you flying back home."

"I'm tired now," Tekla said, packing her food and unrolling a bed roll. "I'm going to sleep."

Ever just sat there and glared. She knew that she had lost.

She wasn't prepared for a battle with a stubborn child like Tekla. So she rolled out her bed and prepared herself for a cold night in the middle of an abandoned road.

But sleep never really came. Every time a bush moved, every gentle gust of wind, every chirp of a cricket had her jumping in fright. Tekla slept soundly, something for which Ever was resentful. She felt responsible for the girl, which was partly why she was so jumpy. She was worried, too, about the dragon clans and the goblins. Would Tekla know how to handle that kind of situation? Perhaps it was a good thing she had decided to come along, as Ever did not know what to do. Still, as soon as Ever could convince Jesper to help her, she would see to it that Tekla returned to Akim and Lia safely and promptly. Until then, she decided to use the girl's knowledge as best as she could.

As the sun began to rise, Ever gave up on the idea of sleep and began to roll up her bed roll, strapping it securely to her pack. Then she looked over at her unwanted companion and rolled her eyes. She walked over to the girl, who was still sound asleep, and kicked her awake. The girl moaned a few times before rubbing the sleep out of her eyes.

"Hey," she protested.

"It's time to go," Ever said coldly, picking up her pack and stepping forward to continue her journey.

"Hey, wait!" she protested again, hurrying to pack her things. "What about breakfast?"

Ever's stomach growled, but she was too proud to admit her hunger.

"I don't have time for that. If you'd like to eat, fine, but if you wish to travel with me, you'd best not slow me down." She was already quite a few paces ahead of Tekla, but the girl heard every word and sprinted to catch up.

"What business do you have that is so important, anyway?" she asked.

To that, Ever truly had no response, so she only kept quiet.

The two walked in silence, both brimming with questions that they didn't ask, choosing instead to continue the disagreeable behavior. And so the day went on, just as quietly as the day before. Ever allowed them to stop for food once when the sun was at its highest in the sky, finally succumbing to her own hunger after hours of walking. The next time they stopped was late in the night, for a light dinner and sleep. Tekla had wanted a fire, but Ever refused, more for the sake of being disagreeable than for the sake of safety. The night went better for Ever, and she was able to sleep soundly. Tekla, however, rose the next morning feeling restless and cranky. Although it made Tekla far more disagreeable, Ever showed a petty smirk at the thought of the girl's misery.

As the sun began to rise high the next day, Ever could hear that they were approaching civilization. Her stomach began to twist and turn. Tekla's question rang in her mind like a taunting sound. What business did she have with the elves? Would Jesper find her quest as important as she found it?

Probably not. She would have to convince him with lies. She wanted most to see the Isola Ruins, and so she would begin by convincing him to take her there. After that, she would venture through the rest of the world by herself if she had to. Without Tekla, as she did plan to ask Jesper to arrange an escort for her return home.

"We should probably set some things straight," Tekla said. "We need to know what to say if they ask us who we are or what we're doing."

"What do we have to set straight?" Ever challenged. "You have your business and I have mine."

"Okay, but what if they ask why we're traveling together?"

"Tell them you wouldn't leave me alone."

It was clear that Tekla was attempting to get some information from Ever.

"Look, I'm not a dumb child like Tamari. I know you have some sort of news for the elves, and I demand that you tell me. My family took care of you, and now you help me take care of them."

"If you were so concerned about your family, perhaps you should have stayed behind to protect them. As it so happens, I have no news that concerns Ioka. Quite frankly, I'd be shocked if anyone even knew the village existed. Perhaps it is even too small to be called a village. Anyway, I plan to see that you are returned to your family before anything else even happens, so you will never know what business I have."

"And I plan to see the downfall of Terrisino, and since my will is clearly stronger than yours, you're going to have to deal with it and tell me what you know."

Ever stopped and turned on the girl.

"Do you have some sort of hero complex? Do you truly believe that you, a child, could do anything to stop the most powerful sorcerer that the world has ever seen?"

She was taken aback, but recovered quickly.

"Every great history starts with one brave soul. If I die creating a better place for my brothers and sisters to live in, and a peaceful world for my mother and father to grow old in, then that is a sacrifice that I am willing to make. And if you're not courageous enough to do so, then get me an audience with the elves and then *you* may see *yourself* out of my way."

"And what qualifies you for such a quest?"

"I am not sure," Tekla began, "that anyone is ever really qualified. I have done my training with Ramaz. He has taught me as much as he knows about the sword. I know very well how to survive in the wilderness. And I am prepared to die, if I must."

"Why would you say such a thing?" Ever asked. "Don't you think that your family would want you to spend every last minute at their side?"

As she said it, Ever began to feel guilt spread through her body. She realized that she was in a similar position. Her family had seen the end, they had seen war and sickness, and they all depended on each other. They all loved each other. Although unrelated by blood, they were family. And yet, here she was, telling this girl to stop saving her own family and instead sit by their side. At least Tekla had been trying to do something for her family. Ever knew that she was only doing it for herself.

Tekla studied Ever carefully. Although she knew nothing about the girl, there was a reason that she had chosen Ever. It was true that Tamari had brought in travelers all the time. And some of them far more sturdy-looking than Ever. She could have gone with any of them and her survival would have been less of a gamble. But there was something that told her that Ever was important. Ever was the one that she needed to follow. And if that was the case, she needed to get Ever on her side.

"I have been out before," Tekla said. "I have been preparing for this journey. At first, I did not know what I was preparing for, I simply thought that one day I would travel to a bigger village, perhaps a city, and I would meet a man. But I no longer care for such trivial things." She took a breath here, trying to gather her thoughts. "I had gone to Sandy Brook. It isn't far from Ioka. It isn't terribly far from where we are now. It's a safe part of the world. Living near Brisdale means that we are constantly living in peace. It's a wonderful feeling. I had gone there only to meet someone. I had gone there just to see if I liked the people. But just on the outskirts of the village, I saw a small group of orcs. There were only four of five of them. Filthy creatures, they were. They dripped in grime and mud. I could see their teeth from where I had crouched behind a bush. They were such a horrid green color, I was shocked that they were still in their mouths at all. One of them was missing a hand, and another was missing his arm clear up to his shoulder. It didn't seem to bother them at all. It was as if those limbs were not even necessary to them. They were all just sitting there, laughing and grunting in their piggish language. I didn't understand any of it. They had clearly made camp for the night, eating around a campfire and laughing. I was scared to move, because I knew that they would kill me and I had left my sword with Ramaz. I also did not believe that I could take that many by myself. But when I realized what they were eating, I ran as fast as I could, straight back to my home."

"What were they eating?"

Tekla paused, looking deep into Ever's eyes as she tried to make her understand her urgency.

"People."

Ever gasped. Tekla nodded.

"Things will only get worse in this world. Already, these things are beginning to happen on our side of the river. On the safe side of the river. I cannot sit back and wait for orcs to come to my family's doorstep for dinner. Because they will. It won't be long now. No, I will not sit idly by, I will make the first move. I believe, Ever, that you are important, and I will see to it that you accomplish your goal… Because I believe we have the same goal."

Now it was Ever's turn to be taken aback. This girl, although no more than a child, was prepared to lose her life if it meant taking down the sorcerer. Ever wasn't sure, though, if that was her goal as well. In fact, she had only just been brought into the world beyond the cave, and she was not sure if she could say she truly knew her goal anymore. Ever continued walking to hide her shock and gain composure.

"I truly have no news for you," she said without emotion. "I can tell you that Terrisino is the reason that I was left orphaned as a child. His orc army, as far as I have been told, wiped out my entire family, my entire home. A small group of us fled, and so I have lived out my life in hiding." As she spoke, she began to realize how angry she was that she had the chances of a normal dwarven life taken away from her. She began to realize that was precisely what Tekla was fearing for herself and for her family. She felt sympathy for her, and more than that, she felt compelled to learn more. Was Tekla perhaps right about her importance? Otak's speech rang through her head. His words of warning, of an evil world. But also his reasoning for letting her go. *The world could use a heroic girl like you.* Perhaps it could, but certainly she couldn't do anything alone, as Tekla could not, either. "I will take you to see the elves, and we," she emphasized, "and we shall see what is to happen after that. I do not know where I will go, or what I wish to do. And if our wishes do not align, that is where we separate."

Tekla fell silent, clearly not having expected that much honesty from Ever. Ever's concentration went to a cart that was passing by them – the first they had seen on their three day journey. The walking was coming to an end.

"Thank you," Tekla said as Ever gave a nod to the driver of the cart. She was watching him wearily, but saw nothing but curiosity in his eyes. Ever dropped her voice to a low whisper.

"I can get us in with the elves, but you need to help me handle the other conversations. Being hidden my whole life has somewhat marred my skills."

"Deal."

As they walked, more and more people began to stare. Some of them, Ever noticed, had pointy ears, and some of them did not. None of them, however, ever presented a challenge or a glower, or any kind of negativity. Ever was absolutely stunned by this. The two places she had visited were filled with one race that the dwarves hated so much and another that the dwarves found useless, and both times she was greeted with pleasantries. Surely there was no sign of Terrisino in these lands. There seemed to be no mistrust or anger in these people.

"We must be nearly there by now," Ever said with growing anxiety.

"There's a bridge we must cross first," Tekla responded. "The elves always build their cities behind rivers."

Her feet were aching and her stomach was empty.

"Let's stop and eat what little we have left. Brisdale isn't going anywhere, and I do not wish to discuss our matters when I am faint with hunger."

Wordlessly, Tekla agreed. She set her pack down by the side of the road and unwrapped her food. Ever watched her as she chewed it without tasting any of it.

"What's the matter?" she asked when they had both swallowed their last bites.

"How are we to convince the elves of anything?"

Truly, Ever did not have an answer to that.

"They don't think much of human travelers, and you and I look of even less concern than two normal human travelers."

"That is true," conceded Ever, "but you must never give up before you try. Already we have gotten farther than I could have thought possible. The words will come to us when we need them."

Already, Ever was beginning to know what she was going to have to sacrifice in order to get the attention of the elves. Two small human girls would not be very successful in igniting a rebellion against Terrisino. But Ever was no human.

"Come along, then," she said, now more anxious than ever to get the whole thing done.

II.

Brisdale was a beautiful city. Upon crossing the bridge, Ever was stricken by the splendor of it all. The cottages where the elves lived were magnificently structured. Each one looked different, but somehow uniform. Each one was big enough to fit two of her clans inside. They were built on white stone, carefully laid to form a sturdy place for the families inside to live comfortably at peace. Each had blue runes carved into the wooden doors. Tekla told her that those were believed to bring protection to the inhabitants, each carefully hand carved by educated elves. Every elf had the opportunity to read and write, many going on to be great scholars. Ever was jealous of each one of them. She would love to have learned to read the dwarven script, to understand the stories that were carved into the walls of the cave of her clan. She longed to have been educated in any proper way, not given advice throughout her life as she had been. She wished that she could read the elven runes, or even the map from Akim. But she knew that it was silly to dwell on such things. The past was the past.

Ever noticed that no other races besides the elves appeared the minute that they had crossed over the bridge. The looks they received from passersby were no longer strictly curious; they now held suspicion and worry as well. Tekla had told her not to pay any mind to them. Simply keep her eyes up and walk through as if she had every right to be there. It made her worry that perhaps the elves were not the most welcoming folk. But Tekla assured her that they were going to be well received.

In the center of the city, the palace stood tall and proud. It was visible from any point in the city, so it was easy for Tekla to lead the way through the streets even though she had never actually been inside the limits. The palace was more beautifully made than the cottages, and surely made them look pitiful in comparison. The bottom was made with the same white stone as the cottages, but after the first floor, there was white marble that stretched into pointed arches for many more floors. Each floor had fewer arches than the last so that they made a larger point that formed the whole palace. At the seventh floor, they finally combined into one single arch that tipped off the whole building. It reminded Ever of a giant crown. Green tinted windows lined the walls and arches, and water trickled down from the top arch all the way down to the moat around the palace. Ever gasped in awe.

"Are you sure this is the right place?" Tekla asked, filled with a new found doubt spurred on by Ever's surprise.

"Of course," Ever said in confusion. "Is this not the palace?"

"This is the palace, alright," Tekla said. "But surely this friend of yours… Must be somewhere else."

"Absolutely not," she answered. "He's royalty."

"He who?" she asked in doubt. "I need to know details."

"The elf that we came to see," she answered only half attentively.

"You never said he was royalty."

"You never asked. How do we get in?"

Tekla rolled her eyes, frustrated with Ever's constant withholding of information, but led her to the bridge in the front of the palace. They crossed the moat – which was filled with big fish, Ever noticed. She wondered if they served as protection or decoration. They reached the gate and were halted by a couple of guards, each just as beautiful as an elf should be. Their fair skin shined in the sun, as did their long blond hair, which was braided with elegance. Each wore a silver chain mail gown that was adorned with blue robes. They carried spears in their hands, but Ever had suspected that they were more proficient with the bows and arrows that slung carefully over their backs.

"State your names," one of them demanded. He had a very long, pointed nose, which was the only thing – beside his voice – that Ever found displeasing about him.

"I am Tekla Pavalandish of Ioka, and, um, this is Ever... Um..."

"I am Every Trolly," she said, hesitating only momentarily on her dwarven surname. She thought it best to disguise it as she disguised herself. "Of Ioka." For that, she earned a sidelong glance from Tekla. More lies about her origins.

"And what is your business with the palace?" the other elf asked. Ever found his rosy cheeks much more pleasing than the other elf's angular nose.

"I need to speak with Jesper, sir," she answered with as much politeness as possible. The elves looked at each other.

"Have you news?" Rosy Cheeks asked.

"No," Ever told them, "I've come to ask a favor."

"Why would you ask something of the adopted prince," scoffed Pointy Nose, "rather than the high king?"

"I do not know the high king," Ever simply stated. She noticed that the elves were cautiously curious, but not altogether suspicious of the two girls.

"What do you expect the adopted prince to grant you?" Pointy Nose sneered.

"If you don't mind," Ever said gently, "I'd like to keep that between myself and Jesper. And my companion," she added as an afterthought. She didn't much like that they kept referring to Jesper as nothing more than adopted royalty, as if he wasn't important enough for legitimate recognition. An afterthought himself among the royal family, and yet, dedicated enough to do the labors of common folk such as hunting. But she could see that asking for him was the very thing that eased the elves weariness – as though nothing concerning the adopted prince could be of terrible importance. The elves nodded to each other and Rosy Cheeks disappeared behind the gate, reappearing in minutes with a third elf. He was taller, with darker hair. He carried no weapons or chain mail, adorned instead in a brown robe with vines patterned in the hems.

"Zellen," Pointy Nose addressed him, "please escort these young girls to the court and see to it that they speak with Jesper the adopted prince."

Zellen gave a nod and beckoned the girls to follow him beyond the gates.

Everything behind the gates glistened just as the elves did. There were pillars stretching from the floors to the tall ceilings, covered in an elegant script that Ever once again wished she could decipher. The script glowed blue, giving the feeling of magic. The marble tile was pristine and didn't seem to take footprints, even though Ever knew that her boots must be a mess. There were beautifully carved marble statues lining the walls which Ever assumed that they were of the royal family and their ancestors. The court room, however, seemed devoid of all of the splendor. The marble tile was gold, the walls were white. There was a polished brown table in the center, long and oval. Zellen pulled out two of the seats and prompted the girls to sit, and they silently obeyed.

"I shall summon the prince."

That was all he said before he left. They weren't left alone, however. Before the big, heavy doors swung shut, two guards stationed themselves inside. Ever was sure that guards did not simply stand at every closed door in the palace. She knew that, although they had made it in the palace, they had not earned anyone's trust, no matter how weak and silly Pointy Nose considered them.

"To think," Tekla said, clearly just as awe stricken with the place as Ever was, "I am in an elven palace! Father would love to see this!"

Ever paid her no mind. Although she would have loved for Vek to share in the splendor as well, she was here on business. She waited patiently for Zellen to return with Jesper, but time seemed to trudge on and on. She began to fret.

Just when she was certain that Zellen had forgotten them altogether, the tall doors opened and Jesper walked through. His eyes went straight to hers, the golden brown irises gleaming with excitement and confusion. He was even more breathtaking in his home than he was in the woods. He wore long, dark green robes decorated with gold vines embroidered in them. His dreadlocks had been cleaned up and added to them were now beads, some wooden and some gold.

"Ever," he said as she took him in, "what are you doing here? Haresh, Hathlan, you may go," he said, turning to dismiss the guards. Reluctantly, they left. Then Jesper turned back to Ever. "Who is *this*?" he asked, brow furrowed and tone a mix of things that Ever could not pick out.

"This," she said through gritted teeth, "is Tekla. My, um, companion."

Tekla rolled her eyes at Ever's title for her.

"I am Tekla Pavalandish of Ioka," she stood and introduced herself in a more fitting manner. "It is a pleasure to make your acquaintance, your highness." She curtsied low to him, and suddenly Ever felt as though she had been accidentally disrespectful to Jesper. She did not know proper etiquette. She felt very uncomfortable, but Jesper simply waved Tekla off and sat at the table next to them. Ever had expected him to take one of the grand, decorated chairs at the opposite side of the table, but he sat right next to her instead.

"Okay, Tekla of Ioka. Why have you come all this way?"

"I have a quest to propose to you," Ever began. "I wish to

find my father, and then to find his killer."

She had hoped to enlist his help without revealing too much about the situation until strictly necessary.

"I see. A quest most valiant. And why do you seek my help?"

Ever contemplated for a moment. She wasn't sure that appealing to his ego would work. He didn't appear to be looking for recognition, and besides, as the "adopted" prince, he sure wasn't accustomed to receiving it. She decided to be truthful instead.

"You're the only person I know outside of my clan. You know the land and its perils. I only know a handful of stories that I have been told, and I have no map to follow."

"And what are you hoping to achieve with this quest?" he challenged her.

To that, she didn't really have an answer. She wasn't entirely sure that there was anything to be accomplished at all. She wasn't even sure why she felt compelled to that mission at all, save for some bitter feelings of having grown up as a myth. She was eternally grateful when Tekla spoke up.

"Look, elf," she said with a harsh tone. "Everyone on this side of the river is at risk of losing their lives. She might be attempting to avenge her father with this quest, but I am going to protect my family. Step up for your kingdom and protect the elves of Brisdale."

That seemed to strike the right chord. Instantly, he changed from relaxed and curious in his demeanor to defensive and battle ready.

"I protect my people every day," he argued with her.

"So you've gone to battle?" she further challenged. "You have an army? An alliance? You could start a war?"

"Yes, I very well could, should I have reason to."

"Good," Tekla declared with a sly smile. "I am going to tell you exactly what Terrisino will do to everyone on this side of the river, and you will then be moved to join our mission."

"You want me to wage a war on the Great Sorcerer?" he almost exploded with surprise, clearly not having expected the name of Terrisino to come up. "There is not a force on this earth that a child like you could use to get me to risk the lives of my elves for your childish endeavor."

"Then let me show you," Ever jumped back in. "Come with me, for a small journey. Come and see what the Great Sorcerer," she nearly spat the title, "has done to my family, to my people. Let me show you who I am and where I come from. Then you will know that we need not only your army, but many more forces to aid us, else the sorcerer continues to kill until there is no one else."

The promise of information to Ever's mysterious identity piqued both of their interests. Jesper had spent long days, over several months, wondering who the girl in the forest could have been. She was the biggest mystery that he had come across. The temptation of knowing where she came from was hard to deny.

"Just a small journey," Ever said again. "A few days, for you to see for yourself and decide your next actions."

"Just a journey," he began, "to the place where you were born?"

"No," she said. "I never lived there. I was born on the run. I want to take you to the place where my father died so that my mother and I could flee."

"What is the name of this place?" he asked.

But Ever would not answer. Instead, she looked at him with an even stare as she let the temptation sit in his mind for a minute. He looked back at her, refusing to give in right away. But as he stared into her expressive eyes, he longed to be at her side. He longed to know her history, personal and otherwise. He longed to be with her for as long as he could get away with.

And besides that, leaving behind the attitudes of the elves for a while was always a welcome benefit.

"We'll set out in the morning, then."

Ever could not hide her shock at his decision, nor her fear. Truth be told, though she could understand that the end of Terrisino was necessary for the survival of the races as Tekla had told her, she had actually hoped that he would not care to bring in his elven army after the journey.

"I will see to it that you are given a room to sleep and a meal as well. Then I shall prepare our horses and we will leave at first light. I don't suppose you two have come all this way on horse?"

Both Ever and Tekla shook their heads. Ever had never ridden a horse in her life. It wasn't particularly the dwarven way. But she knew that, despite her fear of the creatures, she was going to have to ride without protest. She had to hide her secret for a little longer.

"I thought not. Surely we have a couple that we can spare. I shall call for Zellen to show you to your chambers."

Once Zellen had shown them to their rooms, Ever immediately collapsed on to the bed. The white sheets were silky and smooth. The mattress was perfectly inviting. She was sure that she was never going to wake up as soon as she fell asleep. She took off her armor and made her way to the bathing room that Zellen had shown her. She finished stripping there and filled the bath with warm water. She was going to scrub every last bit of dirt off of her body so that she might be better fit for the presence of elves.

After thirty minutes of hard scrubbing in the warmth of the water, Ever finally decided that it was time to get out. In the steam and relaxation of a long bath, she hadn't realized that someone had come in and taken her dirty clothes and replaced them with plain white sleeping garments that fit perfectly. It was no more than a simple white robe, but it made her feel inadequate somehow. She was an intruder among elves, a simple dwarf dressed in elegance and passing herself off as human. She was a fraud. She stood in front of the glass and looked herself up and down. She decided to add braids into her dark hair. It was short now, but she was determined to follow the intricate designs of the elves. She wove a braid on the top of her head, letting the rest of her hair fall on either side. Then she took the hair on the sides and wove them into two smaller braids above her ears. It wasn't as fancy or as well done as it should have been, but it gave her a little more comfort. She went back to her chamber to sleep, feeling already more rested.

And then immediately on edge again. Food was waiting for her on a tray by the bed, but so was Jesper.

"You have a beautiful face underneath all of that dirt," he told her, looking at her in full. She felt suddenly naked and crossed her arms over her chest, as if that could help, and blushed so deeply that she almost wished for the dirt back on her face to hide it.

"Thank you for agreeing to accompany us," she offered.

"I would have gone with you no matter what. Risking my army is another subject, though, and one that I will certainly not take lightly. But I will hear you and your friend out. Is she… part of your clan?"

"No," Ever laughed and sat on the edge of the bed. "Her family helped me out a bit as I was on my way here, and she invited herself for the rest of the way. At first, I was going to ask you to also arrange an escort home for her, but now I think she might be of some use."

"What changed your mind?"

"She has a goal, and I think that it is mine, too."

"The end of the Great Sorcerer," he stated. She nodded her head. "Well, then, Ever, I must confess that I have sent for a companion as well."

"Is that so?" her interest piqued – as well as, she realized, a hint of jealousy.

"Indeed. That is why I have come here so late. She is originally from Shodalea, but has been living in a village called

Abrya on the coast." He paused then, watching her carefully. "Have you heard of those places before?"

Ever shook her head in confusion. He seemed to be hoping that she hadn't heard of them. He let go of a breath that he had been holding.

"She, too, has the same goal as you and your companion. I am taking her as a sort of advisor. Will you allow that?"

"Sure," Ever said, seeing no reason that she could not, but also getting the feeling that he was hiding something from her.

"Good. Thank you. Now, I must be off and you must eat and rest. Tomorrow is going to be a long day. And Ever," he said, already at the door but turning to add one last thing, "you can't tell Tekla where my advisor is from just yet."

He left without waiting for her to give her word.

* * *

Jesper had made sure that the girls were fed that morning before they went to the stables. Ever tasted the sweetest apples she thought to be in existence. Some of them were raw, and they were very delicious, but she found the baked ones even more pleasant to the taste. They had been baked with honey and sugar, and some had been baked into a chewy bread. There was another bread dish, in the shape of a flat pancake, and filled with a custard and berries of different types. The tastiest of all, though, and the most fulfilling, was the waybread. It was flat and square, and very bland to the eye. However, when she finally reached for it and took a bite, Ever discovered that it was anything but bland. It was sweet like honey with a hint of citrus flavor. She had hoped that the elves might give them some for their journey, but did not ask for fear of seeming rude.

After breakfast, both the girls felt satisfied and ready to begin their quest. Zellen led them off to the stables where Jesper was waiting for them. He had already prepared the horses for them, their saddles awaiting a rider. He was whispering to a muscular, white steed when they came up to him.

"This is Andale," he told them, breaking his gaze from the horses. "He had been my faithful companion for many quests. This is Ezaria," he led them to another white horse, a mare with brown streaks woven through her mane and tail. Tekla mounted her immediately, obviously having ridden before. "And this is Minx. She will be your mare, Ever," he said as he showed her the solid black mare. Ever gulped, not quite sure how to mount the beast. "And this," Jesper said, calling her attention away for a moment – for which Ever was relieved, "is my companion and advisor, Teava."

Tekla looked at Ever, her eyes widened with – something. Surprise? Fear? Ever could not tell. But when Tekla did not see the same look reflected in Ever's eyes, she immediately felt betrayed and Ever knew that she would hear about it soon enough. Teava spoke, interrupting the look of betrayal.

"This is my steed, Phantom," she said, addressing the black, saddleless steed by her side, "and my servant Seg."

Seg was a small man, coming up to the midpoint of Teava's thigh. His skin was so white that it was nearly translucent, and it stretched so thinly over his body that his entire skeleton was nearly poking through it. His big, very round head seemed to bob on his scrawny neck. He had very little hair, which revealed his big, pointy ears. Could he be a shrunken elf, then? But his big eyes, which took up nearly half of his face, did not seem very elven at all, nor did his small, thin, pointed nose or his cracked lips below. He was exactly the opposite of Teava, who stood tall and slender, dressed in black knee high boots, black leggings, and a long black shirt with red hems and sleeves that hugged her biceps before dropping loosely in red fabric that hung off her forearms. Her face was breathtaking. It was petite, but her expression was aggressive. Her high cheekbones were a pink contrast to her white face. She had long, black lashes and liner around black eyes. It seemed almost tattooed around her eyes in an intricate pattern. The black color of the liner matched the black of her hair, which was held back in one long braid. It didn't look like an elven braid, though. It looked almost scaly, like the tail of a fish. Ever thought that she was the picture of both beauty and power. And, with a stern expression, she was ready to get straight to the point.

"Now that we are all acquainted," she said, "shall we set off, then?"

Without waiting for a response, she mounted Phantom. Jesper mounted Andale, leaving Ever to panic. She was short, like a dwarf, so simply getting her foot in the first stirrup was hard enough. To her utter embarrassment, Jesper dismounted and came to her aid. He put his hands on her hips – sending a warm tingly feeling through her body that made her blush – and easily lifted her atop Minx. She mumbled her gratitude as he remounted his steed.

"We need to go west," Ever said, addressing the whole group, "towards the mountains."

She knew that she was being vague with the destination. That was with purpose. She was going to hide her identity as long as she could. Tekla did not show any concern on her face, but Jesper looked at her with confusion. Teava, however, looked as though she had already figured out the secret. She raised one perfect brow, all seriousness in her expression. However, to Ever's great relief, she did not say a word.

Riding proved very difficult for Ever. The other three more experienced riders seemed to have slowed down considerably to accommodate her. She jostled up and down, several times losing her balance and nearly falling. The others, she noticed, were completely steady on the backs of the beasts. She could already sense that her rump was going to be sore for days. She tried to sit tall like her companions, squeezing her muscles in effort, but even at the slow pace that they were going, she was hunched over to keep herself on the horse. Teava had slowed even more to trot at her side. Ever gulped, not wanting a conversation while she was struggling to ride. Especially from a girl who rode so easily bare backed on a steed that barely looked tame.

"Jesper has told me all about your quest," she informed Ever.

"Uh-huh," Ever replied, keeping her focus ahead of her. She had expected Jesper to do as much. He said she was his advisor, after all.

"He told me how you met as well."

Ever looked ahead at the other half of their group. She was sure that they were out of ear shot. That was just fine with her. She didn't quite know if she trusted Teava yet, and she didn't want to have all ears on this conversation.

"He doesn't know who you really are, does he?" Ever did not give her a response. "He said you talked of a clan. Are they like you also?" Once again, she did not offer a response. There was a brief pause. "I did not think so. He has left his kingdom for your vengeful quest. Don't you think you owe him a bit of honesty?"

"Does he know everything about you?" Ever finally opened her mouth, offering a cold challenge. Teava did not respond, which prompted Ever to continue. "Does he even know who *you* really are? It seems to me as though you have secrets of your own to keep from him."

"He knows exactly who I am and why I left," she replied, her anger seething in her voice. "He is my friend and I am his, do not ever doubt that. That is exactly why I don't like you. Secrets are not kept among friends."

"He will know mine soon enough," Ever replied.

"You mean when we arrive at the ruins of the dwarves?" she hissed at Ever. It was such a menacing sound that Ever visibly shuddered. "You think that you can hide from everyone, but let me assure you, *dwarf*," she hissed in a low whisper, "keeping secrets does not get you far in the company of an honest elf."

She left it at that and trotted far ahead with Seg struggling to hold on to her just as Ever was struggling to hold on to Minx. So Teava knew her secret. At least she knew how to get there and

Ever could let someone who better knew the land lead them to the place she wanted to be.

They continued their trot, occasionally slowing their pace for Ever's sake. She knew that taking the horses was supposed to quicken their travels, but she wondered if they were actually making any better time at all than if they went on foot. She tried to appear as though she were riding with ease, looking around at the scenery that surrounded them. The land had grown barren. There was no one on the road after they had crossed the bridge leaving Brisdale and eventually the crops had become dead all around them. The few trees that were around them sprouted no leaves nor any fruit, and the bushes had dried up and detached from the earth, now just blowing around in the wind like withered and dried up dancers. The ground beneath the hooves of the horses was packed down firmly, cracking in several places. It was thirsty. For some reason, the deadness and desperation in the land around them is what told Ever that they were going in the right direction. Once the sun had set completely, Teava declared that it was time to make camp, claiming that the horses of the elves required some rest. Ever was sure that the horses were not the sole reason for Teava's decision. Quite frankly, she could have blamed it directly on Ever and that would have been fine by her. She desperately wanted to rest and give her sore rump a break from the jostling.

They settled down and Teava started a fire, for which Ever was grateful. She never started a fire on her journey thus far for fear of being spotted by something she was not prepared to deal with. The warmth was something she had missed. Ever did feel a slight pinch of inadequacy, however. Teava had started the fire so quickly. Ever had been perfecting the technique for her whole life, and it still look her a minute or two. Teava started the fire in the time it took Ever to blink. She wasn't even sure how that was possible. But she wasn't going to question a meal next to a warm fire.

To Ever's great delight, Jesper had, in fact, packed the

waybread for their journey. He passed a piece around to everyone. Ever curiously watched Teava. She almost thought the girl would deny the food. She seemed impervious to average daily needs. But she took it, breaking off some for Seg, and ate the rest.

Seg was by far the more interesting of the two. He took the bread and examined it in his long, bony fingers. He put it up to his nose to smell it, then stuck out his very pink tongue to taste it – and immediately cringed away from the food, making the most disgusted expression that Ever had ever seen. She wanted to laugh, but held back the urge. Seg looked around him, searching for – for what? Ever thought surely there was nothing around this place. He went a few steps away and spat on the ground several times to create a mud. He then used his bare feet, which were also bony and seemed too big for his ankles, to stir his spit into the dirt. He picked up the mud with his fingers and placed it on the bread as a spread, and then happily devoured the morsel. Ever's face wrinkled in disgust. Why would anyone ruin the golden honey taste of the waybread with foot mud? It was sickening to her.

Once they had eaten and settled their weary horses, the matter of riding lessons was brought to the attention of the group by Tekla. Ever was devastated with embarrassment. She was right in her earlier assumption that she had been slowing down the group despite the horses. Actually, because of them. Jesper attempted to blow off Tekla's observation, but the other girls wouldn't drop it.

"She rides like that thing does," Tekla said to Jesper, pointing at Seg.

"Seg is a superior rider," Teava came to his defense. "He only needs a beast of an appropriate size. Ever's kind has not ridden since the dawn of time. It is not in her blood, nor in the blood of her kin."

She gulped, watching as Jesper eyed Teava with a look that begged her to expand on her statement. To Ever's relief, Teava looked away, choosing to focus on stroking her own steed instead.

"We can't afford all the time that her riding has cost us today. This is only the first stop of our journey," Tekla informed the group.

"It could very well be the last," Teava negatively countered her. "We shall see what you two have to say. I doubt very much that it might be impressive."

She was angering Tekla, trying to provoke her in some way. It was working. Tekla was much too proud for her own good.

"Look here," Tekla stamped her foot. "I could care less of what you have to say or choose to do. I did not ask, nor was I asked, for you to join us, and we certainly do not need you."

"Do you realize the power that I can bring to your little quest? What can you, a meager little farm girl, possibly do without me?"

"You're not capable of aiding anyone. Your kind is concerned only for your kind. If that were not true, you would have stopped the sorcerer years ago!"

"The sorcerer," Teava countered, "was not our problem. We stay to ourselves. He was on our side of the river and in your kingdom when he first made known his darkness."

"And immediately thereafter, the elves and men turned him away and chased him off. He fled to your side of the river. He could have been stopped there, he could have been killed or forced into another land, but you let him build up his kingdom."

"I did no such thing!" Teava yelled. "You cannot put the fault of the world on the shoulders of one. You cannot blame someone who was just a child!"

"Can't I?" Tekla pushed her. "It seems as though that is what we are all doing today. You should call this stop, right here, your last, and be on your way in the morning. Better yet, do not let us sleep with you – be gone now!"

The girls were both becoming so angry that they were turning red and Ever feared that Teava might take Tekla's last words to heart.

"Stop!" Ever yelled. "I will take riding lessons, and Teava will come with us. The matter has already been settled. Now, we need to rest before morning.

Everyone went to bed on edge, save for Teava who declared that she would be taking the first watch of the night. She settled against her steed, and Seg curled up at her feet to slumber. Ever had a feeling that she wouldn't sleep at all, but she knew that, as long as Jesper stayed, Teava would not wander off in the middle of the night.

Ever almost wished that she had not stopped Teava from arguing. It had sounded as though Tekla knew something about Teava's past. Now Ever was burning with curiosity about who Teava was, about this power that she could bring to the quest, and, most importantly, why she and her people never bothered to wage war against Terrisino if they did, as Tekla had said, have the power. Ever did not like Teava one bit. She seemed like a spoiled princess with a bad attitude. But she knew that she was going to need an army if she truly did plan to bring down Terrisino and win back the pride of the dwarves. For that, she needed Jesper, and Jesper was going to lean on Teava's advice. Thus, she needed to make Teava want to fight as well. Besides, perhaps there would be a way to use Teava and her mysterious power as well.

Ever slumbered peacefully by the fire. Her dreams came far and few between, and by morning she did not remember any of them. She woke up slowly, stretching her arms and rolling her ankles. All of the previous day seemed to have melted away, save for the soreness in her rump from the horse. She was the first to wake, aside from Teava, who Ever did not see in the camp. Seg was curled up around Phantom's legs, snoring as massive snot bubbled up and popped from his nose. Teava would not have simply left behind her companions, Ever knew this, so she deduced that she must have been somewhere near. She looked around the empty expanse and wondered how far Teava would have strayed from her companions. There were some rocks further off, some of them big enough to duck behind. That must have been the only place that Teava could hide.

But when Ever wandered over, she found only Teava's weapons and robes piled up behind the rocks. Ever only stood there staring. What could the girl have been doing? Momentarily, she imagined Teava running around the barren land in nothing but a braid. Had the girl lost her senses? Surely this could not be Jesper's trustworthy advisor. She began to retreat to the group to tell them of her findings. She knew that Tekla would enjoy hearing of the apparent madness of the advisor – a dismal thought, but a true one, Ever knew. She was sure that telling Jesper would upset him, he might even leave the group. But they could not afford to be led by a loon.

"Up, up, everyone up, now!" Although Ever's mouth was open to say nearly the same thing, it was Teava's voice that spoke the words that stirred everyone. She jumped and turned to face a fully clothed, out of breath Teava. "There are goblins coming," she informed them. "Too many for their average mischief. Something must be further off, something chasing them, unless they are mad enough to attack. Either way, we must leave. Now."

"What's behind them?" Tekla asked. "Orcs?"

"Something loud. It was too far off for me to get there and back in time. We could take the goblins, I'm sure, but not whatever is behind them."

Teava had the group all riled up now, hurriedly packing. Teava swung easily onto Minx, and then just as easily pulled Ever up to sit behind her. She gave her no time to protest, barking orders at everyone and commanding Phantom in a tongue Ever had never heard before. Seg climbed up the limbs of Minx, much to her annoyance as she tried to kick him off, and hung himself off of Ever's back. Teava then kicked the horse into high gear, forcing Ever to hold tightly to Teava's back. Just before they left the campsite, Ever heard the faint but definite sounds of armor clanking on weapons. She had almost thought that Teava had made up the story to get them to move.

They rode through the land at such a fast pace that Ever nearly fell off several times. She was relieved, though, not to have the reigns in her hands. She was able to concentrate solely on not falling off, rather than dividing her attention between that and directing the horse. She tried to ignore the fact that the situation was quite degrading. They rode like that for hours with no break. Finally, as the sun was getting low in the sky once more, the elven horses began to slow. The riders all dismounted to give them a break. They continued to walk forward, though. Teava had informed the group that their destination was only a few hours ahead and they would rest there.

The walk was a great relief to Ever's sore body, even as she grew anxious about the approaching ruins. She walked silently, keeping Minx's reigns in her hands now to lead the beast. She was close enough to hear Jesper and Teava's conversation, and by no means was she above eavesdropping.

"… sure we've outrun them?" Jesper asked in concern.

"They're only goblins," Teava responded. "We've left them in the dust. I can check, though, it you'd feel better."

"Best not," Jesper answered quickly. "Tekla knows what you are already. I don't think she's told Ever, but it's best not to confirm anything yet anyway."

There it was again – Teava's secret past that, evidently, only Ever would not know about. It seemed unfair that Teava knew about her but she would remain in the dark about Teava. Lucky for her, though, Teava felt more pressing matters than Ever's own secret to discuss.

"These girls might be simple farmhands, but they might be on to something bigger with this quest. I'm not even sure they are aware of what they are stumbling on."

"What do you mean?" Jesper asked.

"I am positive that those goblins were running from something. The question is, what is bad enough to drive them out of Marzur?"

"You think the girls know?"

"No," she answered, "I think they might have a lucky guess. Terrisino wiped out Isola a quarter century ago. He's been quiet since then. Perhaps something went wrong, something that we don't know about. Perhaps he's been regrouping all these years, and now he is ready to fight again. There's been far too much peace in these lands for far too long."

"What do you believe happened?"

"Truly, I could not say. I only have guesses to offer, but I suppose that my best guess is that he's been building up to something. He wants to come in and take us all out in one fell swoop. He doesn't want us to have a chance to fight."

"You think he's stronger now," Jesper said as a statement rather than a question, asserting her thoughts for her.

"Yes," she confirmed.

"Do you propose, then, that we join our armies with their quest?"

"I propose that we learn more first."

"How?"

"First, we let Ever take us where she wants to be. I believe that she needs to see what has been left there, and I also believe that there are secrets there for everyone to learn." Ever couldn't hold back a grimace – Teava was referring to her dwarfism, and she was not prepared for Tekla or Jesper's reactions. "Then, I propose that we go see my sister."

Jesper was stunned.

"You think that she would help us?"

"I think that she would be so obliged if we were to tell her of a goblin stirring. They belong to her, and she would not like to know that someone was threatening her system."

Jesper fell silent then, considering the peril. He did not seem too keen on the idea.

"It would take too long. We would have to go down to the

docks in Irodhesi, then cross the land from Woodbridge, through Ranton – which is far too close to Terrisino for comfort – then we would have to make it through the forest of Forsride, and all of that to merely hope that we are granted entrance into Zagnoula. Even if they let the three of us through, you are the hold out. They surely won't let you back in. That's many months of journeying for only a small chance of success. By then, Terrisino might as well have wiped out both of our races."

"If we ride from here to the Siren Sea, it will take us directly to the outskirts of Forsride. It will take us five nights in all, even with Ever's riding skills."

"We will not go there," Jesper gasped as his face paled. "It is far too dangerous."

Teava glared at him in a serious manner.

"I don't know what it is about this girl that you will go wherever she asks on whatever ill-conceived quest she sets before you, but you should know that she isn't what she says she is," Teava argued. "She might be no more than a child, and one who can't ride at that, but she's sturdy enough to make it. I can't say the same for the farm girl, but who among us wanted her here anyway?"

"We will not put these girls in danger," Jesper countered, ignoring Teava's snide comment about Tekla.

"You asked me along as your advisor. That is what I am advising."

"You're advising me to put innocents in direct threat."

"They're no longer innocent. They've decided that for themselves."

They fell silent then. Jesper was dead set against the idea, but Ever was in agreement with Teava. If Jesper decided that he would have no part in the quest, then Ever would see to it that Teava led on without him. She knew that Tekla would feel the same.

* * *

Night had fallen as they reached the edges of the Isola Mountains. Ever could not hold back a gasp of awe. The mountains were tall and expansive. They were gray in color, which made the thick layer of fog around the top seem perfectly at place. The fog seemed to drip down the mountain, giving it an air of mystery. Ever was eager to see what was waiting inside. She made the small mistake of asking Teava how they would get inside.

"Why on earth would we go through a graveyard?" Tekla asked scornfully. "Let's go around. It would probably cut time anyway, none of us knows the layout."

"You simpleton! This is where she's been taking us," Teava responded with just as much scorn.

"She's taking us to her family's home, not a tomb!" Tekla exclaimed, failing to put two and two together.

Jesper was quicker in his thoughts, though. His jaw dropped as he turned to Ever. His eyes had shot wide open, to the point where Ever wondered if they might fall out of his face.

"You're a dwarf?" he asked her, completely befuddled.

"You're an *undergroundling*?" Tekla exclaimed, turning her disgust now to Ever. For some reason, Teava came to her defense.

"And you're a *farm girl*," she reminded Tekla, demeaning her as much as she did Ever.

"And you are nothing more than a smug, fire breathing, sorry excuse for a dragon!" Tekla threw right back and Teava.

"You're a dragon?" Ever asked in shock, her own face now mirroring Jesper's as she was finally let in on Teava's secret. She thought it odd that she had been walking by the side of a dragon. She was sure that they were supposed to be big, monstrous beasts – at least, that's what the dwarves had led her to believe. Now she was confused all over again as she was reminded of how little she really knew about the world.

"How could you not know?" Tekla asked, feeling ill at ease

and angry. "Did you not notice her ears? Her eyes? Her name? She travels with a goblin for heaven's sake! You allowed her to come with us and you didn't even know?"

"Yes, I am a dragon, and you're a dwarf, he's an elf, Seg is a goblin, and she's an idiot farm girl," Teava summed up the conversation. "Are we going to argue, or are we going to find out what you came here to find out?"

"She's right, Tekla," Ever told her. "It doesn't matter who any of us are – at least, not to me. We've been united for some reason, surely. You can turn back now if you'd like, but I have much more traveling to do."

She turned toward the mountain, then, leaving Tekla to decide if she wished to travel with a dwarf and a dragon still.

"Ever," Teava said, reaching out to stop her. "You need to know that it is not a pretty sight inside that mountain. We cannot stay long and we cannot be seen. Truly, I don't know what you hope to gain from this, other than heart break, though I do understand the need that you feel. Are you sure you are prepared?"

Ever gulped, now unsure. Still, she nodded her head.

"Very well. Who is with us?" Despite knowing her secret now, everyone agreed. Teava took the lead, striding toward the stone gates ahead of them.

"You're a dwarf?" Jesper repeated, having silently absorbed the argument. Ever gave a solemn nod, to which his only response was silence as he turned again and lost himself to his own thoughts.

As they approached the mountain, Ever was once again taken aback with the beauty of the world beyond her small little mountain home. Carved into the rock on either side of the steel gate were intricate runes that glowed behind the thin layer of fog at the bottom of the mountain. She could not read any of them, of course. The gates themselves were in shambles. Pieces of metal were scattered all about, and Ever had to watch her step so as not to have her shoes pierced by the rusted pieces. At one point, those gates were forged both for beauty and protection. They were formed into perfectly symmetrical and identical shapes. Clearly, whatever had crushed them had done so with brutal force.

"Orcs," Teava informed the group, picking up a rock that was covered in a dried up yellow colored substance. "They probably had a troll with them. I can't imagine what else could smash through a dwarven gate like this one."

"You know a lot about the dwarves," Ever said, "don't you?"

"I was here when they were at their best," she replied, "and after they fell. They were not my friends, nor did I ever stay long. I only came here on business."

They walked past the gates. The inside of the mountain was cold. The air was empty, even void of a draft. It felt ominous and unforgiving. And, Ever realized, it felt dead. She began to fear that she was leading them into a graveyard, just as Tekla had called it.

"Stay in the shadows," Teava told them, moving toward the wall and motioning for everyone to follow her. Ever wished that they could light the torches that hung on the walls, but she knew that Teava would not allow that. It seemed as though she knew what was ahead waiting for them. They pressed on in the dark, where Ever was unable to see what wonders her ancestors had made. As they passed the empty corridor, Ever knew why.

The corridor was empty, but the rest of the mountain was bustling with activity. There were dwarves! Everywhere! Excitedly, Ever jumped forward, ready to be united with her people and tell them of the clan that fled – but Teava held her back. Ever looked up at her, almost began to scold her. But her eyes implored Ever to take a closer look. She stifled her protest and turned back to the cave.

The dwarves were pale, a sickly gray color. Their long beards and hair seemed to be thinning to near baldness. Their eyes were sallow, sunken in… No, they were gone altogether. Black pits rested where their eye balls should have been. They were marching around as if on a mission, but Ever realized that they were mindlessly working through one single task, as if it was all they knew how to do. They were dead, she realized. Dead, just as she had always known, but dead in a way that she had never imagined possible.

Teava led the group further into the mountain, careful still to stay in the shadows. They walked into the next room to discover a factory of sorts. Dwarves were banging hammers on hot metal, the furnace roaring nearby. Each dwarf had a small job, and each of them completed it quickly and thoroughly, seeming not even to notice when sparks flew into their faces or when they slipped and hurt themselves, even if they lost a finger. It was a weapons factory.

Ever quickly realized what had happened. It was Terrisino's magic. She wasn't sure how it was possible, but he must have been powerful enough to seal the dwarves in such a terrible fate. He must truly have been powerful beyond anything that Ever could have imagined. He had trapped the dwarves after death and was using their forgery skills to make weapons. Having seen enough, she backed away and retreated to the empty corridor. The others followed her.

As soon as she was no longer in the danger of being seen by the undead dwarves, Ever began a sprint. She fled as fast as she could past the corridor. She ran past the destroyed gate, not pausing to look at the great workmanship. She ran past the horses. Finally, she collapsed on the ground. As her hands went to her face, she let out a wail of grief and tears flooded down her face. She had heard the rumors from Jesper. But never did she expect that her people would be forever bound as immortal slaves for Terrisino. She mourned for her father, once a great and mighty warrior, now trapped down in the mountains with the rest of their kin. She wept for the smaller dwarves, the children who did not escape and were not spared such a treacherous fate. She bawled for her guilt, as she was given a lucky escape that freed her and spared her life, and kept her in the dark about the true fate of her kin.

She vowed that there would be vengeance for her race. She vowed that she would see Terrisino fall and the dwarves would be set free to rest in peace. She vowed that she would be the one who would deliver the final blow to Terrisino, ending his tyranny as well as his life.

She realized that she had never really understood why she wanted to go on this journey, nor did she ever fully want to be a part of Tekla's mission. But she understood it now. She understood why Tekla followed her out of her quiet village for this quest. She understood why Jesper needed an advisor and why Teava chose to think critically about each and every step. They were not playing a game, and that moment was the last moment of pleasure that Ever would have on her journey. They were on a mission, and the man on the enemy side was far too powerful to take the quest lightly. But that did not matter to her in that moment.

She would kill Terrisino, the Great and Terrible Sorcerer.

As her sobs quieted to a softer hiccup, Jesper finally placed a comforting hand on her shoulder. Tekla offered her condolences. Ever ignored them both, in no mood for the pleasantries, and turned to Teava.

"What do you know of my race?" she asked.

"They were the most skilled artisans and blacksmiths in the land," she told Ever. "Their weapons and gates were the sturdiest, the most durable in any battle. I can only assume that this is the reason that the sorcerer did not let them die peacefully. The weapons made here certainly must be meant for the orcs' use. Perhaps that is the reason why he has been silent for so long after such a victory. He is collecting armor for his warriors. You should rest now, as we have a long road ahead of us. You girls were right to suspect a move from the sorcerer on the horizon. I only hope that we have seen it with enough time to warn the right people and to save our homes." She paused momentarily before glancing back at Ever. "I am truly sorry for the pain that has been brought to you and your kind."

They set up camp right where Ever had collapsed in tears. She wiped away the salty water from her face and laid her head on the bedroll. She did not sleep that night, her eyes always watching the mountain. Her mind was in disarray.

* * *

The Kingdom of Shodalea

Kylon returned home from her flight. She had been keeping watch lately, afraid that her guards might miss something. It took time away from ruling her kingdom, but she'd prefer that to death.

She wasn't entirely sure that she had anything to fear at all. The dragons were the fiercest creatures in any land. Although they preferred to take on the human form, when they did change into the beast, they were taller than six horses stacked on top of each other, with muscle bulging throughout their bodies. The tail of a dragon was a serious weapon and some, like Kylon's, were even spiked. Their teeth were as long as a human was tall, and their fire breath was potent enough to cause massive destruction. It made their goblin servants look like a joke in comparison. They had the strongest defense against anyone who dared to attack. They mostly played offensive, however. If someone possessed something that the dragons wanted, be it gold, land, or simply power, the dragons took it, and usually by force. Never in their history had they lost a battle, but few even had the chance to fight. Most enemies simply buckled in fear when a dragon or two came near and surrendered whatever was demanded of them. It never took the dragons a lot of effort to win.

But Kylon knew that Terrisino had been stirring. It started when several goblins came knocking at her gates, offering freely their eternal servitude. The dragons were not a clan that one willingly served. Kylon suspected that they were seeking the safety of the dragons. She began to investigate and truly found most disturbing news.

Legend tells of a creature more brutal than anything alive. It is death itself, and it cannot be killed. It has the appearance of a cloaked shadow, and rides a black horse that oozes putrid filth from its eyes, nose, and any wounds. It is the purest form of evil, its weakness unknown. Its name is the Vehsi. Kylon had seen three such creatures in recent nights. She was not even sure if the dragons could take on the man sized death beasts.

Kylon had known about the death of the dwarves when it had happened. She knew that they were trapped as eternal slaves for Terrisino's army. She knew and she had done nothing. The dragons lorded a certain amount of power over every single being, including Terrisino himself. No one dared mess with them, knowing full well that the battle would be the lost before it was even conceived. It had given the dragons a hot head, it seemed, and they did not intervene in the affairs of others, save for when they took something. It gave Kylon an uncaring attitude when the dwarves ended as they had. But if Terrisino might have come up with a way to trap the dragons as he had the dwarves, Kylon could only imagine that the world would burn in the flames of Terrisino's wrath. Something had to be done, beginning with the Vehsi.

* * *

Soon, Ever had composed herself completely and was able to sleep. It was, thankfully, a dreamless sleep. She had worn herself out to the point where she fell into the deepest slumber of her life. The next morning, her eyes felt red and sore, and her face felt dried up from the salt of the tears. She had to splash her face with a bit of drinking water. Then she was ready to join the group and discuss their next move.

"We have to get the elven armies," Tekla stated loudly, so as to be heard over all the other voices, "and take down Terrisino now! He won't expect it. We must go back to Brisdale, and maybe the elves of Sedona might lend an army as well."

"You will be the death of us all," Teava hissed.

"We will never get past the orcs of Ugroryx and Towhorth," Jesper humored the girl's childish naiveté rather than scold her. "Not all the elves in the land could do it. We know already that they have dwarven weapons. There could be thousands of other secrets that we have not yet uncovered. We'd never live to see Terrisino in person."

"It would be a surprise attack," Tekla countered. "They'll be unprepared."

"The orcs live at the ready for war. The surprise advantage would last to kill a hundred orcs before they slaughtered a hundred elven armies."

"We need to talk to the dragons," Ever broke in quietly. Everyone heard her despite her small voice, and they all stared, awaiting further explanation. "Teava is right," she began, trying to sound like she knew what she was talking about. Really, she was only basing it off of hearing Tekla and Teava argue over what Teava was. "They are powerful. We can go further with the dragons than we can with the elves, dwarves, and men combined. We must return to Teava's homeland and pray that they hear us out."

She looked to Teava. Even though it had been her plan and Ever simply repeated it, she did not look happy to hear the proposal. Teava looked around the group, expecting protest. No one spoke, perhaps too stunned by the idea of fighting with dragons, so Teava took that as opportunity to move forward.

"If anyone does not agree with Ever," she said as she packed her things, "then please, do not let us hold you hostage. Go home. Maybe we shall be reunited again one day. Maybe the world will no longer be free by then. The decision is yours, but do not hold us back, either. Ever is right, it has become clear to me. I will fight with her. Flee now, if you must."

She turned to face the group and see who had begun to flee. But she was taken aback momentarily. Everyone had packed and mounted their horses in the time she had given her speech – even the dwarf had managed to climb her mare.

"We need to ride to the Siren Sea," she said after a brief pause to regain her composure. She turned and began to ride without giving anyone a chance to argue.

"We can't go there," Tekla gasped. Her face paled.

"If anyone does not agree with me, then please," Teava repeated her earlier sentiment, "do not let me hold you hostage. Go home." This time, she did not look back, knowing that everyone would be following her despite their reservations about the destination.

The ride this time was filled with anxiety. Jesper had given Ever some tips on riding as they went, which helped ease their troubled minds a bit and made the ride a lot smoother for Ever. The morning passed in a small amount of time, it seemed to the group. Before long at all, Ever saw a fire in the distance. Or, perhaps, it was just the smoke left over from a large fire.

"What's that?" she asked Jesper, who was fixated on the destruction with a sad look in his eyes.

"The city of Ardonia," he answered softly, melancholy in his voice.

"Do we ride through it?"

Everyone looked to Teava.

"If it is Terrisino," she said, "they might already be spies. Perhaps he has no use for a city of men, though, and has already granted them eternal death."

"There's plenty of use for a city of men," Tekla argued.

Ever rolled her eyes.

"Maybe we should investigate anyway," she offered. "Even if we stay far away. We should know the state of the city. Perhaps it is information we could use."

Teava seemed to agree and urged Phantom forward.

Upon approaching the city, it was obvious that the destruction was relatively recent. There were still fires burning in some of the buildings. Not a single cottage or even market stand had been left untouched. Even without entering the city, the group could see right away that there was no life, nor undead life, within the city limits. They had halted just outside the perimeter, and stood watching the flames dance and transform into giant plumes of smoke above them. Tekla shed a tear for her fallen kin. Jesper touched his hand to his forehead, and then his chest, the traditional sign in the elven kingdom for sorrow and prayer. Even Teava, who Ever would have thought unmoved, bowed her head in respect.

And so they stood, respectful and quiet, mourning with Tekla, just as they had for Ever.

Until a sudden movement in a bush behind them caused everyone to jump into readiness, alert hands flying to their weapons. Teava beat everyone to the punch, flying off of her steed in a swift backflip and unsheathing her sword as she landed right on top of the culprit. Ever could hear his startled cry of pain, and in seconds Teava had him off the ground where he had crouched, her sharp shining sword lying precariously against this throat as he pressed against her. He could not even gulp in fear, for the movement it caused would make her slit his throat.

"P-p-please," he said. A mere human, Ever realized. Perhaps a lucky escapee from Ardonia. "I mean no t-t-trouble."

"Who are you?" Teava hissed. Ever and Tekla had yet to recover from the shock of Teava's quick capture, but Jesper was already off his horse and searching the other bushes. He pulled out a woman from one not too far. She refused to walk, or even stand up, so Jesper dragged her out by the hood of her worn out brown cloak as she kicked and screamed. "Shut her up," Teava yelled. Her presence itself scared the girl into silence. "Who are you," she repeated, "and are there any more?"

"N-n-no more, miss," the man answered. "My n-name is Cassio Laham, and this is M-M-Merenda Di Meo. We're actors.

Well, she's my ap-p-prentice. We saw the orcs, but we d-d-didn't go help. We waited. We ran."

"Let the man go," Jesper said. "He's going to soil himself. They are no threat."

Teava's stature loosened, but she did not completely release him.

"Orcs? How long ago?"

"A few nights. Maybe a week. I don't know. I lost track," he admitted. "They came and stayed for a while. I would have gone back, but... But they were eating my entire crew."

Cassio was almost in tears, making his rugged good looks somewhat ironic. His muscle was clearly not gained from fighting, but maybe from stage setting often. He was no warrior. Merenda, on the other hand, looked like she could have put up a fight. Her muscular body rivaled Teava's, and the fire in her eyes showed that she was complying only because her friend was captive against Teava's blade.

"Terrisino," Jesper said, his fists clenching. "He is going to pay for the pain he's inflicted on these families." His eyes flickered to Ever. Her pain in the Isola Ruins was not forgotten to him.

"Yes," Cassio said, his tone taking on a lot of courage that even he seemed surprised by. "They ate my children. We ride to his kingdom and return with his head."

"Let him go," Tekla told Teava this time, her eyes alight with a new plan. "Perhaps we need all the friends that we can get."

"Two humans will do nothing for us," snapped Teava, "when even their own soldiers could do nothing for them."

"She's a sorceress!" Cassio pointed to Merenda. "We can help you plenty!"

"Cassio!" Merenda hissed, and rightly so. Teava's grip tightened on Cassio's throat again.

"W-what I mean is," he stuttered, fear trickling down his face as his courage dissipated, "her sorcery could compliment your prowess quite well, m-m'lady."

"Or she will turn on us the minute I release you," Teava countered.

"He's far too cowardly," Tekla told her, "and she'll do only as he says, else she would have already let you kill him."

"What use do we have for a coward?"

"We have little use for him," allowed Tekla, "but she could get us places."

"Her loyalty lies with him," the blade pressed on his throat, causing a droplet of blood to roll down his neck, "not with us."

"B-but my loyalty could lie with you," Cassio begged, "if you just release me." He tried to squirm out of her grip, but it only caused a bit more blood to leak.

"Release him," Jesper commanded firmly. He had been staring into Merenda's eyes and, in fact, still was, reading into her mind. Teava looked at him now, shocked.

"They could be spies sent after us."

"They aren't," he stated simply, eyes on Merenda still.

"Terrisino has eyes everywhere," Teava reminded him. "As your advisor –"

"As your commander," he countered quickly, finally turning to face her, "I am telling you to let go of him." He waited, eyes now boring into Teava's. She began to slowly and reluctantly release the man. The minute he was free, he dropped to the ground and choked, hands flying to his neck. Pulling them away, he examined the miniscule amount of blood and paled, closing his eyes promptly and breathing with exaggerated concentration. Ever almost wished that Teava had killed him. He seemed as though he would be worse to deal with than Tekla. "They are not spies. They are people without a home now, and they will come with us. Won't they, Cassio?"

"Y-y-yes sir," he answered, still not fully recovered. "Thank you, kind elf master."

Jesper ignored his gratitude.

"Besides, we have no reason to fear Terrisino as of yet. He

has no idea who we are."

That did not reassure or please Teava. She answered only with a glare.

"Precisely right, Master Elf," Cassio replied.

"You can call me Jesper. This is Teava of Abrya, Tekla of Ioka and Ever also of Ioka." Ever did not miss the fact that Jesper had withheld both her own and Teava's own actual origins. "We are off on a dangerous road. I will give you the option; you can make yourself a home in this rubble and never speak of us again, or you can follow behind us without question."

"Where would we go, master Jesper?"

"That, my very lucky friend, is a question. I believe I asked – very nicely – that you refrain from such things. You see, in times like this, you cannot trust a man you just met – especially one who just watched his entire city burn down while orcs dined on the flesh of his family and did nothing to stop it."

Cassio's face fell in shame.

"Of course not, master elf," he halfbreedered.

"So what, then, is your choice?"

For a small second, Cassio looked to Merenda. She portrayed nothing happy on her expression. The anger that pressed in her glower only worsened when Cassio gave his reply.

"We will follow you, master elf, wherever you go. We will offer our most sincere loyalty and our best defense," he said, knowing that he had no home left and fearing to be left to fend for himself. Cassio was, as Teava had put, a coward, and he wholly relied on the aid of other people for his survival. "If only, sir Jesper, you allow me one quick run into the city. You see, I need my props if I am to truly offer assistance."

"We don't care for your entertainment," Teava snapped, annoyed to her core.

"It's too dangerous to risk the flames," Jesper ignored her. "We must press on."

"Sir elf, I must implore you to find a way," Cassio begged.

"I'll do it myself, it will take just a few minutes. You see, I am no great elf, nor do I know alchemy, but I have talents that lie elsewhere. I beg of you, master Jesper."

Jesper rolled his eyes, but conceded anyway.

"Teava, go and fetch his things. It's far too dangerous," he added when he saw that Cassio was about to protest, "for such a delicate man to go in. I'll stay out here and keep the rest of them safe. Cassio, draw her a map."

Jesper turned, willing to say no more on the subject. He walked a distance away from them and took watch at a place where he could see the most. He was very formal in stature, clearly expecting his orders to be carried out without delay. Teava gritted her teeth but did as she was told. She dashed off into the city and was soon invisible behind the smoke.

Ever studied Merenda, willing to see what Jesper had seen in her that made him fight his own advisor just to keep her around. At first, Ever saw only the what she expected of those that carried the human form. She had long dark hair that waved in disorder, tied behind her head in a leather strap with loose locks hanging pretty much everywhere. Her white skin showed no freckles or blemish at all, save for red cheeks. Her high cheek bones accentuated the heart shape of her face. Her dark lips were full, and behind them stood perfectly straight white teeth. She was absolutely stunning in a natural way. Perhaps that was all Jesper saw in her – surely his elven eyes appreciated such beauty.

But then Ever looked below the girls thick, black brows and straight into her pale, ghastly blue eyes. She was stricken by the odd color, and horrified when she saw the images behind them.

Suddenly, the images were no longer behind Merenda's eyes – or maybe Ever had simply looked too deep and was pulled into the images.

She ducked as a dragon – at least ten feet tall and red in color – nearly flew into her. Turning, she saw it light an entire village aflame in one simple breath of fire. Innocent villagers ran in every direction, screaming, most of them lit up like live candles, until they fell and were engulfed by the flames. Brown, muddy, and bloody creatures came from behind Ever, paying her no mind at all. They hissed, grunted, snorted, and yelled as they ran past. Some had pointed ears, some had no ears at all. Their teeth seemed to have been filed to a point, weapons that never left their bodies, and some had slit tongues. Some limped, some ran on all fours, but they all had this in common: they were foul, disgusting, and ugly. Somehow, even though she had never seen one, she knew that they were all orcs. They squealed past to the village, where some people had escaped, and some had put out the fire on their own bodies – only to be devoured by the orcs, dead or alive. Suddenly, there was another high pitched squeal, so disturbing that Ever shrank to the ground, covering her ears and screaming, making her own high pitched sound. She tried to turn, slowly opening her eyes, to see the source of the hideous noise. Her heart fluttered in sporadic and painful bursts when she saw it.

There was a horse, black from tip to tip, and sitting atop it appeared to be the embodiment of death. It was dressed in a black cloak, its hood over its head. It seemed, however, that it did not have a face at all. It was simply a shadow beneath the hood. It raised its black sword into the air as dozens of dragons followed its command, flying in from behind the rider and lighting ablaze everything in sight. Even some of the orc army fell to the flames.

The rider screeched louder and louder, higher and higher. Ever's own screams were the only thing contesting it. She tried to crack her eyes open again, unaware that she had closed them in pain, and saw the rider slowly lower his sword – only to point it directly at her.

Kill the dwarf.

The words seemed whispered in the air, swirling around her like a gust of wind from the wings of the mightiest dragon.

"Ever!" it screamed, and her body was being pushed this way and that as she struggled. "Ever!"

And the scene was gone, replaced by the oddly welcoming sights of the burning Ardonian city and her friends, shaking her as hard as they could as she continued to stare at Merenda's now blank eyes. Ever was now crumbled on the ground, her throat red hot with flames. Jesper was on one side and Teava and Tekla on the other. Cassio crumpled in fear away from her, clutching a trunk to his chest while Merenda coolly stared at Ever.

"What's with the screaming?" Teava demanded. "I nearly had to leave the actors things behind." The way she spat the words made it clear that she had thought about leaving them behind out of spite.

"What happened, Ever?" Jesper demanded. "What's wrong?"

"Yes, talk to us," Tekla plead in a desperate voice. "That was bizarre beyond what I can deal with."

"I know what you saw," Merenda spoke ominously. "It has not yet come."

"What do you mean?" Ever begged, hardly able to get the words out of her throat. Jesper handed her the drinking water, which she gratefully swallowed. "Who was that?"

"That," Merenda began, "was a creation of Terrisino, a tale of legend, thought by most to be no more than a myth. Like yourself, it seems."

Ever gulped. Already her secret had been uncovered.

"What did it want with me?"

"You carry something," she told Ever, "that it needs to destroy."

"What do I have?" Ever made a show of throwing her daggers on the ground and emptying her sack. "I have nothing so important! It can have it all!"

"You carry the fate."

"What does that mean?" Ever begged.

"I cannot tell you. I do not know."

"We have to keep going," said Jesper, rising and pulling

Ever up with him. "We have to get you to a safe place."

"And you think a safer place is the Serpent Sea?" Tekla laughed sarcastically. "What if they kill her there?"

"We need to get to the dragons," he replied.

"Yes, let's cross to the dangerous side of the river," she began incredulously, "and at the most dangerous point, and while we are at it, let's find shelter among the most dangerous creatures in the land. That's precisely what I think of when I want to be somewhere safe."

"There are creatures far more worthy of that title," Ever replied ominously, receiving a terrified glance from most of the group.

"The vision did not take place near the water," Merenda told them. "If we are careful, we should pass without trouble."

"Oh, so now the witch girl is a part of 'we'?" It was Teava's turn to be incredulous.

"I do not receive visions without divine intervention," Merenda stated frankly. "The fact that I have been gifted with the knowledge of the fate means that my deities have given me the task of keeping it out of the hands of the enemy, who seems to have received the same knowledge. She will be hunted," she continued, looking into the eyes of every member of the group, save for Ever who shied away from such contact, "and many attempts will be made for her life. She has been chosen to carry the fate, and we have been chosen each for specific reason to guard her. This is no task for the faint of heart. Can you bear the burden you've been appointed?"

"You, then, are convicted to stay with us?" Jesper asked with a little uneasiness. He had expected them to come along simply because they were without home, not because they believed in the mission.

"I have known for some time," Merenda stated, "that I was going to leave Ardonia. I have known that something was going to come and lead me away. I have been told enough through the visions I have seen. It seems that I have finally been shown where I need to go. I will stand by the dwarf."

Her somber tone calmed down the tempers and nerves of the group. Everyone stood a little taller, even cowardly Cassio, as each member vowed themselves to see the succession of the fate.

And so began the alliance of men, elves, dragons, sorcerers, and dwarves, united to end the greatest evil that would be seen even in the lives of the immortal beings.

III.

The Kingdom of Shodalea

Kylon was being rushed to the dungeons. On a routine lookout, some of her guards had found something peculiar. Having been informed of the moving goblin armies, they took no chances and grabbed the short, stout creatures. They had found them on the northern edge of the Fardocain forest, just across the river. They mistook the creatures for goblins from high up in the air, but soon realized they were something else entirely.

Upon entering the cold rock walls of the dungeon, Kylon could hear the creatures arguing for their freedom, as if they did not realize that they were being held captive by the dragons. She was led to their cell where they were chained to the wall in ankle and hand cuffs. Once she emerged from the shadows, the creatures quickly fell silent.

They were both short, neither reaching five feet in height. Their bulky armor had been removed and piled in the cell. Kylon realized that it had been crafted with precision, the metal work the best she had ever seen.

"I have been delivered two dwarves each with their own brain," she addressed them curiously. Her words sparked anger in the fatter, red haired one.

"Dwarves are smarter than you think, you filthy lizard. Just you wait and see."

"Thiflar," the black haired one warned his friend.

"I did not mean to offend you," Kylon said in a tone that made it obvious that she did not care if she had. "I only meant that the minds of the dwarves have not been free from Terrisino for a quarter of a century."

"That's preposterous," Thiflar grunted. "We would sooner die than be part of his evil. Which is precisely what we did."

"Yes," she allowed, not caring to waste time arguing with them. "Which begs another question. How is your existence possible?"

In answer, Thiflar merely spat in her direction and struggled against his chains. Kylon turned then to the dwarf with the better temperament.

"I am Kylon of Shodalea," she told him, "queen of the dragon clans. Forgive me for these rather unpleasant circumstances in which we meet," she said without bothering to see if they would forgive her. "Tell me, how shall I address you?"

He paused only briefly, and decided to cooperate – after all, the dragon seemed to know more about the dwarves than he did.

"I am Vek Rockheart of Isola. This is Thiflar Steelhand."

"Well, then, Vek," she said, "it seems I have a myth in my dungeons. Do you mind telling me precisely how that is possible?"

Vek thought only momentarily before deciding that honesty would be the best approach when dealing with a dragon queen.

"We fled when the city began to fall," he told her. "There are thirteen of us total."

Thiflar gaped at him, unconvinced that revealing secrets was better than death.

"A well-kept myth, for nearly a quarter of a century," Kylon reveled. "Why should you choose now to come out of hiding and risk your secrecy?"

"One of ours is gone. We were searching for her when

your, er, friends picked us up."

"So there is a lost dwarf amongst us, is there? These are troubling times for secrets to be wandering out in the open."

"Precisely," Thiflar hissed. "So if you'll just free us, we'll be on our way to find her."

"I'm afraid, master Thiflar, that won't be possible. You see, by accident or otherwise, I have under my care the only beings who have ever escaped from Terrisino's wrath. Have you ever wondered, while you were holed up wherever you were, why it was so important for him to demolish the race of the dwarves?"

"Well, of course we have," Thiflar scoffed at her. "It is because we are the greatest warriors there has ever been. We were a threat to his tyranny."

Kylon laughed.

"You cannot fault the dwarven folk for their pride. But no, my boy, not quite. There is a tale of two lines of heritage in the dwarven kingdom. Neither of the lines is purely dwarven. One line is mixed with the potent blood of a sorcerer, and the other with the strength that flows in the blood of a dragon. Perhaps it is only a myth – I'm sure you could not even think of a dwarf mixing races, much less two doing such a thing, just as I would have presumed that my dragons would honor their duties before love. I have been proven wrong only once before. I no longer know if the myth is without truth. Think of that power – a dwarven sorcerer, or a dwarven dragon. Either standing alone – what a creature to behold! But imagine if the blood of all three ran through the same veins. That is what Terrisino feared.

"His power grows every day, and with it his monsters. There is no saying that the dwarven halfbreed would have been proven strong enough to stop him, but imagine the fear he had when first the rumor surfaced. Surely, were you in his position, you would have done the same thing. I know I would have."

"That is a great story," Vek began, "but neither of us comes from a line that was tainted with the blood of another man. So why continue to hold us if we are of no use to you?"

"Oh, sweet Vek, never put yourself down in such a way. I'll make use of you yet. Just be thankful that you'll be safe from the forces stirring outside my kingdom… for the time being, that is."

Leaving the dwarves with her last cryptic warning, Kylon returned to the shadows. Fear suddenly sinking into the feisty dwarven hearts, Thiflar and Vek frantically thrashed against their restraints.

* * *

As the group of mismatched races walked around the flaming city of Ardonia, Ever couldn't help but be shaken up. She was going to be hunted by the beast with no face. Her specifically. She shuddered, the warmth of the flames having practically no effect on her chilled body whatsoever. It was maddening to her, too, that Teava had begun to act different. She wouldn't even look at Ever since she and Merenda had shared the vision. She was stiffer and more angry than usual, if that were even possible. She knew something. Ever didn't quite realize how she knew, or why she would not offer to help Ever with whatever fate she evidently possessed, but Ever knew that she knew something and had decided, for whatever reason, not to share it with the group.

Going around the city rather than through it had been taking a significantly bigger amount of time than Teava or Jesper had hoped. During that time, Ever and Merenda had not locked eyes once. It was on purpose, as Ever surely did not want another vision like that. But she was still left with the image of the girl's pale blue eyes. They were beautiful, and for some reason they made her think of the dwarves that she had left behind.

What would they think of her now, she wondered. A real adventurer. The only think to be done was to kill a troll, this giving her a real entitlement to her family name.

Her dead family.

She would have to complete her mission of vengeance, for she needed to tell the others what had become of the dwarves at Isola.

She shivered again at the thought of her slain kinsfolk, left for slavery rather than rest.

But her somber thoughts were finally cut off when Teava and Jesper halted the entire group. Ever finally caught up to them, having fallen several steps behind to be alone with her thoughts. She heard the reason for the stop before she saw it.

They had not yet reached the Siren Sea, but now impeding their path, just a short distance from them, was an orcish pack snorting loud enough that the sound reached the group long before they were close enough for the orcs to see them. The light from their fire revealed slime and mud on their bodies, glinting off of it like a diamond made of rubbish. The smell was equally disgusting. It was the smell of rotting carcasses and mold. Ever had to hold back a gag. Worst of all was the scene above the fire pit. Turning on the skewers were the unmistakable shapes of human torsos. Ever was able to keep her gag from escaping her mouth, but the more delicate Cassio had to turn away to be sick.

"Who is armed?" Teava asked. "And further, who can fight?"

"We're going to fight?" Cassio asked appalled. Ever almost thought he was going to be sick again. "Can't we go around? They've not seen us yet."

"It is quicker to kill them," she replied curtly. "There are not many, and besides, whatever we kill not cannot kill us later. You may wait in the bushes, if you wish."

"With all due respect, m'lady, I can fight." Cassio palmed the sword as he spoke. "I just do not think it is in our best interest as of yet."

"The orcish brutes will die. Tekla," she summoned the girl, passing her a short sword. "Anyone with courage, we go now and show them no mercy." Ever drew her ax as Merenda and Jesper began to fit their bows with arrows. "Let none escape, lest they might alert Terrisino to our existence." Cassio drew his weapon and Teava lifted hers high in the air. "Fight for the fallen!" she yelled as they began to charge forward, rushing into the pack.

The first orc fell to Teava's sword, as she sliced his head off with ease. All the orcs were now alerted and scrambling.

Ever was immediately surrounded by more than she could count in a single glance. She swung her axe, taking down one of them as its guts splashed back into her face. Quickly, she hefted her axe from the dead torso and swung it as she turned, putting more power in the movement and taking down two orcs at once, severing both torsos in half. Hearing a piggish grunt behind her, she turned again, bringing her axe straight up and down on his head. Behind him was another – but Ever had no time to pick up her axe before the orc fell dead. An arrow to the eye. Risking a glance in the direction from which it came, she saw Merenda preparing to launch another. It went straight through the heard of an orc that had approached Ever's side. Merenda bid Ever to pay attention.

She turned and thrust her axe into an orcish pig. And another. She was quickly becoming drenched in sweat and orc blood. She plunged for more of them, now closing the gap between herself and Teava. Both backing into each other, they fought with their backs pressed together. The orcs began to thin out, the ground littered with their bodies. Soon, Ever could see clearly the arrows that plunged into the bodies of the remaining pigs. The last one fell to her axe.

The group stood on edge, catching their breath and searching for any stray orcs. There did not seem to be any. Merenda and Jesper gracefully hoped down from their battle stations, bows still in hand and eyes darting in search for any runners.

"Is anyone hurt?" Ever panted, her eyes landing immediately on Tekla's bloody arm. *I cannot return her to Akim damaged,* she thought, her vow still fresh in her mind. She rushed over to examine her. The gash was made by the steel of the orcish weapons. They were heavy and able to easily amputate an arm. Tekla was lucky that it was little more than a deep gash. Ever did not feel the same luck. "Who taught you to fight?" she demanded. "Your father extended a great kindness to me, and I do not intend on returning the favor by letting his daughter die." She began to douse the wound in water. "The orcs are infested with nasty infection. Do you think their weapons are not also infested? You may be lucky not to have lost your arm, but what when you develop gangrene?" She would have continued to scold her, but Merenda pushed her aside, taking Tekla's arm in her own hands. She let one hand hover over the wound as she closed her eyes and whispered something in a tongue that Ever had never heard before. Neither had Tekla, it seemed, as her first instinct was to pull away. She was held firmly by Merenda's iron grip.

Slowly, her words began to fade, and her eyes reopened. In amazement, Ever watched as the wound began to seal itself.

"What did you do to me?" Tekla demanded.

"I told you," Cassio said, examining his own freshly healed wound, "she's a sorceress."

"So one of you isn't completely useless," Teava said bitterly.

They bickered over the battle's body count but Ever turned her attention away from them and back to Merenda, looking her in the eyes at long last.

"Thank you," she told her. "For saving me and Tekla both."

"I told you," she began. "The deities have chosen me to protect the one who carries the fate. I dare not let them down."

Ever nodded gravely, sensing the girl's loyalty and devotion to the cause. She realized that Merenda was of value to her quest.

"We need to keep moving," Jesper said, putting out the orcs' fire and tipping their skewered food onto the ground. "Let's try to end this before it goes too much longer."

The horses had stayed away from the battle, but now rejoined the riders upon Teava's call. Seg came back with them, clinging on to Phantom's back leg as the steed trotted gracefully back to his master.

"The sea is not much farther now. We will make camp after we cross it."

Ever gave her mare to Merenda and Cassio and rode behind Jesper on Andale. The ride was easier that way, clinging to the elf who had ridden most of his life.

* * *

Ever was glad when the remainder of the journey to the Siren Sea went was uneventful. The adrenaline of the first battle, for those of them that it was, indeed, their first, was only just wearing off. They were beginning to ache where they had been bruised. Any amount of riding was becoming increasingly hard for Ever, so when they approached the sea and Teava announced that it was time to dismount, she could not have been more pleased.

The first thing that Ever noticed was that it was more of a marsh than a sea. The water did not look terribly deep, and there was plenty of green land throughout it to step on. It was murky water, and it was covered in green plants. The air directly above it seemed to be thick with a misty fog.

"We will travel through fast," Teava announced, "and do not look into the water."

"What's in the water?" Cassio asked with a great deal of fear in his voice.

"The sirens," Merenda answered ominously. "Creatures of the dark, half woman, half fish. They lure you in with their sad songs and beautiful faces. They draw you far into the water. Once you are beyond the safety of the land, their beauty is transformed into something so hideous, you would swear that you imagined it all. They suck your body dry of blood and devour your flesh."

"We cannot go through there," Tekla gasped, her face drained of color.

"All that may be true," Teava said, casting an annoyed glance at Merenda, "but if you do not look at the creatures, we will never have to find out for certain. We set off now." She turned to the sea. "Do not look into the waters, do not listen to the songs. Keep your thoughts straight ahead of you, and we shall pass to the first stop quickly."

Ever's heart was filled with fear and dread, but she knew that this was the path that her destiny was leading her, for whatever reason. So she took a deep breath and stepped forward, following Teava's lead into the marshy sea.

She tried to stare straight ahead, watching the swing of Teava's pony tail. But the first step she took plunged her ankles in cold, watery mud, and she gasped unsuspecting as she looked down to see the marshy water swim around her feet before she could catch herself. The water, although murky, was somehow still translucent and she knew the faces of the sirens would be easy to see.

It's their trick, she thought, quickly lifting her head to focus on the journey that was ahead. She kicked through the mud. Every time the tall grass blades touched her wrists, she couldn't help but jump in fear. Merenda's words were enough warning to paralyze her into focusing ahead.

Something was living in the water with the sirens. Ever could feel the long, thin body pass around her legs and swim away every now and then. It gave her the creeps. She wanted to run as fast as she could, but she knew that Teava had set the pace as slow as she had for a reason. There was too much danger to quicken the pace. Each step she took threatened to force her to slip into deeper waters. There would be no stopping the sirens from devouring her flesh then.

The air began to hum. It was just a soft hum at first, but then a melody formed.

And then words, and Ever was able to understand them.

A sad song. It was a song of stolen souls and a horrible slaughter. It was the story of the siren's people. There was mirth before. But now their kin were enslaved.

Just like the dwarves.

"It's such a sad song," Ever told Tekla in a hushed tone.

"It's a happy one," Tekla argued. "It's hopeful."

"Don't you hear it?" Ever asked, amazed that Tekla had heard any hope at all. "They were enslaved and slaughtered. That is not hopeful. It's a tragedy."

"What? No. They're singing of overcoming their hardships. They are talking of their treacherous queen, but they can stop her. They want our help."

"You're wrong," Cassio interrupted, evidently having eavesdropped. "They're singing of a lost lover. They are missing his warmth. They are calling out to fill the void."

"You're all wrong," Teava pointed out loudly, having also heard them. "They are singing a spell to each of us individually. It works at our inner thoughts and calls to us by our specific situations. Do not flatter yourselves as heroes or lovers. They only intend to lure you into the waters, just as Merenda has already told you. Do not hear the words. It is merely the first step to your eventual doom. Concentrate on your own thoughts."

Another trick of the sirens. Ever tried to listen to Teava. She didn't think about the song. She didn't even think about the enslaved dwarves that the sirens were using against her. Instead, she thought about Teava's mesmerizing swords. Weaponry seemed reasonably safe to think about. She thought of the glow. The silver metal from which it was crafted seemed to give off a white glow around the blade when the sun caught it. She thought of the intricate patterns wrapped around it. Before, she had merely thought of them as decoration, but now, knowing that she was a dragon, she wondered if there was more to it. If they were inscriptions of some kind. She wondered if the blade that Teava had given to Tekla had the same inscriptions, and if that was why a simple farm girl, as Tekla truly was, was able to wield it so well. She wondered about Teava's own fighting style. She was graceful, each movement made in a purposeful way, as if the art of fighting was a dance to her.

The snake like thing in the water passed around her ankles again.

Think of something else, Ever old herself.

She wondered about their destination. She had gone to see the elven kingdom of Brisdale, and it was filled with awe striking sights. She had gone to see the dwarven kingdom, which was once built spectacularly into the mountain. And now she was going to see the dragon kingdom. Oh, if only her clan could see her now, what stories she would have for them!

"There is something in the water," Cassio said, stricken still with fear.

Ever wished that Teava had done away with the coward, but still, she was glad to have someone else mention the very thing that she was fearing.

"The Sarpa," Merenda informed him, seeming to be the one who liked to inform the group in general. "A creature that, too, can get into the minds of its prey. He will trick your mind into thinking your friend is the enemy. You will hack each other into tiny pieces that he can then eat. He likes to separate the limbs, but keep the head in tact so that he can see the fear in your face. Thank your deities that he is not hungry today. There is nothing you can do to defend yourself from him."

Most of the company had gone silent during her speech, the fear already sinking in. Teava and Jesper were the only ones who kept walking without paying mind to Merenda and instead merely watching the sky ahead. They must have already heard of the Sarpa. It made Ever wonder if they believed that they could conquer it themselves.

Or who it was that they were willing to sacrifice for the

cause.

But such thoughts were distracting to Ever, and she had to rid herself of them. She chose instead to take Merenda's suggestion and be grateful that he was not hungry.

The company continued to slosh through the marshy waters, occasionally coming upon a piece of damp land that stuck out from the shallow waters. Ever was grateful for those parts, which gave her cold feet a chance to air out just a bit before being plunged back into the icy water. Her toes had become painfully cold and then numb altogether. She found herself thinking about that rather than the sirens songs, which did not help her cope with the discomfort, but it was better than the alternative.

They all turned as they heard a loud splash behind them.

"Cassio!" Merenda screamed as he plunged face first into the waters. She ran to him, but Jesper caught him first, by the collar of his tunic. Ever chanced a look into the water and saw something that would haunt her nightmares.

The creature had changed in an instant, at first a beautiful woman with sad eyes and a fish tail for the lower half of her body. But when Jesper pulled Cassio away, she changed her human half into a terrifying thing – her true form, Ever recognized. It was blue and scaly, to match her tail. Her hair was gone, giving light to a bald head like a snake woman. Her eyes were red, with no pupils and no white around them. The scariest part was her mouth. No longer did the soft, kissable lips show. Now it was simply an opening that showed teeth sharpened to a point and a tongue that was split down the middle. The songs in the air were no longer sweet, no longer soft and sad. Filling the air now was a shriek so horrid, Ever had to cover her ears. Everyone did, except Cassio, who was struggling against Jesper to reach the siren.

The waters began to shake, the tender earth below their feet seeming to shake with it. The sirens were all screaming, abandoning their ruse. Ever did not have to look to know that they were all changing into their true forms. The calm she once had walking through the waters was now gone.

"Run!" Teava yelled, struggling to be heard over the screeching. She went to Jesper and together they worked to drag Cassio.

Ever and Tekla needed no other instruction. Clutching their ears to their heads, they broke out into as close to a sprint as they could manage through the mud. Merenda dragged behind, worry for Cassio clouding her will to run to safety. Seg and the horses had already gone very far ahead, their wild instincts already rushing them into madness.

As the water quaked and sloshed, drenching the company from head to toe, the sirens reached out of the water, grabbing hold of whatever they could. Luckily, as they tried to grab at the ankles of their victims, they merely passed right through as if they were beings of the spirit realm, unable to touch those who were not under their spell. That did not stop Tekla from screaming at the top of her lungs every time it happened, adding to the shrieks and chaos around them.

"It's Cassio they want," Teava yelled, struggling to be heard over the noise. "He's still under their spell! Faster!"

The group struggled to obey her command. The faster they went, the harder the mud tried to pull them under. Twice, Ever tripped, only to quickly right herself lest she should end up the sirens secondary meal. Looking back at Jesper and Teava, she knew that Cassio had messed up in a bad way, and she feared that it was only going to cause someone to forfeit their life to the sirens. As she watched him thrash and fight to be in the water with the fish beasts, she silently prayed that it would be his life that was forfeited and not either of the brave souls that were currently fighting for his life.

They ran for what seemed like an eternity. Ever felt the mud drying in her boots, and the breath wheezing down her throat like a dry fire. But at last, she could see a stopping point. It was a flat land and relatively dry at that. Ever and Tekla both broke out into a sprint and did not stop until they could not feel the quaking below their feet. They both fell to the ground, struggling to reclaim their breath.

Merenda did not stray too far from Cassio. She did not dare to help him, fearing for her own life. Finally, after much more struggling, everyone in the group had made it to safety. All of them walked further into the land.

After they had all made it ten feet in, everything suddenly stopped. The shrieking was over. The water stilled. The quaking halted. Finally, Cassio collapsed in Jesper and Teava's grasp, forcing them both to stumble towards the ground. Jesper swooped up the weak man, cradling him like a child, as they walked further yet onto the land.

"It's an island," Tekla gasped with a sudden realization.

"It's not a big one," Jesper told her. "So long as the spell on Cassio stays calm here, we shall find rest very soon."

And so they did, all but collapsing onto the ground the very minute that Teava and Jesper agreed that they had found a place far enough from the water on all sides to be safe. Grateful for the reprieve, Tekla and Merenda immediately made for the food in their packs. Ever was more concerned with emptying her boots of the mud that caked them and finding a massage for her sore feet. Teava warned them not to get too comfortable and reminded them of how close the water was still. She said that she had no clue how long the spell on Cassio would last; it could be gone already, or he could merely be asleep until he was close enough to hear their calls again. Either way, they would not be entirely safe, she said, with the weak will of the man until they left the sea behind them altogether. She and Jesper had a short discussion during which she informed him that eyes would be on Cassio at all times and she would take the first watch. Ever knew that Teava had thought the very same thing about forfeiting Cassio's life that she had. Perhaps, if Jesper had not been there, she would have cast the man into the sea herself. As far as Ever was concerned, that was the second time that Jesper had saved his life – a debt the man could never repay, and a gift that Ever wished would stop being given to him. Merenda stayed close to him as she ate and prepared her bedroll. She was most likely guarding him from the company more than from the sirens, despite the people that just saved his life. And, again, despite that fact, she was most likely right to do so. Ever knew very well that they were only as strong as their weakest member. Unlike Tekla, this man could neither fight, nor listen to instruction to keep himself alive.

Ever was exhausted emotionally, but certainly not able to sleep. After rubbing the soreness from her own feet, she tried to start a fire. It was nearly impossible with the moisture that still soaked the ground. Ever had a feeling that all plant life and wood on the island would look the same. Jesper came to sit beside her, grabbing her arms gently and pulling her away from her task.

"If it were possible to start a fire out here," he told her, "Teava would have already done it."

Ever's dwarven temper flared.

"You know, she's not the only one who is capable of basic survival skills."

"I know," he chuckled with amusement. "I know how strong you are, Ever of the Survivors." A term of endearment, she knew. He was telling her that she was strong because of her survival when the dwarves fell, even though she had not even been born when it happened. "I only meant that she is a dragon and breathing fire is second nature to her."

"Right," Ever said, her temper subdued along with her will to start a fire so that the group could dry their clothes. They would have to deal with being clothed in wet clothes for the night, she supposed, and chills in the morning. With any luck, they would all make it out of the Siren Sea alive and without fever.

Jesper noticed her shiver and sat closer to her, wrapping her under his warm elven cloak along with him. It was only a thin piece of cloth, but it had kept his clothes dry underneath and provided Ever with a lot more warmth than she would have thought such a thin material could have provided. She was grateful to shrink into his embrace.

"The sirens…" she began, unsure how to continue her curiosity. She paused, trying to think of a way to ask him what she wanted to know.

"The sirens…?" he prompted her, nudging her shoulder just a bit.

"They sing to each person based on… on what?"

"They seek to appeal to everyone with a song of a tragedy that speaks directly to your soul. They find what part of your soul will most likely pull you into the water. For the weakling Cassio," he said, dropping his voice so that Merenda had no chance of hearing, "it was his ego. Tell him he could be the lover of a beautiful mysterious creature and his lust will have him diving head first into the depths of their bellies."

"And what was their song to you?" she asked timidly. "What did you hear?"

It took Jesper a long minute to respond, and Ever could feel his embrace stiffen with tension. She thought at first that he would not respond at all, and she almost regretted her question.

"They sang a song that was similar to yours," he answered finally. "I lost my family, too. They sang of their slain brothers and sisters. They pled for their god to take them back to that day, so that they might die with them. They pled for the chance of vengeance. They mourned the loss and sung of how they want to know who they truly are, and forget about the life that they've pretended to live for so long."

"Surely you cannot wish that," Ever said, sadness coloring her tone. "To have died with them. Even I do not wish that."

Jesper smiled at her. It was a sad smile, even if it was reassuring in some manner.

"I did," he admitted. "Elves, you see, are cursed with an immortal life. Before, when it was still fresh in my mind, I longed to be with them. I could not bear the thought of an eternity living when I knew that my younger kin were robbed of life. I felt guilty, as though I should not have been spared. I have since grown a great deal," he said more cheerfully. "I know that the wound I incurred should have killed me, but it did not. There is a reason for that, and I have sought every day to learn that reason, and to make sure that I honor the gift I was given when my life was spared."

He had begun to sit taller, his embrace becoming more protective of her. Ever wondered if he thought that she might be the reason that he was spared. Perhaps he thought that he was to protect whatever fate she carried. She thought that perhaps that was the reason that they were drawn to each other from the start.

"What happened to them?" she asked. Immediately, his mood darkened.

"A sorcerer slayed them in our own home. His enchanted blade pierced through the hearts of my brothers, my sisters, my mother, and my father. It pierced straight through my own, as well," he said, pulling his clothing aside to show her the scar that never healed as an elf's wound should have. It was the only mark that interrupted an otherwise perfectly sculpted chest directly over the place where his heart beat. "I died, for only a moment. I was able to see my brothers and sisters, scared as the light took them away. But it left me behind, and I was sent back to my body. It was days later that I woke, no longer in my own home. Queen Elria had found me laying among the corpses of my family, a boy of only four years old, barely breathing and still bleeding. She took me in. I was lucky for that, as she is among the best elven healers. She cared for me until I had regained my health, and then she adopted me into the royal family."

Ever did not ask further questions. She remembered the way that he was referred to as the adopted prince by the other elves. Most of them would not even use his actual name. Instead they used the scornful title to remind him that he was not royalty, despite everything he did for them. She knew that he already felt as though he was living a life he was not meant for, and felt it wrong to make him talk more of it. So she changed the conversation.

"What do you think they sung to Teava?" she asked in a quiet voice, hoping that the dragon would not hear.

Jesper looked at her intently, assessing her body language before asking questions of his own.

"You fought back to back with her. That required a great deal of trust from someone who you met in such uncertain circumstances. And you've let her lead us through a dangerous path. Tell me, my dwarven friend, what do you see in her?"

Ever contemplated his question carefully.

"I see a strong leader, and one who is worthy of my trust. I admit, I do not always like her rude behavior, and I do not always agree with her," she said, leaving out her agreement of Teava's assessment of Cassio. "But I am still drawn to her in some way. I feel as though we were meant to be on this journey together. I feel connected to her somehow, though I cannot figure out how. I think she must feel it, too." Ever recalled the hushed conversation she shared with the dragon, one where Teava revealed that she knew Ever's secret.

Jesper contemplated her response, his eyes wandering to Teava as she stood at her post. He knew that Teava did not share her secrets lightly, and as her closest friend, he should not, either. But he had sensed a connection between the girls as well.

"I cannot tell you what they sung to her, as only she heard it, and I assure you that she will not be telling anyone," he began. "But I can tell you what I think they might have sung about, based on my friendship with her. She, too, lost her family, but not in the way that you and I have. They cast her away. Once a princess and heir to the crown, she was faced with a choice and chose incorrectly, according to her family. The dragons are very strict on certain subjects. On the subject of love and family, they become quite heartless, ironically. There is but one story, perhaps no more than a legend, of a dragon choosing love over the dragon principles. That dragon would have been banished."

"Who did he love?" she asked.

"The story does not say," he answered. "Only that it was not a dragon at all."

"Oh," she said. She knew that any race did not take kindly to mixing blood with another race, but she could not imagine a family turning down its own child because of it. "And she fell for a man who was not a dragon, then?"

"Oh, no," he said with a wicked and playful grin, "she's a dragon, all right."

"Oh," Ever said in shock, her own eyes now going to study the girl at her post. "Oh."

"And what do you think of her now?"

Ever continued to stare at the girl. She understood her cold and bitter behavior just a bit better now. She understood why the girl would not trust whoever she met, leaping instead to the trust she had in her sword first. Abandonment was not something that one could recover from fully, especially when all she did was love another woman.

Ever shrugged, looking back at Jesper.

"I think she is Teava," she answered him. "Nothing has changed."

She could see the relief on his face, clearly glad that she had received the information so well, especially when it was not his information to have revealed.

Now that Ever had learned more about her traveling companions – all but the mysterious Merenda – she was ready to sleep. She shrank further into Jesper's embrace, unwilling to let his warmth go, and closed her eyes, hoping that Cassio's, too, would remain closed until morning.

* * *

The night passed without event, neither from Cassio nor from the sirens, nor from any other outside threat. That was the advantage of making camp on an island directly in the middle of one of the most dangerous species home – no orc, evil sorcerer, or any other being would dare cross through to pose a threat to them. Jesper had woken before Ever, and when she woke, he was still caressing her. In minutes, everyone was stretching and waking, save for Merenda, who had relieved Teava of her duties sometime in the night, and Cassio, who was just as asleep as the waters were still.

"Does anyone have more food?" Tekla asked. "I'm starving."

Ever shook her head.

"I left mine with Minx."

As it turned out, the horses had most of their supplies still. Teava was the only one who hadn't left everything with her steed, though she did admit that Seg had most of her food. She took a small loaf of elven bread from her sack and everyone ate a small piece of it.

"How is this supposed to be enough?" whined Tekla.

"It's elven," Jesper told her. "You'll just have to trust that it will fill you up. You won't even notice a hunger."

"But what about tomorrow?" she demanded. "Or the next day? How long is this journey anyway? The bread won't fill us up forever."

"Seg will have the horses gathered on the other side of the sea," Teava told her. "He knows his duties and he will not abandon them."

"He's a tiny goblin, and they are four huge beasts. He cannot handle them all!"

"They are four tame beasts," she argued. "Just trust in Seg. And, if he fails, and you die of starvation before we come to the next town, we will make sure your body does not go to waste and our bellies do not stay empty."

Ever could tell from Teava's eyes that, despite the wicked words and the grin that went with them, she was only kidding.

Still, the threat of being fed to her friends was enough to shut Tekla up. That was just fine with Ever, who could not tolerate the whining of the weak human girl.

Before they set off, Ever went to check on Tekla's wound from the orcs. There was not a mark left behind, no sign that she had ever been hurt. Whatever magic Merenda had performed on her had erased the wound completely. She knew that she was in Merenda's debt for that, but she did not care to admit to it. She supposed that, since Merenda had saved her companion, she would promise to do her best to keep Merenda's companion alive, too. So long as he cooperated.

That would prove to be a challenging task. The very second they set foot in the water, with Jesper holding Cassio's body over it, he woke and began thrashing once more. The waters mirrored his movements as if he controlled them. The sirens began to shriek and wail, demanding their rightful kill. The entire company shrank back to the camp site.

Tekla immediately began complaining again, fearing for her own safety. Even after Teava pointed out that she would starve for sure, Tekla stuck to her complaint and her decision to stay on the island, awarding her an eye roll from most of the group.

"Teava," Jesper approached, "she's right that we are risking our lives. At least, with Cassio in our midst we are."

"What are you suggesting?" demanded the weary Merenda.

"I am suggesting," he said, motioning with his hands for her to calm down, "that Teava takes him across through the air."

The suggestion created a rumble from the group. Ever remained the only quiet one. Jesper had to snap at them to make them to get their attention.

"It's the safest way. With him across, the spell should be broken and the rest of us can travel unhindered. It's either that," Jesper said, eyeing the sorceress, "or we risk letting the sirens take him."

"I'm not playing ferry to a man who is determined to get us

all killed," Teava argued. "Let the sirens have their dinner for all I care. I am not a beast to be ridden."

"No one said you were," Jesper tried to calm her. He seemed to be the only level headed one of the group. "This is simply a one-time necessity."

"Why can't she take us all?" Tekla countered. "It seems far safer than anything else. The dragons are far too selfish a creature. We could have finished this journey a long time ago."

"I am not a beast to be ridden," repeated Teava, with heated malice. "Do you not realize the power it takes to transform? Some of us do not even know they have such a capability as they have never been close enough to the dragon heart to discover it. This is a power that cannot be used lightly. Why don't we get on your back and you can carry us across?"

"I am not trusting my master to a dragon," Merenda finally put in her word.

"Thus, this argument is moot anyway," Ever spoke up. "If we do not go, we will die here. If we take Cassio across, he will surely die, and I do not doubt that more of us will follow in his wake. Teava, I trusted you to take us this far, now I will trust you to know your duty. Merenda, you will have no choice in the matter. If Teava kills him, I assure you that he will be met with a kinder fate than what the sirens would deliver to him. And Tekla," she said, her eyes already rolling, "just shut up!"

Jesper, pleased with her rant, smiled at her before turning to Teava.

"Will you do it?"

It took her a few seconds, during which she stared at Ever, and Ever felt their connection grow stronger at that moment despite the dragon's anger. Finally, if a bit begrudgingly, Teava nodded her head. She handed over her sack to Jesper, barely even looking at him. Then she began to take off her swords, choosing to hand those to Ever. Looking her in the eyes, still holding on to the weapons, she held Ever's attention.

"I hope you will not need them," she told her gravely, "but I know you will know how to wield them."

Wordlessly, Ever strapped them to her back the way that Teava had worn them. They felt much lighter than she had expected. Teava then began to empty her daggers, handing those to Jesper. She shed her cloak and her outer wear, also leaving them with the elf. Underneath, she wore a tight fitting red suit that looked like it was made of scales. Then she closed her eyes and began to whisper in a strange tongue that seemed familiar to Ever somehow. Before long, she was covered in a blue mist that grew and grew. Everyone began to back away from it, not wanting that particular magic to touch them. It seemed threatening to them.

As it got bigger and thicker, the company watched in awe, all except for Jesper who had seen it before, and Cassio, who was unconscious away from the sirens. In minutes, the mist began to clear, revealing Teava in her dragon form. Ever's neck had to strain to see the head of the dragon, which was high enough that she wondered if Teava could touch the clouds. She was a dark crimson red, the color of blood. Her claws were as long as Ever was tall, coming to a sharp point at the end of each toe. The horns on her face, coming out at the side where Ever could only guess her ears were, pointed straight back. Her long tail ended with more horns, giving Ever the impression that Teava was always meant to fight.

The dragon snorted, unimpressed by the company's awe. She grabbed Cassio with her talloned hands and opened her long, spectacular wings, which Ever saw were black underneath. Before taking off, she cast Ever one last look with an eye that matched her human form, right down to the black liner that Ever thought had been tattoed for beauty when they first met. With one powerful flap of her glorious wings, she lifted off into the air. The rest of the company had to fight against the gust to keep their own ground.

The minute that she flew over the water, the sirens began to screech again, calling to their food. The water began to tremble, as well as the soft earth beneath them.

"We need to get back!" Jesper called out. They retreated back to the spot where they had camped. There, they would have to wait for the waters to quiet, and hope that meant the mission was completed successfully.

Jesper began to fold Teava's things and carefully pack it in her sack. Ever felt the weight of the swords on her back. They were certainly not as heavy as her axes, but they came with the weight of Teava's words. Ever could not understand what she had meant. She knew that she had permission to use them, but why would she wield a weapon that she did not know when she had axes that she had been trained to use since she was old enough to learn? Why would Teava choose to give them to her?

She felt as if the dragon knew something that she was not telling Ever. She knew something about her that Ever herself did not know.

After a little over an hour of waiting, the waters became calm. The company could only hope that Teava and Cassio both made it to the other side unharmed. Either way, they knew that it meant it was their time to cross the waters. The walk began exactly the same as it had before. Ever's ankles were met with the cold sensation of muddy water and her ears were met with the sad song of her ancestors.

Ignoring the melody was easier the second time around, maybe because this time she knew what would happen and what it would mean for the whole group. Or maybe it was because the sirens were not trying as hard. Ever noticed that the song was not as loud as before and certainly not as persistent. She assumed that it was because they were mad at having lost their hard earned meal. Or perhaps it was because they had gotten it after all. Whatever the cause, it seemed to make the whole group travel even faster through the eerie waters.

There was something else that gave Ever a sense of urgency. She did not know exactly what it was, but she felt something in the air, something looming over their heads and threatening their journey. She had picked up the pace without even realizing she had done it. She was now at the front of the group. Paranoia had elected her the leader, and she felt frustrated that the rest of the group wasn't feeling the same sense of urgency and threat – especially Merenda, who should have felt eager to be reunited with Cassio. Ever eventually got too far ahead of everyone else and had to stop and let them catch up.

When she stopped, she could not help but think of the water that she was standing in. The soft mud beneath her boots had caved in slightly from her weight, allowing the water to rise just a bit higher. She could feel the sirens ghosting through her ankles, and it sent chills up her spine. The tall grass that grew in the wet marsh was getting thicker and ticking her calves, like fingers urging her to come closer – which only made her want to leave sooner. The air around her was clouded with a thin fog, which threatened to close in at any moment. Perhaps that was the only reason Ever had even stopped to wait for her group, the fear of losing sight of them and ending up lost and alone outweighing her need to run away.

But then she realized what was so different about their second trip through the waters. There was no eel like creature wrapping itself around her ankles, no more of the Sarpa sniffing them out. She tried to take comfort in that. The Sarpa was gone, leaving them to peacefully wade though the waters in hope of avoiding the sirens song. She tried to think of it as a positive thing, as they no longer had to worry about becoming the snake-like fish's next meal. She tried to calm her heart rate and her increasing paranoia, but no matter how hard she tried, she could not shake the feeling of evil. She could not rest easy and walk through the sea at a leisurely pace. She was growing more anxious the longer it took her friends to come near enough to her that she could begin running again. She knew, in her very core, that something was going to happen, and the longer they stayed in the ankle deep muds in the middle of the murky sea, the quicker she could sense a danger approaching.

Still, her paranoia was not shared by anyone among else in the company.

Once Jesper was at her side and the girls just a few feet behind them, Ever began walking again. She tried to convince herself that there was no immediate danger. She tried to gauge Jesper's sense of the situation. He seemed to be walking calmly enough, worried only for the two that kept falling behind. Still keeping pace with him, Ever decided to voice her concerns.

"The Sarpa is gone," Ever told him. "Is it because he lives only on the other side of the sea, or is it because something else is much closer? Or perhaps he's had his feast on our friends?"

Jesper glanced back at the girls, shushing Ever as he did so. Merenda and Tekla were busy watching their own paths, not paying any mind at all to the conversation.

"He's not left us," he told Ever in a hushed voice. "I sense it, too, Ever. You cannot show them our suspicions, though," he said, speaking of the weaker girls. "Merenda should know already, but her powers have not alerted her to anything. It would not help to send them into a panic."

"Then why are we not moving faster," she argued anyway, "if you feel it, too? We need to leave this place. I'm beginning to wonder if you were right to begin with, and we should have taken the long way to the dragon kingdom."

"I was not right," he said, only sort of reassuring her. "Merenda's vision has shown me that. There is a great danger that lies beyond these waters. For whatever reason, we have been brought together to put a stop to it. Time is of the essence, no matter how treacherous the road might be. Whatever the Sarpa lies in wait to do to us will be no measure to what will lie even further ahead of us. We must be stronger than each trial we face."

She knew that he was right. There would be no end to the dangers that would be met by the group. Even so, she could not help but think that they were naïve not to try to out run the current one that was threatening them; nor did she agree that they should not alert the girls to such a danger. Let them think of escaping from the Sarpa's trap. It would allow them to better ignore the dimmed songs of the sirens that called for their dinner.

But she decided to trust Jesper, forcing her pace to match with his and her breath to keep an even pattern. She decided to let him lead them with his own decision making, and hope that it was worthy of being called a prince among the elves, adopted or not. She decided to lean on his extended knowledge of the land and wisdom in years.

The ghosts of the sirens began to retreat, the songs growing dimmer and dimmer, until they were all but gone. Ever could sense that the danger was nearly present now.

They trudged through the waters and when the sun began to set, Ever finally got her wish and they moved faster. The air had gone completely silent, save for the breathing of the group. It was an eerie feeling. They would not make it through the waters without meeting the enemy. Instead of cowering, she decided that she had to prepare for the oncoming battle. She kept one hand on her axe, making sure not to alert the girls, even though she still believed that that would have been the proper thing to do.

The clouds above them began to thicken. A storm was rolling in. They would be lucky to make it out of the waters before the rain came. Their clothes were already wet and cold. Ever felt like they were being threatened by Mother Nature herself. It would either be the Sarpa or pneumonia what would take their lives. She didn't see a third option where they made it out alive.

Fight, she thought to herself. The third option was to fight, to survive against all odds. Her people had done it before. She knew that she was capable of it still, and she felt that Jesper was right – they were chosen for this burden for a reason. Surely that meant that they were all strong enough.

Or were they? Ever's mind went back to Cassio the Weak. Cassio the Cowardly. He had yet to prove his worth to the group.

"Something touched my leg," Tekla gasped in surprise. Ever suddenly froze in her tracks, locking eyes with Jesper while Tekla squealed in disgust. "What was it?"

"Ack!" Merenda jumped in the mud, making a splash as she landed. "It's fish! It's so gross!"

"What kind of fish would live here?" Tekla muttered.

Jesper and Ever had not yet moved, still gauging the situation. But suddenly, Ever felt more than the slimy skin of a fish. She felt teeth graze her calf.

"Run!" she yelled, ushering the girls ahead of her. "Run far, and run fast!"

For Tekla, panic was never more than a heartbeat away. She needed no more instruction. She splashed through the water, pushing past Merenda, in a mad attempt to escape.

Merenda was a different story. She chose instead to draw her sword and face the enemy.

"There shall be no more Sarpa when I am through with you!" she called out with ferocity.

Ever readied her axe and searched the water for the enemy, her plan to flee having failed at the hands of Merenda's feisty spirit. Jesper's bow was already notched with an arrow, its wielder also aware that there would be a fight rather than a flight.

The Sarpa wound its way around the legs of each of the warriors, forcing a scream from Tekla each time it passed her feet. The other three concentrated on its patterns, unable to see clearly where it was in the murky water.

And suddenly, having selected its first victim, it shot ten feet into the air in front of Ever, hissing at her face as it unhinged its jaw. The sight of the sharp teeth coupled with the surprise caused Ever to jump. The tight grip on her axe was gone, and her weapon fell to the ground, instantly lost in the murk.

As the Sarpa aimed and lunged directly at her face, she jumped into the water. Before she recovered, the Sarpa was already recoiling for another strike.

But mid strike, he stopped and hissed with a shriek. He turned to face his attacker, revealing an arrow lodged along his long snake-like body.

Merenda seized her chance and leaped onto the beast, latching onto its long neck. She lifted her sword, ready to slice its neck, but it was of no use. The beast was throwing its own body this way and that, trying to throw the girl off. He succeeded at least in forcing her to slide down, slipping too far to cause any real damage to his throat.

By the time he had dislodged her enough, Jesper had sank two more arrows into the beast's body. Ever, now fully recovered, could see that the elven weapon was not causing enough damage to the beast; it was no more than an annoyance. She searched the waters for her axe, knowing that now it would be sunken into the mud. She was frantically splashing about, and the Sarpa took notice. His sights were once more on the dwarf, and she was without weapon. The beast hissed and prepared itself for another strike, this time ignoring the arrows that were being shot into its scales at a rapid rate.

Ever took a step back, unsure how to proceed, and lost her balance, falling backwards in the sloshy mud. She could not stand up again in time as she struggled in the mud, which meant that she was an easy target.

The Sarpa began to launch its strike. It was mere inches away from the dwarves face when instinct kicked in and she reached back for the dragon blades, taking one in each hand and swinging them to the front of her body. She brought them down in an X formation, creating a scissor-like function. The force of the Sarpa's strike was met with the strength of dwarven muscle as Ever closed the makeshift scissors in the beasts neck.

The action severed the beast into two parts, both falling limply to the water. The murk turned a deep red, tainted with blood.

Ever could only sit and stare, the swords still in her hands.

An instinctive weapon that she knew nothing of had defeated the beast that terrified her from the minute she set foot in the water while her own weapon had abandoned her at the start.

Her own weapon!

She put the blades back in their sheaths and searched the waters once again for her axe. Upon finding it, she turned to see the group staring at her with jaws hanging open.

"What?" she said, offended and at the same time eager to leave again.

"The swords…" Tekla started.

"They glowed," Merenda finished.

"Aren't they supposed to do that?" Ever asked in confusion, recalling the glow she saw when Teava fought the orcs.

"Not always," Jesper said, his brow furrowed in thought. "They respond to some people, and not others. I once thought that Teava was their master. Perhaps I was mistaken in this thought."

"Can we save that for another time?" Ever asked, her mind still stricken with urgency. "It won't be long before the sirens return, and I'd really like to be gone before they – or this storm – have a chance at getting to us."

Jesper conceded, acknowledging that she was right, though he would certainly discuss what he had seen with Teava. And surely, it did not take long for the sirens to begin singing to them again. This time, however, each one of their minds already engaged in the battle they just witnessed, freeing them from the sirens' temptations completely.

IV.

They made it safely out of the waters and found Teava on the other side. She was still in her dragon form, pacing back and forth. She stood still as they approached and waited for Jesper to retrieve her clothing before transforming back into her human form.

Merenda ran to Cassio the minute that she could see his figure behind the giant beast that was Teava. He was still passed out but his slumber now seemed peaceful rather than spell bound. Teava retrieved all of her weapons, including the swords from Ever, who handed them back without words, simply too tired to tell her what had happened.

Jesper and Teava then broke off from the group to discuss things that Ever could have easily guessed. They looked at her every now and then, so she assumed that he was filling her in on the glowing swords – and perhaps she was filling him in on whatever secret she knew of Ever Trollkiller, of the lost kingdom of Isola, survivor, against all odds, and certainly one whose existence – and therefore whatever secrets came with it – had been well hidden for the duration of her life. She was annoyed that Teava might know something that she did not, and even more bothered that she didn't bother sharing that information, especially given the circumstances of all that had happened. But she did not concern herself with any eavesdropping – too tired at that moment to put too much effort into caring.

She surveyed the land around them. The ground was much softer than it was on the other side of the sea, perhaps offering a better place to camp than what they had been used to. However, they were just as out in the open, which felt less safe on this side of the river than the other. She would not feel comfortable or rest easy if they made camp there, especially so close to the Sarpa's lifeless body. She felt that they should be far away from the evidence. Luckily, Teava did, too.

"The horses aren't too far from here," Teava announced, breaking away from Jesper. "I had Seg keep them far enough that they would not be disturbed by my size, but close enough not to hinder us too much. I cannot wake Cassio, so a few of us will have to go and fetch them while the rest stay and watch him. Ever?"

She looked up at the dragon, wishing that she could stay where she was. But Teava beckoned her to follow. She obeyed without comment.

She was dismayed when Jesper silently opted to stay behind with the others. They must have discussed this plan as well. Perhaps Teava was not going to keep her secret from Ever for much longer.

"Have you heard the legend of the dragon heart?" Teava asked when they were away from the group.

Ever noticed that Teava had slowed her pace as soon as they were out of ear shot from the group. She wasn't ready to have a conversation like the one that she knew was about to come.

"No," she answered plainly, knowing that her disinterest would not dissuade Teava from speaking her piece.

"The dragon heart," she began, "is not a real heart. It's a relic, hidden in the depths of the Zagnoula Mountain. Few have ever had the honors of laying their own eyes on the relic, but there it dwells, safely hidden from anyone who means it harm, but powerful enough to wake the spirit of any dragon. We call it the dragon heart because it is what keeps our species alive. To be sure, the dragons would live on without it. They would still bear dragon children, who would pass the dragon blood to their own children, and so the race would continue. But without the dragon heart there to awaken the dragon within, the race would be stuck in the human form. All things that come from the dragon spirit would be lost. And so, in time, the race of the dragons would forget who they are, perhaps not even know that they have the blood of a dragon running through their own veins. Eventually, the dragons would fade, memory becoming legend, and legend becoming fairy tale. The dragons, no matter how pure of blood they were, would appear to be no more than humankind – both to the world around them and even to themselves.

"With the dragon heart safely hidden where it belongs, every dragon of the Earth of Eald can benefit from it. Of course, you must be close enough for it to awaken the dragon spirit, but after that, you can use your powers as often or as little as you want. Mind you, the amount of energy it takes to transform can be exhausting unless you're near the relic. But there are many more benefits of keeping close to the relic. It has healing powers. Things that you could surely do on your own, but it speeds up the process and produces a stronger outcome. That's why most dragons opt to stay close enough to feel its presence, be that in Zagnoula, Shodalea, or any other place relatively close. You know when you're close enough because you can feel it in your veins."

"Why are you telling me this?" Ever asked, unsure if she was interested or annoyed.

"I think it is good for anyone to know. Jesper tells me," she said, casting Ever a sidelong glance, "that in your – what did he say? Twenty-three years? – you have lived in the mountains of Inunia, and never, until you went to him in Brisdale, did you go further than the forests of Fardocain. Is that true?"

"Yes," Ever said, not knowing where she was going with the question. She seemed to give Teava the answer she was looking for, though.

"It is good, then, for you to learn legends that are not strictly dwarven, as I'm sure those are the only tales you were told as a child. You never know when you hear something that might be useful you."

Ever decided that Teava did have a point. Any knowledge she had would only help her out.

"So, will this dragon heart fix Cassio?" she asked. Teava responded with a dry chuckle.

"Will it lift the spell? Probably. But fix him? He's beyond that."

Although Ever agreed with her completely, that wasn't entirely what she was getting at.

"So humans can feel its power, too?"

"Everyone can. Dragons simply feel it in a greater way."

"And sorcerers?"

"Yes… Why do you ask this?"

"What if Terrisino tries to take it?"

"He would fail miserably, and probably die in the process."

"In the vision I had with Merenda," Ever began, "the dark creature was commanding the dragons."

"The dragons are a proud people," Teava responded. "But we are not stupid. I will tell Queen Kylon of your vision, and she will be sure that the dragon heart is more properly guarded. I assure you, Ever, my kind will do everything they can to protect themselves."

Ever was satisfied with this. She began to grow curious of other things.

"What will happen when you take us there?" she asked. "You chose exile. Surely they will not receive us well."

It took her a couple beats to answer, and when she did, Ever could hear the sadness in her voice. Ever almost wished she hadn't asked, hadn't upset her.

"If I were alone, they would not let me past the mountain. They wouldn't admit anyone else, either. Actually, anyone who comes near the clans with me runs the risk of losing their life. In their eyes, I've chosen the most despicable thing I could have, worse even than killing one of my own. But we have information, like the goblin sighting. Like the vision. Those things will at least get us into the palace to see the queen. But we have a secret, too. I have not been the only dragon exiled for the decision that I have made." She stopped to take a breath, preparing herself to reveal something of herself to a girl that she would never have chosen to associate with before. "I chose a love that goes against tradition. The dragons do not choose your partner for you, but you are expected to pick an appropriate dragon. I feel as though I have picked the appropriate dragon for myself. If it had been a male, I would be queen right now. But I chose the love of a woman.

"There are other dragons that have gone against tradition, dragons that we no longer remember, which could mean that there are dragons in the world that do not know the power that runs in their veins. There are dragons who have picked the love of a human, or an elf, or anything that is not a dragon. They bear offspring then that are neither purely dragon, nor purely the other species. The power of that offspring, then, could be great. But the offspring might never know of the power themselves, if they never come close to the dragon heart. I believe that I have found such an offspring. The dragons are too proud to think that they should keep tabs on the exiled dragons' family lines, which means that there are too many secrets out in the world now. Legend tells of one such secret that will save us from evil. I do not know that I have found that specific dragon halfbreed, but circumstances lead me to believe that, at the very least, this halfbreed is important."

They began to approach Seg and the horses then, so Ever let the subject drop. She wasn't quite sure what Teava was talking about anymore anyway. All the talk of legends and relics and magic only reminded her that she had absolutely no idea what was going on.

Seg was standing in the middle of nowhere, it seemed,

holding the reigns of Minx and Ezaria, while Andale stood nearby, his own reigns hanging over the ground, and Phantom stood as if he was guarding the group. Although Seg was the only one who could speak at all, Ever knew that the one who was in charge was Phantom – his strong presence holding the group under control. As soon as he saw Teava approaching, he relinquished the role of leader to her.

Ever took the reins of the mares from Seg, who then ran to Teava's legs. They began the short walk back to the group. It was silent at first, but curiosity quickly got the better of Ever.

"Who is she?" she asked, hoping that Teava truly felt the connection that Ever had felt between them and that she thought Teava had felt as well. "Your dragon," she added for clarification.

Teava did feel a connection, but it wasn't as familial as Ever seemed to feel. Still, begrudgingly, she humored Ever's questions. Perhaps more because she missed her lover than because she felt the need to answer the nosy dwarf. Teava could feel the need to say her name.

"My Salora," she said, the name rolling off her tongue like sweet honey. "We left to Abrya shortly after we were exiled from the dragon kingdom. It was her choice. She likes living in a small village, away from most everyone. It has grown on me as well. It's quiet. We're left alone."

"Her family didn't want her, either?" Ever asked. She sensed Teava's mood darken and immediately regretted her question. "I mean – "

"No, that's not quite how it happened," she answered. "Her family was willing to keep it a secret. But as the former heir to the throne, I thought that it was time for traditions to change. I should have waited until I was actually queen. Then there would not have been much that anyone could have said. But I got cocky and impatient, and I wanted everyone to know about Salora. I was immediately exiled, and her family then had no choice, as her secret was out then, too. If they hadn't turned her away, the whole family would have been banished. Because of me, she lost her family."

Ever reached out her free hand to comfort Teava, but then thought better of it and let her hand drop back to her side. The rest of the walk was quiet after that as Ever contemplated the strict traditions of the dragons. Vek had never told her stories like that of the dwarves, but she wondered if they were the same way. They certainly were proud of the fact that they were dwarves. Perhaps there were no dwarven "halfbreeds," as Teava called them, as Ever doubted any dwarf would choose another race to lie with. But would a dwarf go against tradition the way that Teava had with Salora? And what would the other dwarves do in response? Surely they would not have turned on their own kind. That seemed worse than a love that was not approved of. Love should not need approval anyway, Ever thought.

They rejoined the group, and Teava was immediately cold again. Ever knew that her short time of friendship, or something that resembled it, was over. They decided to set off right away and stop at a nearby village to find an inn to sleep in. Merenda made the point that sleeping out in the open with Cassio might not be a good idea. She reminded them of the goblin army that was making its way to the dragon kingdom. She didn't want to have them catch up to the group, especially if that meant that whatever they were running from would catch up as well. Ever doubted that any village would offer much in the way of defense, but welcomed the idea of sleeping on a bed anyway.

As they began to approach the Baia Village, she could see pretty quickly that she was wrong about the defense. From the cities and villages she had seen before, she thought that they had all lived pretty humbly, minding their own business and trusting the other settlements to mind their own as well. Perhaps that was because they were surrounding the peaceful elves of Brisdale, and on the calmer side of the river as well. This small village seemed intent on proving that its size should not fool anyone. They had built stone walls around their perimeter, which seemed sturdy enough to keep a troll busy. Atop those walls stood sentries, even at this hour in the night. Below the walls were wooden posts, sitting diagonally to aim at visitors, and sharpened to a point. They lined the walls as far as Ever could see, save for the spot where the door was. Approaching that door, she saw a smaller door inside it, where the guards posted on the other side could open to reveal only their faces as they questioned the people entering their village.

This company was treated no differently from any other. The door inside the door was opened to reveal a bearded man with a gruff voice.

"State your business," he demanded.

"We seek a warm bed to lodge in for the night," Teava answered.

The man looked over the group, his eyes resting for a moment on Ever, on Jesper, and on Cassio. Ever wondered how much he was seeing. She thought that perhaps Jesper should have covered his pointed ears as Teava had covered hers. Though, she doubted a head scarf could have hidden his elven presence.

"What's wrong with your friend there?" the man chose to demand, selecting from a plethora of questions Ever was sure he had prepared already.

"He's fallen under a spell," Teava answered honestly. "We're on our way to save him."

Ever did not miss the information that Teava was selecting to leave out. Their destination, for instance, as well as what spell he was under and who had cast it. Or the fact that what she had said was not their direct mission.

"And what," the man began, "does an elf have to do with it?"

"He is our friend," Teava answered.

"Elves do not make friends with men," the guard replied. "If that truly be what you are." His eyes shifted back to Ever, whose height must have made the guard question her race.

"That is not altogether true," she answered. "The elves of Brisdale have peacefully ruled over the men of Thaedal and its surrounding villages for thousands of years. Our friend here had chosen to help us with his elven remedies until we are able to find someone to break the curse."

The guard took a few minutes to respond to this, his gaze shifting constantly from Ever to Jesper and back to Teava. Teava never offered more information than directly asked, and the man never knew exactly what his suspicions of the group were, thus never asked the right questions. Finally, deciding that he was only being overly cautious, he allowed the group entrance into the village as he opened the heavy, bolted door.

"Welcome to Baia Village," he said half-heartedly. "The inns are that way. You'll understand when I ask you to stay no longer than you absolutely must."

Teava nodded gravely before leading the group in the direction of the inns. Ever felt the man's eyes on their backs as they walked away but refused to look back. She was beginning to feel paranoid about people that might be able to guess that she was not human.

The group found lodging for them and their horses, quickly, and settled in for the night in a cozy place called the Dancing Deer Lodge. They paid for food for the horses and for themselves. The inn maid brought them warm porridge after they had set their belongings down.

The porridge was too thick for most of the groups' likings. They could nearly slice it with the spoons, and it was quite chewy. But no one was complaining as they devoured the food, enjoying the freshness of the meal even if it was not the best. Coupled with the comfort of an actual bed, they felt like royalty.

* * *

Ever was woken in the middle of the night by a strange sensation. She felt as though something was watching her. But when she looked around, she saw only Merenda, sitting up tall in her own bed, searching around the room as well. Ever did not know if it was safe to speak, or if Merenda was feeling the same thing as her. Merenda was the first to speak upon hearing Ever wake with a gasp.

"We should not have come here," she said ominously. "We have made it too easy for the evil to find us."

"What do you mean?" Ever whispered. "What's coming for us?"

"What's going on?" Jesper said groggily, just waking from his own slumber to see the two girls upright in their beds.

"Wake the others," Merenda commanded him. "We need to leave this village."

As if on cue, screams sounded from outside the open window. It was enough to wake Teava and Tekla, and after the second scream, the group was arming themselves with the weaponry that they had cast aside in the night. Jesper was the first to finish, leaving the room and instructing the others to meet him at the stables as he ran out the door.

Once they had all donned their gear, they set out after Jesper.

The minute they stepped outside of the inn, Ever saw exactly what had caused the terror in the villagers. There was a tall, hooded figure, seeming no more than a cloaked shadow. He was grabbing the villagers by the neck, holding them up to eye level, and boring into their minds. Some would writhe in pain and agony as he did so while the on lookers screamed in horror, running as fast as they could, or else frozen in place.

Merenda gasped in horror, seeing the same thing that Ever had.

"Take Seg," Teava told Merenda, "and hide with Ever. Keep her safe. I will lead him away, then we will meet outside the village. Go!"

Teava then whistled, causing a ruckus in the nearby stables.

In seconds, Phantom came running to her, while stable boys helplessly chased the run-away steed. Merenda yanked Ever out of her trance, pulling her back into the inn as Teava swung herself and Tekla onto her steed.

Merenda, Ever, and Seg were then alone in the small inn, save for the few night employees who were cowering under the desks and tables. Merenda led Ever through the inn's kitchen, where another employee hid behind the pantry. She demanded to know where the back exit was and followed the direction in which the trembling chef pointed her.

"That was the creature from our vision," Ever pointed out as they ran. "Wasn't it?"

"Its name is the Vehsi," she panted back, somehow sounding less terrified as the screams continued. "It searches the village for you. We should not have come here."

"How does it know we are here?"

"Shh," she shushed her as they began to make their way through the confusion and crowds.

Everyone was in panic, no one was running in the same direction. No one seemed to care, either, when they fell onto each other. A rather tall man nearly threw Ever to the ground, barely looking at her as she fell, only glimpsing enough to be sure that he would not trip over her and cost time for himself to escape. Ever stayed focused and alert, darting back and forth between the chaotic villagers. She struggled to keep an eye on Merenda as well as the crowds, but she was determined not to lose the sorceress.

Suddenly, Merenda stopped, forcing Ever to plow straight into her. The sorceress grabbed her hand and yanked her to the left, changing the course. At the very last minute, Ever saw why. The Vehsi had made its round to where they were going. Ever wondered how he had gotten there so fast. She knew that she had just heard screams behind them.

Unless there were two Vehsi.

The screams seemed to echo around the whole village. To

the left, screams. To the right, screams. Behind this building, behind that building, around this alley, down that street, the screaming was everywhere. And they both knew, where there was screaming, a Vehsi was sure to be close.

Finally, lost in the village and unsure where to go, Merenda pulled Ever into an alley with no way out. There was a large garbage trough at the end of it. Merenda ran to it and threw Ever behind it, following in after her. She whispered a spell in a tongue that Ever could not decipher, then touched her hand to Ever's forehead and brought her hand down to her chest before repeating the motion on herself.

Ever felt a heavy fog come over her body, but saw nothing. The fog did not leave, though. She had a feeling that Merenda's spell was to blame but dared not speak and ask what she had done. Merenda seemed focused on keeping quiet and hidden, and Ever decided that it was best to follow suit and keep her own mouth shut. She didn't like the feeling of the spell, but knew that she had no other choice than to trust Merenda.

They sat quietly for hours. The screaming never did seem to fade at all. Ever tried to imagine that that was good thing. It meant that people were still alive. If the screams had faded, then the Vehsi must not be killing.

But that was not always true, she knew. Occasionally, a scream would come to a very sudden end. Ever knew that that meant a neck had been snapped. How could a village that was so prepared for an attack be in such a surprised uproar as this? How had the Vehsi came through without any warning signal sent through the village? An alarm of some sort? How had they gotten past the guards without any damage being inflicted upon them?

But Ever knew the truth. These creatures were not alive. They could not, therefore, die, no matter what the guards tried. All Ever could do was hope that the screams she heard did not belong to her friends. She could only hope that they had succeeded where she and Merenda had failed, and that she and Merenda, too, would eventually make it out.

The screams continued, occasionally bursting out louder as people in hiding were discovered and sometimes subduing when people found a new spot to hide, but never ceasing altogether. Ever knew that the creatures were looking for her. The words of the Vehsi from her vision never faded form her mind. *Kill the dwarf.* She somehow knew that the Vehsi were reading the minds of the people. Somehow they knew she had come here. Somehow they had found her. If they got ahold of one of her friends, who knew she was dwarven, they would be mercilessly killed. Her life would be spared, only if the creatures did not find her in the alley, since the others only knew that she was supposed to flee the village. She did not want their lives to be sacrificed at her expense. Nor did she want to live with the knowledge that the villagers were dying for her sake, either.

But still, the screaming continued. The night had long since passed, the sun now high in the sky. Ever could only hope that the creatures were coming to the end of the villagers. They had to be close to looking into the minds of all the population by now. It was not an incredibly large village.

The Vehsi were determined, though, and soon the sun started to set. Ever was feeling incredibly cramped in the small space and the smell of the rotting food was starting to make her sick. Although the smell was the worst part about where they were, she was glad for it. On top of the fear she was feeling, the smell helped her repress any hunger she might feel for being there for so long without a meal. She worried that hunger noises might draw her away. She didn't understand why she was so special, but she would keep herself alive and see to it that no one who died that night will have lost their lives in vein.

Finally, the screaming was quieting. Most of what was still to be heard was very far away. Ever began to feel safe enough to breath and relax a little bit more. Merenda did not feel the same. She remained tense and alert, her lips occasionally mouthing some words as her eyes closed. She was praying, Ever realized.

And it might not have worked.

As if it was an afterthought to check the alleys, Ever heard footsteps hesitating in the street. In seconds, the culprit had made his decision and walked into the alley. Ever had to bite her lop to hold back a gasp. She had to concentrate on keeping her breathing steady so that she would not become audible. She noticed that Merenda had squeezed her eyes closed tight, still praying. She wished that she had a god to pray to. Perhaps then someone would lay a protective hand over them.

The footsteps grew closer.

Closer.

Ever's heard began to pound harder and harder till she thought that it, too, would become audible and give away her location.

But the creature decided that there was nothing in the alley. With a screech so loud that Ever winced, he turned and fled the alley.

The girls did not move. In fact, they remained as still as possible for nearly an hour after the screaming had stopped entirely. Their hearts only slowed a little bit. Once they decided that it was probably safe enough to venture out, they slowly crept out from behind the garbage bin. Ever did not dare stray far from Merenda, for fear that she would leave the safety of the cloak that she had provided.

The village was clearly in shambles. Widows mourned their dead husbands on the side of the street. Bodies were scattered throughout. The people that weren't crying or dead were clutching their heads, clearly in agony. Some of them moaned, some of them tried to shut out the noise by closing their eyes tightly. Ever could only imagine the splitting headaches that they were all now feeling. Carts had been toppled over, throwing cabbages, fruits, and small accessories from one side of the street to the other on every stretch of every road. Doors were left swung open or broken down, and there were many windows that, too, had been smashed through. The girls very quietly made their way through the melancholy village. Ever, having completely lost her way before they hid, was now very lost, and knew that Merenda was, too, judging by the various turns she was taking.

Then she stopped short, a small gasp escaping her mouth and causing Merenda to stop as well, looking for the cause of Ever's surprise. That was the problem, though. The cause of the gasp wasn't something that was there and shouldn't be, it was something that was not there that should have been. Seg was gone. A panic made its way through Ever's bones. If the Vehsi had gotten the goblin, there would be no doubt that the Vehsi would be waiting for them at the dragon kingdom.

Seeing nothing imminently dangerous in their surroundings, Merenda prodded Ever forward. Ever, her mind flying through the many possible outcomes of Seg's disappearance, followed without truly knowing what she was doing.

Merenda led her carefully through the village. Her own mind was sharply alert. It was true that she was just as lost as Ever, but she kept focused enough to remember the streets that they had gone down and constructed a map of the village in her mind so that she did not lead them in circles. Every street they turned down looked exactly like the last. People littered the paths, dead and alive, and Merenda kept her hand around Ever's arm to keep her from touching anything and giving away their invisibility. She continued forging the way through the now dark Baia Village until she finally found a way that led to the exit. Eventually, they were safely on the other side of the wall without so much as a scratch on their bodies.

Outside the village, things were eerily quiet. Perhaps that was because they had been used to hearing sounds of agony at that point, so any amount of quiet seemed distrustful. Even so, Merenda did not drop the cloak as they continued on.

The rest of the group was not at the point where the girls exited, but Merenda was almost sure that no one had made it out at the same side. Hoping that the others had decided to make a camp and wait for them, Ever and Merenda began to trace the outskirts of the town.

* * *

<u>The Kingdom of Shodalea</u>

Kylon had just received news of Vehsi sightings in villages along the river. It was not just one village, but several that had witnessed the terror of the faceless creature. Based on the time and day that each scout had claimed the sources provided, Kylon had assumed that there were at least four of the creatures plaguing their land. She had hoped that Terrisino had not managed to create an entire army of them, but there were already four now. Four of a creature that she had believed impossible, four of a creature that she knew to be impervious to death, four of a creature that embodied death itself. When faced with an enemy like that, four was an army already. And that was only a number that she had guessed based on reports given to her.

She was pacing the castle wall. She had more sentries posted, but she had the fear still that it wasn't enough. The scholars were busy combing through the libraries, searching for any information that could find on the Vehsi. Kylon was hoping for a weakness, anything that could use to defeat the creatures of legend. All she could really do was hope, though. With a creature of death itself, it seemed like defeat would be impossible.

"Your highness," someone interrupted her thoughts from behind. She turned on him, wrath in her eyes. Her usual glare. The dragon looked passed it as he knelt to the ground. He was clearly out of breath, having just come back from his scouting trip. Kylon was hopeful for good news, then, since he found it too important to catch his breath before coming in her presence. She wasn't sure that she could handle any more bad news.

"Well, then? What is it?" she demanded impatiently.

"There has been news," he panted, "of another dwarf."

"Where?" she demanded, excitement taking over the wrath in her eyes. "Where did you hear this? Where is the dwarf? Is it the one?"

"The rumors have come from the villages of Ranton. I don't know if it is the one, but I can tell you that Terrisino has taken a great interest in it. He must have somehow heard rumors of surviving dwarves. He has sent many of his armies in search for the dwarf. They are currently plundering the villages of Ranton. They must have had word of sightings. They could have killed the dwarf already. Or captured it."

Kylon's heart sank. Her good news quickly turned sour. Without another word to the messenger, she turned on her heels and made her way to the dungeons. Another conversation with Vek was in order.

Down in the dark dungeons, Vek and Thiflar were still exactly where she had left them, leading her to believe that – at the very least - she knew that neither of these two could be the dwarf who was foretold in the legends. That dwarf should have escaped easily with its magical heritage. Not to mention, these dungeons weren't meant to hold a dragon at all, which the foretold dwarf should be.

"Master Vek," she addressed the more cooperative dwarf. "It seems that your lost dwarf friend may not be lost any longer."

"What do you speak of?" he asked, hope filling his eyes. "You've found her?"

"Unfortunately, I have not. Perhaps other darker forces have," she admitted, then quickly realized her mistake as fear set in his eyes, "or maybe she has had better luck than you. No, I do not know what has yet become of her, but it is important that I am the one to find her."

"It's not at all," Thiflar interrupted. "Let us go, let us find our own!" He began to thrash against his chains again, ever the fiery spirited dwarf. Kylon ignored his behavior.

"How many dwarves did you say survived?" she asked, looking only at Vek.

"Thirteen," he answered, far more concerned with being reunited with Ever than with protecting any secrets or escaping.

"There's you two, and the one that fled," she thought out loud. "That leaves ten others. Are there any other search parties like yourselves?"

"No. Some are too old to travel. The others needed to stay behind as protectors for them."

"Is there perhaps another surviving dwarf clan?"

"I mean… I suppose there could be a small possibility, but we could not really know for sure. We're pretty certain that the kingdom was annihilated. Perhaps others left before, and perhaps some were able to flee after us, but that seems highly unlikely."

"And what was this maiden of yours leaving for?"

"To be honest… I can only make guesses. Our oldest member believes that she wanted to see the place of her family."

"From the ruins of Isola, all the way to the villages of Ranton," Kylon pondered out loud. "What could she be doing?"

"Ranton?" Vek said, "She's on this side of the river, then! She's closer than we thought!"

"She's probably been eaten by the orcs by now," Thiflar grunted, always the one with the cynical outlook. "Or she's being tortured in Terrisino's castle. Or stomped on by the trolls. A thousand terrible things could have already happened to her on this side of the river. Just look at us!" As if to emphasize his point, he tugged at his chains.

"You believe she's alive," Vek began, "don't you?"

"I have to believe," she answered. "Because I believe she may be the dwarf of legends. And if she is dead, then I might as well set my kingdom on fire, lest we end up slaves to the sorcerer."

"Then we are fighting for the same cause, are we not? Let

us help you find her!"

Kylon did not grace his plea with a response. Now unsure of what other information he could supply her with, she left the dungeons, satisfied for the time being.

She now knew the trial of the dwarf maiden's journey, and was more curious than ever.

* * *

Once again reunited with the company, Ever and Merenda felt more than ready to leave the Baia village behind them. They felt more than ready to forget the traumatic screams of the villagers. Ever could not help but feel guilty for the lives that were lost on her behalf, simply because she was being hunted. And she could not help but feel guilty for the loss of Seg as well.

"Wherever he is," Teava had assured her, "he will find his way back to me. He is bound to me."

"What if the Vehsi got him?" Ever had argued.

"Then he is dead," she had replied coldly, "but they cannot get in the mind of a goblin. They are not a human species. We are still safe for now."

The conversation that was still fresh in Ever's mind had done nothing to ease her guilt.

They began their quiet march to Zioccard, the next city and resting place, without word. Paranoia had made its way through the minds of the group. Even Teava seemed to have lost her confidence. She swung her head back and forth constantly, scanning the surroundings for any type of threat at all times. Tekla had ceased all complaints that she might have had, for which Ever was grateful. She knew that they would make camp outside the city limits and avoid the population altogether. If the Vehsi were truly hunting them, as Ever knew they were, then they would be too easily spotted inside the city walls.

After crossing the river between the city and the Baia village, they cut across to the east side of the city, hidden well behind the foliage that grew thickly by the ocean. Before walking too far beyond the city gates, they set up camp. Tekla quietly unwrapped some of the elven bread, still not daring to utter a complaint, when Jesper put a hand over hers.

"We won't have enough waybread to finish the journey to the dragon kingdom," he announced, "and anyway, we need information. I think it would be best if a few of us went into the city for trade, and see what the merchants know as well."

"We can't take the risk," Tekla said, speaking softly, as if the trees were listening. She tentatively began unwrapping the bread again.

"No," Teava said, "he is right. We need to know how far, and in what direction, the Vehsi have gone. And we need to know who else is looking for Ever. The city is safe enough. It is a trading point for the dragons. They keep it guarded while they are there. Even if they are not there, the thought of dragon warriors is enough to keep the city safe."

"So, Teava and I will go," Jesper announced, "and you will all stay and watch over Cassio."

"No," Teava said, "I never intended to enter the city. Not now, not before the Vehsi. My face might still be known and we cannot run the risk of being recognized. The queen will be alerted, I assure you. She can be unpredictable, and if she already knows about Ever, she may join the hunt to kill her knowing she and I are both on this side of the river. It won't take long for her to figure out what would have brought me this close to her. No, I cannot go. And you cannot go alone. Take Ever with you."

Ever was startled by her suggestion, and Jesper did not like it any more than she did.

"I cannot bring the very dwarf that is being hunted directly to the slaughter!" he protested.

"On the contrary, they will never see it coming," Teava argued calmly. "Besides that, she does not look like a dwarf. She could pass for a small human, as she did in the village. With ears like that, she could even pass for an elven child."

Ever's hands went to her own ears. What did Teava mean? Surely they were not pointed like Jesper's. Even as she thought it, she felt the small, dull point in the structure of her ears. She wondered how she had never noticed it before. They were not as pronounced as Jesper's or even Teava's, by any means, but they were certainly there.

Something in her heart sank. There was yet another thing about her that separated her from her own kin. Was she destined to forever be an outsider? Was there nowhere for her to belong? Her hands quietly dropped to her side as she eyed Teava. She once again was left to wonder what the girl knew about her that she did not.

"It's too dangerous," Jesper continued to argue, though with less force as he, too, examined her ears.

Merenda had come to Ever's side to pull her hair behind her ears. Evidently agreeing with Teava, she began to fuss with the girl's hair, first running her fingers through it to remove the tangles. She then parted the hair straight down the middle. Then, beginning at the back of the part, she wove a small braid all the way to the front, where she separated it into two smaller braids, using bands from her own hair to fix them into place behind Ever's ears, creating a natural head piece with an elegant braid, as was the elven way. She made sure to tuck enough loose hair behind her ears so that the small points were visible. Then she stepped back to examine Ever's wardrobe and ordered her to take off the dwarven armor. She went to Cassio's bags and dug through them until she found a dark blue gown. She ordered Ever to put it on. In doing so, it was obvious that the gown was made for someone much taller than Ever. Merenda did not seem to be bothered, though. She messed with the bodice, making sure to fit it tightly around Ever's torso. Then she pulled out a knife. First beginning with the sleeves, she made a clean cut from the wide wrist of the sleeve up to Ever's elbow. The gown now resembled an elven cloak. Next, Merenda, much to Ever's embarrassment, picked her up and placed her on a tall rock so that she could examine the bottom of the gown. Once again, making a clean cut with the knife, she cut off the excess material, leaving the gown now looking as though it had always belonged to Ever.

Returning to Cassio's bag, Merenda fished out a kit full of homemade makeup. She wiped the dirt from Ever's face and replaced it with a glossy foundation to match her skin tone. She added a few things to her eyes, and subtracted a few others from her eyebrows – much to Ever's disdain. Afterwards, she took a step back to examine her work. Seeing the looks on everyone's faces – especially Jesper's – Ever wished that she had a glass to see herself in. However, she was also embarrassed to be looked at, and she felt the heat rush to her cheeks.

"I'll go, then," she said.

This time, no one protested. Ever took that to mean that Merenda had successfully made her look like an elven child. She supposed that was the very reason for Cassio's insistence on going back for the trunk with his things in it. She now understood that even the human did, after all, have a skill set to be added to the group. He had taught Merenda the art of stage disguise, and Ever was sure he knew much more.

Ever and Jesper collected a few coins from Teava and began their walk into the city of Zioccard. Luckily for Ever's aching feet, it was not a long trek. But her feet were not the most unbearable part. In her peripheral vision, she could see Jesper watching her. She felt incredibly overdressed and wished desperately for her plain dwarven garments back. At the same time, in an odd sort of way that she had never felt before, she liked that he wanted to look at her so much.

But she pushed those feelings aside. They were not there to discover feelings or admire elven looks, as Ever so often did when she saw Jesper. No, they were there to find food. And, at last, they were approaching the trading carts that had settled outside the city walls.

"I will do all the talking, okay?" Jesper informed Ever. She nodded her submission, and they continued forward.

The first couple of carts were selling tapestries from various lands and garments that looked simple. Ever noticed that every last merchant and customer would cease their conversation and transaction to look at the two companions as they walked by. She felt a panic wash over her, even though the curiosity stemmed only from the fact that elven folk were among them.

"They aren't worried at all," Jesper whispered to her. "That's a good sign."

"But they're watching us," she argued back in a hushed tone.

"That's probably because they have never seen such a beautiful elf maiden," he said, flashing her a crooked smile. She tried to control her face, but only ended up looking like a fool, which, in turn, brought further amusement to Jesper. "Anyway," he continued, "they aren't threatened by our presence at all. That must mean that our... friends... have not yet made it this far."

"So we are safe in the city?"

"Perhaps. But I would not feel comfortable staying for more than a trade or two. We never know when they might catch wind of strangers in Zioccard. Look there, he has dried meats in his cart. Tekla will appreciate that."

They approached a modest cart. The merchant behind it was dressed in simple peasant's clothing and wearing a politely curious expression on his face. As promised, Ever said nothing, allowing Jesper to do all of the talking.

"Hello, there," the merchant greeted them kindly with a thick accent. "It's not often we see an elven pair in these parts." His tone said that he was only stating a fact, but the way his eyes kept shifting to Ever made her aware that he was actually trying to get information from them.

"That's true," Jesper replied in kind. "We like to stay on

our side of the river. My apprentice and I are here merely on business and are on our way back."

"What kind of business is it ye be here for?"

"Elven business," Jesper answered nonchalantly as he pretended to examine the meats. "Say, do you have any poultry?"

"Aye, just a bit," he said, motioning to the selection that Ever knew Jesper had already noticed. Jesper pretended to examine it closer. "These are dangerous times to be taking out a young elfling girl across the river. Ye must have important business."

"Indeed, we do," Jesper said. "But what of these dangers? I have not seen anything."

"There are rumors," began the merchant with excitement, "of a faceless creature that burns the minds of its victims."

"Oh? And where does this creature go?"

"I've heard it has come from the orc dwellings and has made it as far east as the river. Others say it started across the river and made it all the way west to the villages of Ranton. There is no way of telling where it comes from or where it goes."

"You feel safe enough here, then?"

"Aye, business must go on!"

"Indeed. You do not fear that it might be in search of something, and that it might come here to find it?"

"Oh, it is most assuredly in search," he replied. "Rumors of a dwarf wandering these parts."

Ever let out a tiny gasp, to which Jesper responded with a small kick in her shin. She attempted to regain her composure again.

"A dwarf? I believed them to be extinct." Jesper had never given as much as a twitch in his face to show surprise, dismay, or any other emotion he might have felt.

"Aye, I did, too. But if you're to believe the rumors, this one is a savior."

"A savior?"

"Aye."

"What are these rumors?"

"This dwarf, the one who will rid us of the great sorcerer, is to be brought forth by a company who has escaped from the sorcerer themselves. It is to be the strongest dwarf, both in blood and in capability, taught by the very company who survived the evil one's clutches. If I were the evil one, I'd be sending out faceless creatures to kill the dwarf, too. Rumor says the dwarf will be unstoppable."

"And you believe that?"

"Aye," he answered. "I have to, else I should surrender me family to the orcs' dinner plates and save us the fear of running."

"I suppose so," Jesper said, deep in thought. Suddenly, he snapped out of it. "I think we will take the beef instead," he said.

The merchant wrapped up Jesper's selections, including a jar of jam, and Jesper gave him the coins. Then the two began the walk back to the rest of the company.

And Ever was once again left with thoughts that plagued her mind as the merchant's rumors repeated in her head.

She felt certain that she was not this dwarven savior of legend. She was almost angry to have been dragged into the whole ordeal, even if she had gone willingly. She had begun to crave the warmth of the cave in the mountain, and of Vek's embrace. She missed Otak and his gentle guidance and wisdom. She had even begun to miss Marra, despite her cold behavior. Marra was simply honoring her duty to the dwarven race, as perhaps Ever should have, she now realized. Her duty was surely not meant to be seeking a route to the dragon kingdom while dressed as an elven child. If Marra could see her now, she would surely have a few ill words to speak.

"Do not trouble your mind, Ever," Jesper spoke to her, seeing the wrinkle in her brow as she was, in fact, troubled in her mind at that very moment.

"How can you not?" she countered. "If this merchant speaks the truth, are we not then frauds, wandering this barren land, offering its inhabitants false hopes and leaving them instead with terrors of the worst kind?"

"We are frauds, then, are we?" he asked with a raised brow.

"You believe his stories?" she asked. "You believe that I am the savior, and that you have all escaped the Great Sorcerer's evil?"

"I do not understand that part of his story," he admitted. "I suppose that I know Teava has been inside Terrisino's castle, but the others, I cannot say the same. I do not know Cassio or Merenda, and I doubt very much that Tekla has ever been outside of her quiet Ioka village. Nor have I come face to face with the evil one myself. But I do see something different in you. Perhaps I have never met the dwarves, so I cannot speak from experience, but I can say this of you. You do not look like a dwarf should, as your ears are too pointed, your figure too slim, and your body too hairless. You do not fight like a dwarf should – that is not to say that you cannot fight or do not know how to wield an axe. Quite the opposite, actually. You use the axe better than any stories I've heard of dwarven warriors, but I also cannot forget the way you took down the Sarpa single handedly using the unpredictable blades of a dragon, though you were never trained to command them."

He paused in the forest before they rejoined the group and forced Ever to face him.

"You must ask yourself this, Ever," he told her. "Why did you survive the annihilation of the dwarves, before you were even born? Why was it your mother that fought to escape to preserve her unborn child? What gave her the strength to make it to the mountain to keep you in this life? Perhaps she knew of some secret that she was unable to reveal before she died. Or perhaps not. But whether or not you are the dwarf of legends is not really the heart of the matter. It is this: you have been given the chance to change the course of history. Will you take it, or will you go back to the mountain to live out the remainder of your life in hiding? Do you truly believe that is what your mother would have had you do with her sacrifice?"

Ever had no response to offer. She only stood, staring at his golden eyes, and let his words sink in. She knew that he was right. Her doubts were far from quieted, but she had a duty that was far greater than anything that Marra would have guessed. Whether it was her destiny or not was not the question she needed to answer. That question was simply what she was to do next, where she was to go, and who she was to go with.

After all, legends were only legends, tales of the past that have little effect on the present. Legends were only stories told from generation to generation. Ever was not sure if she believed any of them, or if there was a single line of truth to any of them. But she knew that the future was always carved by the choices that were made in the present. She knew that even the smallest, strangest dwarf could make the biggest difference, if only presented with an opportunity. Whether or not she was the dwarf of legends did not matter. What mattered was her choice to rise to the challenge or to hide away as Jesper had suggested.

With a renewed conviction, she set her sights on the mission at hand. She would go to the dragons with confidence, she decided, and seek out the help they so desired. Surely, they did not need a special dwarf to save them. They could rely on the help of the mighty dragons and the valiant elves, who she still believed would fight for them. Terrisino could not stop an army that consisted of such great warriors. He could easily kill a single dwarf, if she were to go alone under the assumption that she was the savior.

But she was never alone. She never had been. Fate had carried her from the kingdom of the dwarves to the safety of the mountains with some of the greatest dwarves that she could learn from. From there, fate led her into the hands of an adopted elven prince, who would fight valiantly for her. Then fate assembled the strangest mix of companions to assist her; an exiled dragon, a strong hearted human, a powerful sorceress, and a human with his own tricks. It seemed like an odd mix, but somehow Ever knew that they were all crucial, even as she knew that she was just as crucial.

She set forth once more, knowing in the core of her very being, that she would be responsible for the downfall of the Great and Terrible Sorcerer.

V.

    She stood face to face with the enemy. He seemed to be taller than the tallest dragon, though he was only the size of a mortal. He wore heavy armor, which seemed excessive in comparison with Ever's blue elven dress. His face was hidden beneath a metal helmet that spiked out on his chin and on either side of this head. The only thing visible was his mouth. His skin was dark, his lips a pretty maroon. It seemed like he would have a pretty face beneath that helmet, but his sinister smile took that away. His teeth had been carved into a point, which might have been the cause for the blood pouring out of his lips.

    And there Ever stood, holding a weapon that she had never seen before. It certainly was not her dwarven axe, and she was completely unsure of how to wield it.

    But that did not matter. She had no time. The sorcerer was already lifting his arms, fitting his bow with a heavy arrow. In seconds, he released the string and let the arrow shoot from the weapon, aiming straight at her heart.

    Ever gasped in pain as she woke with a sudden fright, clutching at the fabric over her heart where the arrow had pierced. But there was nothing there. It had only been a dream. The very same dream that she had been having since they slept near the city of Zioccard. She breathed deeply a few times to slow her heart rate before resting her head back down.

But she saw piercing blue eyes staring at her from just a few feet away.

"A dream," said Merenda, to whom the eyes belonged, "is never just a dream."

"Go back to sleep," Ever told her. She was simply too exhausted to listen to the riddles of the strange sorceress. Ever closed her eyes and felt relief when Merenda offered no further words.

Later that morning, no one seemed to wake with peaceful energy. That was the last night they would spend out in the open. For the next several days, many weeks, possibly, they would be in the thick of the wooded area of the Forsride Forest. Ever felt that they could take some sense of security there, where it would be easy to hide from orcs or goblins or the Vehsi. But she also knew that those enemies could be easily hidden, too, awaiting their ambush.

Could. The enemy *could* hide in wait for a surprise attack. But they would not be in there. No one willingly went into Forsride. Even the mighty dragons, whose kingdom lay behind the forest, chose to fly over it rather than risk their lives going through it.

And yet, a dragon was about to face those terrors, choosing to unite herself faithfully with a dwarf, an elf, two mortals, and a sorceress. Her loyalty had given Ever strength to forge on, though she only grew more terrified with each passing moment. She had never heard the legends of what lie hidden in the trees, nor did she have the courage to ask. She heard the noises, though. She had started to hear them the night before last, and they grew louder and louder with every step she took closer. It was a horrible sound. She had no words for it, save for a terrible, hollow screech that must have come from a giant monster.

It was no wonder that Zioccard was the last city on the map between there and Forsride. She would not have chosen to live where the noises could be heard. It seemed like a poor decision to make a settlement there, where you would be doomed to die. It seemed a poor decision to go through now, where fate would be the only thing that could carry them through.

Yet there they were, preparing to go forward.

Jesper was with the elven horses, relieving them of their saddles and luggage. The forest was no place for them. They had helped the company thus far, and now with a heavy heart, Jesper was preparing to say goodbye to his steed.

"We will meet again, Andale," he told him, stroking the steed's face as he placed his own face on Andale's nose. Ever felt it was such a personal moment that she had to look away out of respect.

He said his goodbye and sent the horses off. All of them besides Phantom, who had no choice but to travel with them. Someone had to carry Cassio through to the other side, where the dragon heart could save him from the sirens' spell, and neither Teava nor Jesper, and surely not the other smaller girls, were capable of keeping him as well as themselves alive through the perils of the forest. But Ever knew that the dragon's horse would carry the task better than the elven horses would. And, though she was not a strong rider, nor did her dwarven nature lend a want for horses, she was sad to see them go. She was sad for Jesper, who had truly loved them. But, as the creature of the forest let out another hallow screech that echoed in the trees, the horses, even the great Andale, fled abruptly in the opposite direction. Ever watched as Jesper stared after them with a heavy heart. She hoped that he would be reunited with his steed before too long.

As they packed up, each of the members of the company were eyeing the forest with weary anticipation. Save for Ever, they had all heard the legends of the forest. There was a great many that seemed to circle the entire Earth of Eald. Nobody seemed to agree on any particular version, but everyone could agree to stay away from it. Even Teava, the great dragon who never seemed to fear the dangers that were laid in their path, did not seem eager to wander into the forest. Having grown up just on the other side of it, she had been taught from childhood to stay very far away from whatever might be living there. She had personally known a dragon who had gone into the forest – a dare, from children who thought too little of the stories. He was one of her closest friends as a child. He disappeared that day, barely more than a ten year old child, and was never seen again. Teava had known right away that he died that day. Whatever legends lived in the forest were strong enough to slay a dragon.

As she finished securing Cassio's limp body to her own steed, Teava announced that it was time to leave. Jesper was the last to turn and follow. Ever held back as they entered the forest until her pace matched his and took his hand in hers, offering some comfort.

"They will find their way back to Brisdale," she told him, "just as you will."

He did not care to discuss his steed, though.

"Where will you go," he changed the focus, "when all is said and done?"

Ever dropped his hand then, shocked by his question. In truth, the thought of returning anywhere had never crossed her mind. She had never been completely sure where it was that they were heading, so she was never able to imagine a next destination.

She thought of the bravery she had when she left the mountain where she grew up, the only place that she had ever known. She thought of the luck she had in finding Tekla's family along the way and a route to Brisdale, to Jesper. She thought of the frightening experiences, too. Experiences like the vision with Merenda, her first encounter with the orcs, and the sirens. She thought of the Vehsi in the village, and the constant feeling of being hunted that came with them. She thought of what lied ahead

– first the monster that was responsible for those wretched noises, and then the mighty dragon kingdom. Neither of those were going to be easy to survive, and yet, she was about to face them head on.

The world from which she had been hidden for twenty-three years was a fearsome place. Perhaps it was one in which she did not belong it at all. She was but a frail dwarven child, after all. And yet, she did not want to go to the place she knew as home. Even before she left, she was anxious to go. Now that she saw that the world needed a savior, she could not leave it. Despite the fact that the mountain was still home to the only twelve dwarves remaining on the map, she did not feel like it was home to her any longer. She would never belong there.

But where, then, did she belong?

"You could come to Brisdale with me," Jesper said, sensing the direction of her thoughts.

But Ever was not sure that she would be welcome there, either. Despite the friendlier nature of the Brisdale elves, they were still not keen on the idea of living among the mortal races. Even Jesper surely would not choose to stay with a mortal.

Ever decided to change the subject. After all, before they even thought of returning home, they would first have to survive the journey.

"What creature makes those noises?" she asked, though she wasn't sure she really wanted to know.

Jesper did not answer right away, and when he did, he had lowered his voice so that the others could not hear him.

Or perhaps so that the beast itself could not hear.

"Her name is Celeano," he told her. "It is said that she was formed from the souls of those who died in the forest centuries ago, though I do not believe that. Most will agree that she is a giant beast like a lion, but that she consists of little more than skeleton and organs."

"Do you believe *that*?" Ever asked.

"I do not understand how such a creature could survive.

And yet, I know that something lives in this forest. I know that the very trees we walk through now have held her secrets for centuries. I know that no one that enters this forest, despite the stories of Celeano's appearance, have ever been seen again."

Ever gulped, her eyes now peering through every tree.

"I do not know if I believe the stories to be any more than fairy tales meant to scare children away from certain death," he told her. "And yet, I know that every story has some inkling of truth to it."

"Why does she cry like she does?" she asked him.

"I have heard stories of a lost child," he answered. "I do not understand how two of these creatures could have been made, nor do I understand how she could go missing, but that is the story."

Ever contemplated this. Perhaps, if the beast was in mourning, there might be a way to console it. If they discovered whatever consolation that might be, it would perhaps spare their journey of some trouble. Should they encounter it, anyway. She hoped that they would not. Yet, she felt eyes on her.

In fact, she was sure it was not only paranoia produced by Jesper's stories. She was almost certain that they were being followed. She felt as though they had been watched the minute they stepped into the forest. She tried to shake the feeling and concentrate on walking quietly.

The forest was really a beautiful place, save for its dark history. The trees grew tall and strong, most of them willows. Their canopies were full and glorious, giving the company full protection from the sun.

And sealing them away from the outside world, a fact that never left Ever's mind. She felt uneasy about it somehow. She tried once again to focus on something else.

The ground cover blossomed with small purple flowers that surrounded each of the willow trees. As they walked further in, the willows' canopies seemed to twinkle with blue lights. It was a spectacular sight, almost magical. It perhaps didn't seem natural, but it was a wonderful sight to wander through. Ever took the time to gaze in awe as each new wonder passed. The curves of the tree trunks that looked almost purposeful, as if made for the ease of climbing. The way that some of the trees glowed more than others. The careful weave of some of the canopies, as if netted into a hammock.

And then she thought that something must have lived there, as it all seemed too purposeful. Something that dwelled in the trees rather than on the ground. Something that was not the beast Celeano. It must have been an equally terrible creature to live side by side with such a beast and survive so well. But it must have been the one to weave the trees together like they were.

She realized that, while she and the less experienced members of the group were playing tourist and ogling over the sights, Jesper and Teava were keeping an even sharper eye out than usual. They had reached much the same conclusion that Ever had, she was sure. She began to watch with sharp eyes, too, though for what, she hadn't any idea.

The wind began to pick up quickly, sweeping the loose hair into Ever's face. She constantly had to hold it back, afraid to miss even the smallest movement. But as the wind got stronger and more fierce, she had a hard time deciphering if the trees moved because of the wind, the beast, or the unknown creature. The beast had become nearly silent, as if taking shelter from the hissing wind, so she was certain that Celeano was not the reason for the movement. However, the feeling of being watched never went away.

As the day wore on, nothing but the slapping of the wind ever interfered with the company. They were slowed, struggling with each step, but never once stopped. Tekla had never even complained about food. Despite her tourist gazing, she was probably just as anxious to leave the forest as the rest of them were. Even without knowing of the possible threat, the forest had a dark and uninviting atmosphere about it.

Teava was watching the impending threat. Unlike Tekla, she had known very well what had been watching them. She saw the curious creature and studied them between the leaves of the trees. She had thought that race to be long since extinct, but she was watching them, however impossibly, dance through the treetops as she followed the group. It was fascinating. Well, not completely. She had to remind herself that the creature was clearly the enemy. From the look on its face, it was not happy to have the intrusion that the company presented. Teava wondered why it had not yet acted on its anger. She knew its kind was good with weaponry, and yet, it simply watched.

And then Ever saw it, too. Out of the corner of her eye, she saw a dark shape jump from one tree to the next. In a second, it was again hidden in the canopies. She could have only imagined it. Perhaps it was the wind making the leaves dance. But she was positive that it was there. Quickly, she walked as close to Jesper's side as she could, her eyes still scanning the canopies, hoping to see it again.

"We're being followed," she told him, whispering as quietly as she could while still being heard above the wind.

"Yes," he said. Ever took her eyes off of the forest to look at him in bewilderment. How had he known and not done something about it? "I've seen her, too."

"What is she?"

"I cannot tell. A creature of the night, I am sure."

"Celeano?"

"No. She is much too small. Much too quiet. Teava believes that she can handle her, should she interfere with us."

"And what do you think?"

"I think that she is not alone."

"There's more?"

"I cannot tell for certain. Watch there," he told her, directing her with his eyes only. She looked. She saw a distinct movement in the canopy, maybe like the weight of something landing, but it could have been the wind. "And there." In the opposite direction, she saw the same movement. She wondered if Jesper's elven eyes could see more shapes than her dwarven eyes were seeing, allowing him to make more of the movements than she had. Still, she understood what he saw. Two creatures following them. But neither of them had made a move.

The day was slowly turning to evening and the company was losing light. Tekla had finally begun her typical complaints of hunger, and reluctantly, though they were still being followed, Jesper and Teava relented to making camp.

Ever did not share her troubles with Tekla or Merenda, allowing them to have a bit of peace in the night. Instead, they talked about the future of their journey, for which Ever was both glad of and nervous for. She was glad because they all talked with an assumption that they would have a future at all, and she was nervous because the journey did not end once they reached the dragon kingdom.

"I know everyone is anxious to gather an elven army," Jesper said, "but I believe there is another whose council we should seek."

"You don't think it wise to fight by the side of your own?" Merenda asked quizzically.

"On the contrary," Jesper told her. "I think, though, that we may not be the ones to convince the elves. Let the dragons travel to the south and speak to the elves. They are far quicker, and far more convincing, than a group of exiles and oddities, such as ourselves."

"Then what are you suggesting, Jesper?" Teava asked with one perfectly arched eyebrow.

"There are tales of a wise sorcerer, who always seeks to fight the good fight. Often, he stays in a cottage near the Empty Sea, keeping a low profile, but watching. Always watching. He has heard of the legends. He knows far more than we could ever hope to know. He could help us. He will help us."

"How do you know someone like that exists," Tekla

snorted, "much less wants to help a bunch of misfits, as you call us?"

"I know he exists," he said, "because he is my friend. And it is also for that reason that I know he will help."

"Who is he," Merenda interjected, "this sorcerer friend of yours?"

"His name is Theodoric."

"We cannot go to him."

Merenda's words felt final. It was as if she had made up her mind for the whole group and her decision would be respected by it. She went on eating as if the topic was through. Jesper was not through discussing it, however.

"You've heard of him, then?" he asked.

"Every sorcerer worth their magic has heard of him," she replied coldly. "Many have sought apprenticeship from him."

"He has never had an apprentice."

"Precisely," came her cold response. "He is never found when sought. He comes only when he means to, and only for his own agenda. He will not do anything for us. Our time is spent better with the elves."

"How arrogantly you speak of your own kind."

"You're one to talk," she snapped at him. "You left the elves as soon as you could, and I doubt very much that you intend to go back. You suggest that we send the dragons to their doorstep, the very beings that instill fright in the hearts of every race."

"Stop this," Teava put in, interrupting whatever Jesper what about to say. "This Theodoric," she said, looking at the elf. "You are sure of his character?"

In response, Jesper gave a silent nod.

"And you feel certain that he is a necessity in our quest?"

He responded with another single, silent nod.

"Then we must split up."

"What?" Tekla and Ever said together. Despite having their reservations about each new addition, neither girl had considered separating.

"Jesper will lead the expedition to find the sorcerer, and the rest of us will follow Ever with the dragons to the elven kingdoms."

Ever liked even less the idea of separating from Jesper, who had been her first ally outside of the mountain. The two shared a look that said the feeling had been mutual. But Teava took no notice, continuing with her directions.

"We must first think of reaching the dragon heart, so that we might all be recovered at long last. After that, we must be sure that we can secure the help of the elven armies. For that, we will need Ever. She is the most valuable piece of information that we have to convince them. Whoever does not wish to accompany the dragons on a journey may stay with Jesper. That choice will be yours. The Empty Sea is not far from here, and it will not be such a treacherous journey."

The group had sobered then. Even Merenda's anger had dissipated. No one liked the idea of splitting up, and certainly no one liked the idea of having to choose. But discussions of any kind ceased then, as the beast Celeano had decided that her silence was over. Her voice now seemed like less of an angry screech. Now it was a saddened moan, as if she, too, was sobered with the group. Still, her noisy return to the atmosphere called the group back to the danger at hand. They were not safe, nor were they promised tomorrow. One by one, each of them put their remaining food away and laid down to get whatever rest they could. All but Merenda, who had been chosen for the first watch, drifted off into a slumber.

* * *

Ever woke with a start. Merenda had choked on a scream, the cause of everyone's sudden awakening.

She was held with a sword to her throat, the culprit snarling at the rest of the group. She was tall, with muscles beneath her black skin that showed her physical strength. She had long blonde hair that flowed loosely around pointed ears. She hissed as the group woke, clearly having planned to take them out silently as they dozed.

Ever gasped as cold metal was suddenly pressed against her own skin. The culprint behind her was much the same as the girl who held Merenda, save that her blonde hair had been tied back in a long braid.

"We don't mean to hurt you," said the girl who held Ever. Her companion hissed again, clearly in disagreement. Ever realized with a start that these were the creatures that had been following them, lying in wait until they were fast asleep.

"Then what do you mean to do?" Teava challenged. Her swords were in her hands and Jesper's bow was niched with an arrow, but neither attacked. They knew that they would cost Ever and Merenda their lives if they did – their response had been quick, but not quick enough.

"What are you doing in our forest?" the girl asked, ignoring Teava and speaking only to Jesper.

"This is not your forest," he told them. "It belongs to Celeano."

"Celeano belongs to us," came her counter.

"How can that be?"

"We have what she desires. But that is neither here nor there. Answer my question."

"We seek the council of the dragon queen. Let our company go. We will be gone in but a few nights, and have no intention of returning."

"It's not that simple, I'm afraid," she said. "For we do not let anyone simply walk through our home with their lives. You see, we have a reputation and a legend to keep alive."

"Then kill us now," he commanded. Ever gasped in shock at his suggestion. The other girl snarled and tightened her grip on Merenda, clearly in agreement.

"Patience, Venea," the girl with the braid told her. "We very well would have," she addressed Jesper, "but you see, it is not every day that we come across one of our own."

"One of your own?" he asked in confusion.

"Indeed. So I ask again. What are you doing in our forest?"

"There is none of your own here," he argued, ignoring her. She played along.

"Oh? Then I suppose we can kill you now." The blade dug into Ever's throat.

"No!" he yelled, jumping forward.

The girl smiled smugly, enjoying every minute of her sadistic game.

"Let's see," she said. "You and I sure do look alike. How can you not be my brother?"

"I am no dark elf."

Dark elves, Ever thought with a chill. She had never heard of them, and surely did not wish to hear more.

"Perhaps not completely," she said, "just as this girl is not completely dwarven, nor is that girl completely human," she said with a tilt of her head in Merenda's direction. "It would seem as though the world had become quite a curious, naughty place. Oh – did you not know?" she asked with feigned shock as the group looked at her in confusion. "Then you have a lot to learn about yourselves. A lot that I know already, it seems. The insight of a dark elf is a strange and powerful thing, you see. Lucky for you," she said, reaching in her bag and pulling out rope, "the curiosity of a dark elf is just as powerful. You are going to come with us now, away from our beast where we can talk." She tossed the rope at Jesper, her grip on Ever never weakening. "Tie them up," she commanded, "and you be sure not to be loose with the knots, else your… *dwarven* friend… will see her end. And be sure that I will know if you are playing any games."

Now with Jesper wearing the snarl on his lips, he slowly lowered his bow and obliged to the dark elf's commands.

He tied the long rope around each of his friends feet, leaving for his own free, and then tied their hands behind their backs with several smaller pieces of ropes, as per the dark elf's instructions. He then handed her the end of the rope so that she could lead the group. Ever tried the knots by rotating her wrists a small bit. Jesper had clearly chosen not to play games, though Ever was sure they could have taken the creatures down easily. They had the numbers, after all.

Ever was also aggravated by the trust that they had seemed to have in Jesper. He was not tied up, and instead given the task of leading Phantom and caring for Cassio. She knew that he would not run when all the others were tied up, as the creatures must also have sensed, but it still put her out. She was angry that the dark elves thought they knew so much about the group. They were right about Merenda, as she was a sorceress and thus not wholly mortal. But they had challenged her dwarvenism, for which she was proud, and also Jesper's elvenism. She could not tell if he was so proud of his own race, but he was certainly no creature of the dark as they had presumed.

She was also exceptionally angry to be in their control, to be led off course to wherever they chose. She hoped that the creatures were not actually leading them to Celeano, whether on purpose or accident. Meeting the beast while tied up in Jesper's knots would be a deadly fate.

But the evil creatures did not lead them to the beast, nor was it ever their intention to do so. They led them not too far off, to a place that they had clearly prepared. Jesper was instructed to tie up Phantom and carry Cassio into their hideout.

The hideout itself was strange. It was little more than a giant hole in the ground, covered at its opening with a trap door made of leaves. Inside, it was littered with bones of all sorts, clearly not from the same person or even from the same race. Ever assumed that this was not where the girls lived, but where they took their guests to. Everyone was told to sit on the dirt ground and no one disobeyed.

"Now, down to business, then," the leader said. "My name is Nika, and this is my sister Venea. Now will you introduce yourselves? Careful, we will know when you're lying, and liars will be killed."

Ever glared at her. Lying was the only safe thing for her, as she knew that her secret was important.

"I am Tekla of Ioka," Tekla piped up, "and my family is surely looking for me by now. You should be careful of what you intend to do."

Her ferociousness only amused Nika.

"Of course they are," she said when she was done chuckling. "But what have I to fear of a farm family from a tiny village? They would not even make it over the river. I do admire your conviction, though. You left your family to save them, did you not? How heroic of you. I only hope that it is not a wasted effort," she added with a sly grin. "But you have not lied, Tekla of Ioka, so I will not kill you yet, though you are of little interest to me. Now who is next?"

Her eyes went to Ever, who immediately paled.

"I am Teava," Teava said quickly, taking the pressure off of Ever and hoping that Nika would forget about the dwarf. It was a useless hope. "Teava of Abrya."

"Careful now, Teava," grinned Nika. "That is only a half-truth, isn't it? And what is a half-truth but a half lie?" She raised one eyebrow as Teava gritted her teeth.

"It is the whole truth," she argued, but continued on to give the rest of the story anyway. "I am no longer associated with Shodalea. I left there long ago."

"Ah, yes," Nika said in thought. "An exiled princess would surely not wish to associate with those who exiled her."

Teava received a few sidelong glances from the members of the group that did not already know her story.

"I heard of you, so long ago. How brave you must have

thought yourself. You stood up for the woman you love. I'm sure it meant a lot to her. What was her name – Salora, I do believe." Hearing the dark elf say the name made Teava want to spit at her face. But she knew better and kept her mouth shut. "If only the gesture had been as well received among your own clan. Do you not call yourself an Emperik anymore? I assume not. But I have no interest in you, either. I'm through with you now," Nika declared. "I'd like to know the names of the half breeds now."

Merenda acted quickly. She knew that Ever needed time to figure out how to respond to the tricky ways of the dark elf. She valued Ever's secret as much as Ever herself did, if not more. She had seen much more than the vision she had shared with the young dwarf. She knew much more than Ever did, and knew that she was meant to protect those secrets from enemy ears.

"I am Merenda Di Meo," she declared, "and I belong to no place."

"A nomad, then? How clever. Tell me, nomad, why do you fear security in making a home?"

"Homes are destroyed," she spat. "The evil sorcerer does not leave alone the smallest village."

Nika seemed deep in thought just then.

"I like you, nomad. You think in the right way. But most sorcerers think that way, do they not? Oh," she added when she saw Merenda's eyes widen, "I know exactly what you are. I have already seen it in your eyes. I do not wish to see more. I do not like your kind. You are little more than witches to me, and you cause nothing but chaos… You are not important to me. So I suppose you, then, dark elf, will introduce yourself next? You are saving the dwarf for last, are you not?"

Through another pair of gritted teeth, Jesper responded.

"I am Jesper of Brisdale."

"Oh!" Nika said in pleasant surprise. "Venea, we are in the presence of royalty! Had I known the dark elf was a prince, I would have cleaned up the hole!"

"It is not real royalty," he said with annoyance, "and if you have already heard of me, you would know that."

"Oh, but my dear prince, you do not know everything that you are!"

"And what is it that I am, since you know me so well?"

"Your blood is mixed with great and terrible things. You are light of the brightest kind and dark of the blackest night. Should you choose to stay with us – and you will choose – we will show you your dark half." Her answer to him was not really an answer at all and it made him even more annoyed. "Now, then, on to the most curious one!" Her attention turned to Ever.

Ever gulped, but decided that she should follow suit and tell the truth. The dark elves seemed to have a certain knack for insight and it felt unwise to lie. Perhaps, at least, Nika might tell her what Teava would not.

"I am Ever," she said quietly, and with a tremble.

"Ever, huh? What a strange name," Nika said, "even for a dwarf. And they were exceptionally strange creatures. Where are you from, then, Ever?"

"I..." she began, uncertain of how to continue. "I don't really know. Isola, I suppose, though I never lived there."

"An Isolan dwarf?" she asked.

"She's lying," Venea finally interjected, her hand going to her sword.

"No," Nika said calmly, "we both know that she isn't."

"It's not possible," Venea argued. "No dwarf could have escaped that annihilation. No one has ever escaped Terrisino."

"And yet," Nika ventured, "someone has. In fact, we are in the presence of three such people already."

"You've seen him?" Jesper broke in with shock.

Venea and Nika both laughed in response.

"We would not be so foolish as to make his acquaintance," Venea said in a smug way.

"Now, now, Venea," Nika chimed. "I'm sure it was not by

choice. The funny thing, though, is that our friend Ever bears no mark."

"What mark?" Jesper demanded. "And who among us bears it?"

"The mark is not something you can see. It is something you can… feel, in a way. You and your friends probably cannot ever see it, because you have not tuned your sixth senses as Venea and I have, as comes easy to the dark elves. Perhaps if you were as in tune to your dark side, you, too, would be able to embrace that sense and know that you bear the mark yourself."

Jesper scoffed.

"Perhaps you are not as good as you say you are," he told her dryly. "For I have never had the pleasure of meeting the Great Sorcerer. If I had, he would be dead."

"I believe that you believe that," said Nika, "however, the mark is there. Whether you know it or not, you have had the chance to rid the world of his evil doings and you chose, for whatever reason, to let him go on. Perhaps you can be dark after all."

"Lies," Jesper seethed.

"Believe what you will," Nika said. "I am still interested in your friend."

"No more," he said. "Let us go."

"Oh, but I don't know what I wish to know. We've only just met. Now tell me, Ever, how did you escape?"

Ever decided that she had to phrase her words carefully. She got the sense that although the dark elves had great intuition, they did not know anything until they were told. Teava's story must have been told throughout the land by other dragons, and surely Jesper's royal family was no secret. Other than that, Nika had not revealed anything of substance. She knew that she could keep the other dwarves a secret if she proceeded with caution.

"My mother ran from the kingdom," she told Nika, "before I was born. She is the one who escaped him, not I."

"How valiant of your mother," she said. "Does that heroic quality dwell in you as well?" Ever did not know how to answer, and so she kept quiet. "You have set off to destroy the evil one," Nika continued, "so I will assume you do. Did you not take into consideration that he is all powerful and you are just a bunch of left over scraps from your respective races? I suppose you have, and merely though yourselves invincible, since you have survived him before."

"What do you want with us?" Teava jumped in, growing impatient with the dark elves' games.

"To be quite clear," Nika said, unperturbed by her bluntness, "I want to know how a dwarf exists at all. And then I want him," she pointed to Jesper.

"Well," Teava said, "a dwarf exists exactly as the rest of us do. Shall I explain to you the act of love, or can I assume you understand that already?" she snapped sarcastically. "And you cannot have him, so we will be on our way, then."

"Quite the opposite. You see, we had to flee our home and our kin. We do not know what has become of all of them, but we grow lonely here by ourselves. We have not seen a dark elf venture into our forest for a long time. He is the only reason we did not kill you. I will have him, and that is all there is to it."

"Look," Jesper said calmly, "no decision needs to be reached today. Help us get our friend to the place he needs to be. Help us get through this forest. He needs the medical attention of the dragons, and he needs it soon."

"And what do I get in return?" Venea asked, snaking her hand around his chest in a way that made Ever's stomach sicken. "There is always a price to be paid in a bargain. We give what you want, and you give what we want."

Jesper gulped audibly.

"Venea grows more tiresome of the loneliness than I do," Nika said. "I prefer information. So, here is the bargain that I propose to you. We will help you get through the forest. In return, you will answer my questions, since I know you have more to tell."

"Yes," Jesper said, jumping to detangle himself from Venea. "Yes, we will take that bargain."

"I was not done. You need both my sister and myself to get through with your lives. Therefore, my sister must get something from you as well."

Jesper stopped struggling against Venea. He already knew what she would demand.

"My sister," said Nika, "needs a dark knight at her side for the rest of her immortal life. Since you are the only dark elf we have seen in a hundred years, you will have to do. If we are to help you and not kill you or your friends, you will be her betrothed."

"No!" Teava and Ever shouted together, while Tekla laughed in disbelief and Merenda stared in horror. Nika ignored all of them, waiting only for Jesper's response as Venea continued snaking her arms around his chest.

"If that is the deal," he began, "then you will not only help us through the forest, but you will help us on our entire quest, as I have much more to do before I am free to marry."

There was a moment of silence as the girls looked at each other. They were communicating without words, as is so easy to do when you have lived with no one else for a century. Finally, Venea spoke.

"I will go with you," she said, "and you will be mine."

So they had reached their agreement. Ever shuddered, both in anger and in repulsion. Jesper had been tricked. Although she knew that he had done it for them, she was still furious that he would now be forced to spend his immortal life with a creature of the night. It was not right.

But what else could she expect from such a species? If they had not accepted the bargain and Jesper agreed to the proposal, the dark elves would have killed them. There was no question of that.

"We will leave immediately," Nika said decisively. "Our tree house is in the middle of the forest, and that is where we will be the safest. We have a long walk, then."

She lowered herself to the ground and knelt next to Ever, who gasped and cringed away. Nika gave her an amused grin, and Ever was shocked to see that it was not sadistic any longer. Nika set to untying the ropes.

"You need not fear," she whispered in a low tone to Ever, "unless you betray us. My sister and I have a very strong sense of loyalty, especially when it comes to family. And your friend? Well," her grin turned slightly more sadistic then, "he's as good as family now."

Once Ever was freed, Nika moved on and she and Jesper untied everyone. Ever rubbed at her sore wrists as she stared after Nika. She was unsure if she could trust the girl. Plots were already forming in her mind – plots of murder. First, she would take out Venea. If Nika killed her after that, at least she would have saved Jesper from his fate with the snake. She was great with her axe. All she really had to do was wait for their backs to turn. If she planned it just right, she could take them both out just as they had planned to take the group out – quickly, quietly, and in their sleep.

But she quickly cleared that train of thought. She did not know enough about the extent of their powers, and she was growing quite paranoid of what psychic abilities – if any – they might have. She did not want them to catch wind of her plan.

And so, their awkward and distrustful walk began. The entire time, Venea never left Jesper's side, and made sure to touch him in some way every minute. Ever felt a seething sense of jealousy. She did not know why. Jesper was not hers. But she felt that neither was he Venea's. That was a proposal that he had been forced into, and his body language clearly said that he did not feel happy about it. And yet, the jealousy she felt only grew to take over her whole mind. She did not wish to kill Venea so much as she wished to *be* her. She wanted to have her hand on the small of Jesper's back, as Venea did. And, more than that, she wanted him to wrap his arm around her as well. That, at least, was one thing that neither she nor Venea had. Jesper was as stiff as a stick in Venea's snake-like embrace. That was the only but of satisfaction that Ever felt from watching the two elven creatures walking ahead of her.

Ever decided that she needed a distraction to take her mind off of the seething jealousy in her thoughts. At the very first moment that she could, Ever pulled Teava aside to ask her about the practical matters of the dark elves. She felt ill equipped in knowledge about this world, and sought after it the same way that Nika did.

"Dark elves," Teava whispered to her, trying to be as out of hearing range as possible, "are mostly just elves, but of the night. They possess the same immortal life, the same heightened senses, and the same love for woodland life. But they practice a certain kind of black magic that gives them this extra sixth sense that they have spoken of. It makes them more dangerous because it makes them one of most cunning creatures in the land. It is true that they have a strong sense of loyalty to their families, as the loud one says, but dark elves are often at war with their own kind. At least, they were. No one has heard of them for a long time. To be quite honest, I had thought them to be extinct. But then," she added thoughtfully, "I also thought the dwarves were extinct. Perhaps endangered is the better word for your races."

Ever thought this over carefully before asking her next question.

"Do you think it is safe to travel with them?"

"I think we have no choice. We cannot double cross them without losing at least one of our own. And if we do not catch them by surprise, they could take out our entire group. Dark elves are trained as warriors from the moment they take their first steps. We are no match for their skills. Fighting is more second nature to them than it is for the dwarves." She paused then, her voice dropping even lower. "Whatever you are planning to do, you should forget it right now."

Ever did not want to take her advice. At the very least, she wanted Venea dead, even if it meant that she had to forfeit her own life. But she did not want to risk anyone else's, and she knew that they had to get through the forest. So, for the moment, she tried to put her plans on hold.

"Do you think it wise to take them all the way to the end of our quest?"

"Do not think that I have not thought of this myself, Ever," she chuckled. "It is my hope that we will not have to double cross them to be rid of them. You see, I already have suspicions in my own mind. New revelations, perhaps. Already, each of us that has taken on this quest knows that a price will be paid, and that death is not out of the question. The dark elves, even if they do not care for our quest, have chosen to join us. They are not simple creatures. They know the ultimate price might be paid by them."

"So," Ever said, "your hope is that someone else will kill them."

"Indeed," Teava said. "But more than that is my revelation. Most folk know the story of Terrisino. He was once an elf who chose the path of black magic. He murdered his family before he rose to power. That is a common motif among the creatures of the night. My idea is that perhaps there truly are more dark elves among us."

"You think Terrisino is one."

"I am becoming convinced that it is a strong possibility."

"How can one be so many things at once?" Ever asked. "He was an elf, and is now a sorcerer, and could be a dark elf."

"Against wiser judgment," explained Teava, "many of the races have mixed before. It is not as uncommon of an occurrence as it should be, as the loud one has informed us. Most of us possess the qualities to perform sorcery to some level, though you or I could never be like Merenda. Even if you had an ancestor long ago with the pure blood of a sorcerer, their blood is not potent enough to carry down. It must be a direct parent. It controls the magic, in a way. However, all dark elves have the sorcerer blood in them, enough to practice a great deal of magic. That further convinces me of my revelation. How else could Terrisino have acquired the magic that he has? How else could he have raised the Vehsi or destroyed your people so easily? I believe that there is much about this world that even I do not know." Here, she paused again, looking on Ever with sad understanding. It was the first sign of empathy that Ever had seen from her, and it took her by surprise. "How terrifying it must be for you."

"It can be," Ever quietly admitted.

"It is my hope," Teava said, "that more than you could ever hope for will be revealed to you once we reach the dragon heart."

Ever appreciated her attempt at comfort, but it wasn't enough.

"You know something about me," she said bluntly. The only response she received was a cold shoulder. "The dark elves know it, too, don't they?"

It took Teava a moment to respond.

"I hope that they do not know what I suspect," came her vague answer. "I think that since you do not know it yourself, they cannot know, either. No more questions," she said, interrupting Ever as she was about to, indeed, ask questions. "This is something that should not be taken lightly. If what I suspect is true, you will find out in due time. But it is a discovery that you must make yourself, without any prior inklings from the dark elves or me."

Ever was reluctant to let it go, but she could see that the matter was not worth pursuing. Teava had said all that she would say now.

* * *

The journey to the dark elves' tree house had not been as perilous as Ever thought it would have been – and, indeed, as Teava had hoped it would be. Everyone made it there safely, including Cassio and Phantom and the dark creatures that Teava would have gladly fed to the beast. As luck would have it, they never came across the wailing Celeano.

The tree house was well decorated, and with many exotic treasures. Ever made the assumption that they had been stolen, perhaps even from the bodies of the brave souls that made the fatal decision of traveling through the forest. The blue lights on the willow trees kept the tree house well lit. Ever was not sure if she would prefer the dark, as it was better to hide in. Still, she supposed, after the time they spent on the ground waiting in suspense for the beast that never came, she was glad to be safe enough, so long as the dark elves chose not to double cross them.

Although Ever had expected at any moment to be double crossed, she was surprised at the treatment that the group received instead. It made her feel uneasy when they were treated as friends rather than captives. They were welcomed into the home of the dark elves without so much as a warning not to touch their belongings. They were never given any snide remarks, or any sarcastic jokes at their expense. Instead, the dark elves seemed almost glad to be hosting a few visitors for once. Ever could not decide if it was a game they played, to give their prey a false sense of security, or if it was truly genuine. The dark elves were excellent at hiding whatever their motive to that behavior might have been.

Everyone had settled in the house and was seated along the round wooden table in the kitchen as Venea prepared a meal for everyone to eat. She seemed happy to be in the kitchen. As she cooked, she even asked about likes and dislikes among the various races, claiming she only knew how to cook for her sister and herself. When she was through cooking, she brought them a sort of stew with meat that Ever did not recognize. She was hesitant to eat it at all, but reluctantly followed as everyone else took a bite. She was most comforted when Nika ate from the same pot as the rest of them had been served from. The stew was warm, which was all Ever really needed to be satisfied. It had been too long since she had had a warm meal. But she noticed, too, it had an earthy flavor that wasn't unpleasant, as she had thought it would have been. The meat chunks, she discovered after a few bites, were made from rabbit. There was a berry taste, too – she thought it to be cranberry. All in all, the dark elf seemed to know how to blend a variety of flavors together to create a delicious meal. Ever had assumed them to eat like wild animals, but it seemed that they also knew how to behave in a society.

Before long, everyone's bellies were full and satisfied, and each of them leaned back in their chairs, feeling ready for a nice long nap. Just then, the flapping of large wings sounded from above, taking away the calm tone of the situation. Ever and Tekla both gasped as they sat upright, startled, but everyone else just listened tensely as the wings passed by. Silence sat in the room until the noise had disappeared completely into the west.

"Was that…" Tekla gulped, shaking with fear.

"Celeano?" Ever finished for her, her own mind filling with fear as she imagined the creature that Jesper had described, but with wings on top of the already menacing picture he painted.

"No," Nika told them, putting both girls at ease for only a moment. "It is the dragons. It sounded like only one. It must be a scout this time."

"They have passed on other occasions?" Teava asked, her interest piqued despite her deep rooted distrust of the creatures.

"Several times we have heard them over the forest. Usually they come one or two at a time. Sometimes, a whole flock of them passes over and never comes back."

"Could they be leaving the kingdom?" Teava thought out loud. "Or perhaps it is an army that has been sent out. I can't imagine that they would feel safer leaving the kingdom."

"I think that it is time you told us more about your quest," Nika said. "It seems to me that you think our world is in danger. And if that is the case, no matter how much you resent our kind, we do live here and wish to be armed with knowledge."

"We have isolated ourselves," put in Venea, her hands finally kept to herself as she put on a more serious front. "For a century, we have lived in the confines of this forest, collecting very little information from whoever dares to enter, and those who dare have become fewer and fewer as the time has gone on."

"Before you, we have not seen a soul for nearly a decade."

Ever began to wonder if the dark elves had been so easy on them simply because they lacked interaction with other beings. She began to think that their oddly friendly behavior could be, in fact, genuine. Loneliness had driven people to do stranger things.

"I believe," Teava answered after taking a breath, "that Terrisino is ready to make a move to conquer us. He already believes that he has wiped out the dwarven race, which bought him time to prepare his armies. But then the rumor of a single dwarf, the legendary savior, surfaced. I have heard it, long before I met Ever. He has probably heard it as well, and realizes that his time is running out."

"You think that he is finally prepared to do the very thing he had sworn to do all those years ago when he killed his family?" Nika asked.

"Yes." Teava's answer was simple, but it brought sheer terror to the faces of most of the company. Once again, Tekla and Ever were the only two who did not understand.

"What did he swear?" Ever asked, her own confusion supplying enough terror without the tension felt from the rest of the group.

"He will wipe out every race that he deems unusable," Teava began ominously, "just as he did with the dwarves. And everyone, dead and alive, will be his servant."

"Did he take the dark elves, too, then?" Tekla asked.

"The dark elves," Nika put in with scorn, "wiped themselves out. That's what happens when a race can never unite itself."

"The race of men," Teava continued, as if uninterrupted,

"will be next. He has no use for mortal souls. Which means the sorcerers will be gone, too. He will only keep the elves and the dragons. The dragons will be his brain washed pets, doing his bidding, killing all he wishes to be dead. The elves will be forced to learn his dark magic and serve him, or die. He will conquer this land and move out to take over the lands beyond the Earth of Eald with his immortal army."

"But you think" Venea said definitively, "that you can defeat him. You think that you have the dwarf of legend."

Suddenly, the dark elves both fixed their eyes on Ever. She sighed. Once again, the weight of the free world was a burden she felt heavy on her shoulders, and she was still unconvinced of her place in the legend.

"I do not know yet," admitted Teava, causing Ever to look up at her. Merenda, too, looked at her. Ever had thought that was the secret Teava would not voice.

"But my vision," Merenda argued, "showed the Vehsi hunting her specifically."

"It did not say that she was the very dwarf of legend, but simply a dwarf that carried the fate. There is another reason I wish to go to Shodalea, and for that reason I may stay longer than I really wish to. And that is to get to the archives. I don't know if she is the right dwarf, but I do believe that she has survived for a reason, and I plan to figure that out."

"How do you expect to get to those archives," began Nika, "as the exiled princess? I doubt very much that your kin will even let you pass the gates."

"I do not think they would disallow it," she answered, "in such a dire time. I have my ways."

To Ever's surprise, Nika did not ask any question about those ways. The conversation slowly ended, and each person was left to their own thoughts. Before long, the weather outside began to change. The soft patter of rain began to thrum against the leaves over their heads. The creative architecture of the dark elves kept their heads dry and never once did the wind knock anything loose. The group decided that it was time to stop talking and get a bit of rest before they began their journey through the second half of the forest.

Ever realized as Venea led them to their sleeping quarters that the term tree house was a humble way to describe the place that the dark elves had built for themselves. She supposed that living out there for a century had probably bred a bit of boredom for the girls, and thus they spent their time with home improvements. The tree house must have connected a few trees together, as it had several rooms within it. And, indeed, Venea led them across a bridge that was not sheltered from the rain. The cool droplets fell on their faces as they entered the next tree house structure.

Within the structure were several more rooms. Venea showed Jesper into one of them, going in only to help him place Cassio on the bed, to Ever's great satisfaction. She led Teava and Merenda into the next, and Tekla and Ever across the hall. Immediately, the girls went to their own separate beds.

The dark elves' homemade furniture was like sleeping on clouds compared to the ground that they had grown accustomed to. In fact, Ever would venture far enough as to say it was better than the elven beds. The wooden frame was carved with intricate designs. The mattress itself was still connected to the trees as they wove themselves around the frame several times, providing a comfortable thickness between the sleeper and the wooden frame. As a passing thought before she drifted to sleep, Ever wondered why the dark creatures had made so many extra beds and rooms for only the two of them. They didn't seem the type to keep company.

Sleep came quickly that night. Perhaps it was due to her exhaustion, or perhaps it was due to the softness of the willow tree beds. Whatever it was, Ever welcomed it gladly. She did not toss or turn once she had fallen asleep, and her dreams were quiet.

But then, all too soon, the snores of Tekla broke into her

slumber. Ever squeezed her eyes tighter, as if it would block out the sound. When that didn't work, she placed a pillow over her ears and pressed down hard. The sound muffled then, and she was happy. She tried to surrender her conscious again to the softness of the bed.

Alas, sleep did not come to her at that moment. Instead, the muffled snores of the girl in the other bed began to change… They morphed into a voice… Ever had never noticed that Tekla talked in her sleep in all the nights she spent with the girl.

But she realized it was not Tekla at all. No, Ever could distinctly hear several voices now. None of them did she recognize. She loosened the grip on her pillow in order to make out the voices.

"We are not safe here," one voice, a female, said.

"No," another female replied. "But what choice do we have? Our father has betrayed us all."

Who were these new people? And what were they speaking of?

"Shh," the second voice hissed. "I hear someone coming."

Ever tensed as fear ran through her body.

Oh, please let it be a friend, she thought. She waited, frozen in place, for the door to swing open. But it never did. And, eventually, the girls began to converse again.

"I could smell it," the first voice said.

"You smelled the poison?" the second one asked with skepticism.

"Yes. In the stew."

The stew? The one that Venea had given them all? Ever gulped.

"Look, I share your fears," the second voice said. "They are despicable, even for our own kin. But poison is not their style. When it's time to fight, we'll know."

"We are not safe here."

"No, but what choice do we have? Our father has betrayed

us all."

Ever was beginning to feel confused. They had just said that, hadn't they?

"Shh, I hear someone coming."

Silence folded over the room for a moment as Ever's brows furrowed together, puzzled. What was this? Who were these girls and, more important, who do they hear coming?

The silence was abruptly ended as the first girl spoke again. "I could smell it."

"You smelled the poison?"

"Yes. In the stew."

The conversation repeated again and again, word for word, tone for tone. A chill went down Ever's spine. She knew that she had to venture a sight of these two very strange girls.

Slowly, so that they would not notice that she was awake, she lifted the pillow just high enough to peek out. At first, she saw nothing but a couple of blue lights. But as she blinked a few times, she realized that those lights were the voices. Or, rather, the beings from which those voices came.

They were tall, like Venea and Nika. In fact, they very much resembled the dark elves, from their blonde hair and pointed ears to their dark skin. The only difference, really, was the soft blue light that was emanating from their transparent bodies.

These girls were dead.

She didn't know how she knew that, but she did. Ever sat up then, unafraid of them noticing her, and watched the scene play out. They stood, the second girl's arms folded over her body as the first waved hers wildly about, desperate to be understood. Right after the second girl claims that she hears someone coming, both fix their gaze on the door for a moment before ducking behind Ever's bed. Except they never hit the floor. They simply disappeared.

The time passed by, and, like clockwork, the girls appeared at the same time as before and began their script again. Ever realized that she was watching spirits, and she assumed that this was the moment right before their death. Whoever it was that never came for Ever to see must have been their killer.

She suspected it was Nika or Venea.

But that was a detail that she might never be given. Something in her told her to leave the room. Perhaps it was the morbidity or the spirits, perhaps just the need for a night walk. Whatever it was, she walked straight past the spirits, knowing they would never see her existence, and into the hall.

That is where she found Jesper, Merenda, and Teava, all out of their rooms, surrounded by the troubled voices of too many more spirits. Wide eyed, Ever tried to focus on each individual scene.

Immediately to her left, a dark elf was swinging his sword frantically, as if he could not see his threat. He grunted with each thrust, but never seemed to hit anything. His sword was never met with resistance, spirit or otherwise. To her right, Ever watched as a girl sobbed on her knees, her violet eyes marred with tears and her blonde braid in disarray. She loudly blubbered, begging for her life. Suddenly, she would stop and fall over, only to get back up on her knees and beg again. In front of her, two dark elves fought each other, the weaker of the two begging the other to come to his senses. He never did, and they ended up killing each other. Further off, a girl sat, laughing hysterically. She laughed for several moments before she reached for a small bottle in front of her, drained its contents, and fell over. It must have been poison, Ever figured. Behind her, another man was mid sword fight. His weapon was constantly met with resistance, though Ever could not see his attacker. Many more lives beyond that were being pled for. Spirits in every direction fighting, ultimately losing, then rising to play out their deaths over and over on every side of her, all the way up and down the hall. They never once acknowledged the wide eyed strangers staring at them from the doorway of their sleeping quarters. Finally, Teava spoke from across the hall.

"They brought us to their slaughter house," she said accusingly. "This is absurd."

"They won't kill us," Jesper answered her. "We will not be met with the same fate.

"How can you still be so sure of them?" she asked him snidely, struggling to be heard over the jumbled chorus of death. "We must get Tekla and Cassio and leave at once, before they come to us."

"They would have fed us to the beast if they had meant for us to die," Jesper stated. "These spirits, they are all dark elves. I believe that many of them are family to the creatures we know. This was their battle, and they've already won. By the looks of most of their wardrobes, they won decades ago. This was personal, we are not."

"Then why make us sleep here?"

"They don't have proper guest rooms," Merenda said with a scoff.

Suddenly, a thought occurred to Ever.

"Why do these spirits disturb out sleep and not Tekla's, or even Cassio's?"

All three studied Ever's face.

"I think," Jesper said, "that is not the question to ask. Rather, we should ask, why have they managed to disturb the sleep of a dwarf?"

Ever looked at him blankly, confused. Merenda tried to clear things up.

"When an immortal being dies," she began, "their soul goes on living, often repeating their downfall, for an eternity. The light of the moon gives sight to those who share the immortal curse, like Teava and Jesper. But it also gives a sorceress like me the sight. Most sorcerers learn the ways of the spirit world early on. You, a dwarfling, are neither immortal nor a sorceress. Thus begs the question… Why were you awoken?"

Suddenly, every single spirit stopped in their scripts, as if they had heard Merenda. The halls fell dead with silence as each spirit turned to stare at the dwarf. Ever's heart sank to the pit of her stomach. They began to chant, perfectly synchronized, their voices seeming loud enough to shake the trees.

"The fate of one seals the fate of many. The destiny of all not clearly written, but death reveals the path of any."

Silence fell over the air once more. The four living souls stood frozen with fear as each other the dead ones only stared back at Ever. Merenda was the first to speak again.

"They're waiting for you, Ever," she said. "They're communicating to you."

Ever tried to gulp, but even that action she could not manage. She did not know what to do. The spirits simply went on staring at her, paying no mind to anyone else. Finally, Ever found her voice.

"Who killed you?" she asked, even though she knew the answer already.

"Our fate is not yours," they answered, ignoring her question. Ever took that as a confirmation of her theory. But it was clearly not what the spirits wanted to talk about.

"Who…" she began slowly, but then rephrased her question. "What am I?"

"You are two bred into one, and together with him, the fight will be won."

"Please," groaned Ever in frustration, "speak plainly! What do you mean? What two am I? And who is 'he'? What is my fate? Just tell me what I need to do! Tell me why I am so important in all of this!"

"You must experience the journey to experience the destination, but understand that the importance is carried within."

Ever was only growing more and more frustrated with the vague answers. She had received enough of those from Teava. If they were not going to communicate clearly, then she'd rather they didn't communicate at all.

"The light of the moon is fading," Merenda told her. "You must find out all you can before they disappear."

"How are we supposed to bring down Terrisino?" she asked in a rush.

"The defeat is not your destiny, but rather the distraction. You must fight to live until the time when your child can take action."

Sure enough, the light of the moon had faded till it was no more, and that was the last of what the spirits said. Ever stood, dumbfounded. Jesper was the first to speak.

"I think what they meant…" he began, trying to think out loud. His face was wrinkled in confusion. But when he was able to collect his thoughts, he almost glared at Teava. "Two bred into one? Have you thought this all long? You believe her to be the legend," he accused.

"The legend," Ever repeated as the words of Teava, spoken long ago, came back to her. She turned to face the dragon. "You spoke long before of a tale of lovers. You said that the dragons were exiled if they found love with an unacceptable partner. Then you told me of a legend of a *dragon halfbreed* that is to save the world," she said, spitting out the phrase that the dragon used as her own temper became heated. "You mentioned that you thought that you had found such a *halfbreed*. And now, here I am, seeing things that a dwarf should not see." Ever's face was turning red with anger, her fists balling up tight and her posture tall. The dragon merely watched her evenly. "Answer him! Answer *me*! That is why you are so desperate for me to be near the dragon heart, it is not? You actually think that I am a dragon, don't you?"

Angrily, Ever waited for the dragon to explain herself.

"I have seen several signs," Teava finally admitted, "the least of which surely includes the spirits here. But even if I was right, you are also a dwarf, and an exceptionally stubborn one at that. Had I told you what I feared, you would have dismissed it entirely. Still, a part of you would doubt your heritage, as you know neither of your parents, and your clan has purposefully kept you in the dark. You would have refused to go anywhere near the dragon heart, lest you prove me right and disgrace your family's name with your own tainted blood." She paused and eyed Ever closely. "Am I not right?"

Ever flinched at her accusation. She knew that Teava was right. The idea that there might be a chance of mixed blood in her heritage to shame the dwarves once more would be enough for her to make sure it never happened, which made her a hypocrite. She had thought ill of the dragons for disowning Teava as they had, and now she was angry that Teava was suggesting that one of her own ancestors chose love over their dwarven race. She was a hypocrite for judging Vek, so long ago, in the cave when he told her that the dwarves didn't like friends of other races. But she didn't want to admit that, even to herself.

"You had no right," she said instead of answering Teava, "to hide that from me. If it was a possibility, I should be the first to know."

"Be honest to yourself," Teava challenged. "Had I told you that Jesper only lured me into this with the mention of a small yet grown woman, and that I thought something else of you from the moment he said it, would you have left Brisdale with us, or would you have gone back to Inunia?"

"If I am a halfbreed," Ever stated through clenched teeth, "then I suppose we shall find out soon enough."

That was it for her. She had taken all that she could take for the night. She stormed back to her room and threw herself on the soft willow bed. It no longer welcomed sleep for her. Instead, she simmered with anger.

Somehow, she already felt like less of a dwarf. She already felt the shame of mixed blood. And why should she? It was Teava's twisted – and very wrong – theory, not hers. But there truly had been signs. The swords of the dragons were supposed to respond only to the dragons, and yet, had she not slain the Sarpa with them? And there was her elven disguise, made most believable by the small points on her ears. Dwarves were supposed to have perfectly rounded ears, whereas dragons did have a point. And her physique – could that really be the blame of hungry winters, or did her heritage have something to come into play as well?

Ever shook her head. Was she really thinking about this? Did she think there was a chance of truth in it? She was a dwarf!

But she did feel a sliver of truth in it. In her heart, she knew that she had never truly been completely at peace with the dwarven ways. As proud as she was to call herself one of them, somewhere in her heart, she knew it wasn't completely true.

Sleep did not return to her that night.

* * *

The Kingdom of Shodalea

Kylon could hear the beast of the forest from her castle in Shodalea. Something had disturbed her – more than usual, that is. It was horrid timing. The orcs had almost finished plaguing the villages of Ranton, several black riders had been creating their own havoc across the map, and the spells… The spells that Terrisino had cast were the worst part of it all. Kylon had very little idea of what had gone on in the outside world, but that was of little concern to her. What was troubling was the magic that was inside her kingdom.

The first day, it rained blood. Kylon believed this to be done by a young dragon, who was dumb enough to play with dark magic, and so excused it as the child's parent's responsibility. The second day, many of her dragons fell into a coma. There were three from her own clan that were not sheltered in the palace, and many other among the dragon kingdom that had been reported to her. On the third day, there came an illness that resembled the historic epidemic of the dwarves. The only difference was that, so close to the dragon heart, the dragons under the spells could not die. Still, it was hard to keep the peace among the fearful dragons. Many of them decided to flee. They took their families and crossed over the forest, seeking out a land where the name of Terrisino was not heard. Kylon supposed that the flight of the dragons could have been the trigger of Celeano's uproar, but the cause was a moot point. The dragons might be fleeing, but they may not make it away safely if the beast was determined enough. For Terrisino, that would just be one more benefit. She understood his plan. In order to take on the dragons, he must first find a way to diminish their numbers. And what better way than to instill fear in their hearts. A good approach, Kylon had to give him credit. His approach was working, despite her efforts to convince the dragons of the peril of separating. Alas, too many of them were choosing the easy way out. Terrisino would be sure to come before every last dragon had fled, but he would also wait until enough had gone. It was all about timing.

That pressure of timing was there for Kylon, too. She had to choose the next move of the kingdom. She could evacuate the remaining dragons. If she chose that path, she would have to force everyone to evacuate immediately, so as not to give Terrisino a chance to carry out whatever he planned to do on those left behind. Her other option was to bring the battle to him, and then he would have the advantage. Not to mention, either way, what was she supposed to do with the prisoners?

Kylon was struggling to choose her plan of action because she was struggling to understand what it was that Terrisino was hoping to accomplish through any of this. What was his end goal? He could not possibly think that he was prepared to take over the dragon minds, as he had sworn to do. The obvious answer was that he was after her dwarven prisoners. The whole world knew by now that he was desperate to find the escaped dwarf and kill him. But what none of the world knew was that she had in her possession two such creatures, though neither appeared to be the chosen one of legend. But even that could not be it, since no one knew what she had been hiding in her dungeons. The honorable and very isolated dragons had not leaked this information. So he had to have wanted something else.

Killing off every last dragon, as he had thought he did with the dwarves, could have been his goal. But only a lunatic would think that possible. No orc has ever slain a dragon. No sorcerer, either, unless the dragon remained in its human form. And that was only one dragon. With an army as small as ten, nothing Terrisino could do could even slow them.

But Kylon knew that Terrisino was smarter than that. He would not dare threaten the dragons unless he could put up a fair fight. Thus brought another subject for Kylon to consider; what did he have up his sleeve? What magic did he discover? Could her dragons truly stand a fair chance with him?

She needed more scholars. She needed people to find out what was going on outside her kingdom. But her people kept leaving. She could not convince them to make the right decision, that there was infinite power in their numbers. They had begun to deduce the same thing that she had – that there was an unknown component in Terrisino's favor that would likely kill them. And so, to them, abandonment was the better option.

And if Kylon could not think quickly enough, she would, too, be forced to abandon the kingdom with the few loyal subjects that remained with her.

VI.

The soft rain had quickly turned into a full storm by the time the company had woken again. In fact, the very sound of the rain pouring on the trees is what had woken them at all. Flashes of lightening lit the sky rather than the rising sun, which was well hidden behind the thick storm clouds.

"We have to stay another night," Nika was arguing to the group when they had all convened for another meal prepared by Venea. "It is far too dangerous to travel in a storm like this. Even Celeano would not be so stupid."

"You threw us in a haunted house," Teava glowered at her with a look that could burn a hole through the girl's face. "If you do not have more livable sleeping quarters, than we will leave today."

Teava had such a way of stating things as if what she said was going to be final. Unfortunately for her, the dark elves could be just as obstinate.

"They are dead," Nika argued. "They can't hurt you. They are not even aware of you."

Teava very deliberately ignored the second half of her statement.

"It does not matter what they can or cannot do, the point is that we will not be staying in those rooms, watching those haunting moments, as if they are something to lull us to sleep."

"What are you talking about?" Tekla demanded.

"Besides that," Merenda spoke, worry in her voice as she held a cloth to her mortal friend's head, "we need to break Cassio's curse. Has anyone looked at him this morning? He has begun to sweat."

"All the more reason to stay and wait out the storm," Nika said. "He should not be traveling in such conditions."

"And we should not be sleeping in such conditions," Teava argued. "We will not sleep with the dead."

"What is everyone talking about?" Tekla demanded again, louder this time.

"Your inferior mortality would not comprehend," Venea rolled her eyes. It was a comment meant to degrade Tekla, and it certainly worked. She fell silent then and settled for simply listening to the conversation as it unfolded.

"She's right," Jesper said. "He was burning up all night. Started mumbling, too, like he was talking to the spirits. We will lose him if we don't get him the proper care quickly."

"The rain is only going to slow us down."

"That's a chance we'll have to take," Jesper said dismissively. "Everyone eat quickly. We will leave as soon as we can."

And just like that, the matter was settled. The dark elves did not wish to upset Jesper. And so, everyone ate the meal without really tasting it, before preparing to leave.

Ever caught sight of Jesper and Merenda securing Cassio to Phantom under the cover of the tree. They were whispering too low for Ever to hear, but with Merenda's concerned look, she had a feeling that Jesper was trying to console her about her companion. It did not seem to be working.

In truth, as Ever got her first real look at Cassio that

morning, she did not think that he was going to make the trip. He was sweating through his clothing. His forehead was glistening, and his hair looked as if it had already been through the rain. His cheeks flushed with heat. His breathing seemed very random – as if he stopped for a while, and then suddenly had to do a lot of it to catch up on the missing breaths. Ever looked around to find Teava, hoping that she might ease her mind as Jesper attempted to ease Merenda's. But Teava was far off.

In fact, Teava was almost completely hidden among the trees. Ever was sure that she was the only one who could see her. She was talking to someone. Ever could not see whoever it was, but she thought that it must have been someone small, as Teava was crouched low. Soon enough, Teava emerged, looking as though the conversation went well. She rejoined the group completely unnoticed, save for Ever, who made the smart decision to keep what she had seen to herself.

The group was ready to leave, at any rate. Everyone had pulled their hoods over their faces as the heavy rain fall leaked a considerable amount through the canopies of the trees. The ground beneath them had already absorbed enough of the rain to create a spongy earth that slowed them down. Still, Nika led them on, with Tekla, Teava and Phantom, and Ever following behind, while Jesper, Merenda, and Venea came up on the rear. Ever was pleased to note that all of the graceful, light footed creatures were struggling in the mud like the rest of them, which made it near impossible for Venea to be her normal vixen self.

The creatures of the woodland forest had silenced themselves that day. Unlike the group, the creatures felt no need to be out in the storm. The only sound they heard at all was that of the thunder. That sound only grew louder and more consistent as they left the tree house behind. Even the squish of their feet on the earth became subdued and lost in the thunder.

Tekla fell back to hover around Ever. She had something on her mind, Ever could tell. Still, she remained silent for quite some time. Ever waited patiently, choosing instead to concentrate on keeping her footing in the mud until Tekla decided to let it out.

Ever found herself wishing that dwarven boots were made of something easier to travel in. The thick leather was great for life in the mountains. It was sturdy and durable. The fur padding kept her feet warm enough. The heavy buckles kept the boots on her feet. But all the same, she wished for something lighter that would not get stuck in the mud. She wished for a material that wasn't so slippery. But she kept her concentration and was able to stay upright. But then Tekla interrupted that concentration when she finally felt ready to talk.

"I think I saw Seg," she confessed to Ever.

That's when Ever lost her footing, nearly falling face first. Luckily, Tekla was quick and was able to catch her arm before she fell into the mud.

"What do you mean?" Ever asked. Although she knew that Tekla was unable to see spirits, she couldn't help but wonder if that was, in fact, what Tekla had seen. After all, she had all but considered the goblin to be dead.

"I thought I saw him when we first came into the forest, but I figured it was just my imagination. But this morning, before breakfast, I know I saw him feeding Phantom – or, trying to, anyway. Horses don't eat worms." She shuddered over the same strange behavior that Ever had been disgusted by when they first met the creature. "And I have noticed Teava sneaking around and disappearing sometimes. I think she knows that he is back."

"No," Ever argued. "She would have told us. Why would she make him sleep out in the cold and rain if she knew he was back?"

"He is a goblin. That's what they do. I think that Teava is planning something. Scheming with him."

"What would she be planning?"

"I don't know. But dragons are cunning, evil beings. We should never have let her in. She might be planning our deaths. At the very least, someone might die because of her."

Ever felt as though Tekla had just punched her in the gut. She could not think of what to say.

"She is and always will be a selfish, vile creature. It's the only way of the dragons. They are all the same. She does not care about us or our quest. She only seeks her own victory in this. And she's leading us straight to the most filthy, corrupt kingdom in the land. Perhaps Terrisino will wipe them out next. I only hope she lets me live long enough to see her race die."

"Stop!" Ever said in a pant. She could not help her near hyperventilation. This terrible race, as Tekla saw it, could be part of her. She was still unable to sort out her feelings about that, but she was done listening to Tekla on the subject. "Just stop. Teava has taken us this far. Jesper trusts her, and so do I. The race you are does not define the person you can be."

She tried to believe her own words. But somehow, she knew that there was some truth to what Tekla had said. She knew that there were certain things about herself that simply came about because she was a dwarf. If she was, in fact, a dragon also, then what traits had she inherited from them? And then there was the more pressing question at the moment – what about Teava? Ever might not have had as much experience with the race as the rest of the world had, but perhaps that was why she was so naïve in trusting Teava. Truly the race was like a snake, lying in wait. Was Teava lying in wait, then? Was she truly scheming?

It must have been Seg, then, that she had talked to behind the trees that morning, and he must be around still, somewhere nearby. What was it that Teava had told him? Ever's stomach twisted with sour anxiety. She tried to push her thoughts about it out of her mind. She tried to believe with her whole being that Teava would never purposefully put them in danger, despite her dragon tendencies. She thought back to the Siren Sea, when she concentrated on her walk to ignore the sirens.

One foot in front of the other.

There were plenty of roots hidden in the mud, anyway, that were easy to trip over. She could not afford to lose concentration on her walk. The rain was refusing to let up, too, which caused her to shiver in the cold. Nika had informed them that they would have to move quickly and rest little, but that they could make it to the end of the forest by sunset the next day. That was encouraging enough for Ever to pick up the pace.

As time passed, stomachs began to growl. Tekla was, once again and true to herself, complaining that they needed to stop for food. Nika would not allow that, though, telling her instead to eat as she walked. Ever took her advice and did just that, sharing her waybread with her whiny companion.

As they continued walking, Ever was pleased that nothing seemed to happen. The Forsride Forest had such negative associations that she half expected everyone to die before coming this far. She had seen the spirits haunting the tree house, but those, she was sure, were the fault of the dark elves solely. And she had heard Celeano, sometimes close and sometimes far, but she had yet to actually see the beast. It seemed that all of the myths surrounding the forest were actually based on the danger of the dark elves. Since they had somehow managed to befriend the elves, they were escaping the dangers altogether. Ever took great comfort in that.

That is, until night fell and they were preparing for rest.

It began quite normally. They walked until they found a place that had enough tree to cover up the ground somewhat and keep it dry. The dark elves rose to the tree tops, searching the branches to find out if they would possibly offer a better place to sleep. They left their bags behind and jumped easily into the trees and quickly disappeared – Venea making sure to take Jesper along. Once they were gone, Teava again disappeared behind the trees. This time, after receiving a conspiratory look from Tekla, Ever quietly followed the dragon.

Staying a safe distance away, she waited. Teava was alone

just then, peering through and around the foliage, supposedly waiting for her company to arrive. It was not long at all until both of the girls spotted a rustling in the trees. Ever held her breath, waiting for the mysterious forest friend of Teava's to emerge. And once he did, despite Tekla's earlier words, Ever was still shocked to see the small, scrawny goblin emerge from the trees.

It was, in fact, Seg.

Now Ever wondered about Teava's lack of care for him after the Baia village. Perhaps he never truly disappeared. Perhaps Teava always knew where he had been. In that moment, she realized that her mind had begun to turn on Teava. All it took was this very small situation for her to have the very same suspicion as Tekla had – the dragon was a schemer at heart, and perhaps she needed to be exiled from the group. Perhaps she should have asked Jesper more about the creature before so readily agreeing to allow her in the quest. If only she had not been so naïve.

She was not close enough to hear the quiet whispers of the scheming couple, regrettably. Yet, she dared not move any closer, for fear of being discovered. Instead, she simply watched. Seg was holding a burlap sack that Teava must have given him – Ever had seen her carry it before. She did not notice its absence, but that must have been what happened. He passed it to her without opening it, so Ever was unable to see that was hiding inside of it, but she was able to make out its shape. It was a round object, and by the way the two were handling it, it was also delicate with a light weight. Ever knew that she needed to see its contents. But the two were separating and fear told Ever to leave. She needed to be back at the camp site before Teava.

She did not make it in time. The dragon maneuvered through the mud more easily than she had. When she arrived, just minutes later, Teava was already waiting, arms crossed with suspicion in her eyes. Tekla was sitting against a tree, looking anywhere but at them. Ever thought very quickly and pretended to wipe her hands on her pants and adjust her belt as if she had just relieved herself. Teava squinted her eyes. She clearly did not buy Ever's performance, but she let it go and went back over to her own things. Ever went to sit by Tekla.

"More waybread?" Tekla asked loudly enough for Teava to hear, as if there weren't other, more pressing matters.

"I'm full," Ever said, almost matching her volume. "Best save it for morning."

"Good point," Tekla said, turning to face her back to Teava as she packed the bread away. "What happened?" she whispered without looking at Ever. Ever did the same.

"Goblin gave her something," she said in a rushed whisper. "Something big. In her bag. Don't know what."

Tekla struggled to keep herself composed.

"She put something in the dark elves bag. Venea's, I think."

"Did you see?"

"No," Tekla was able to say before the rustle of trees disrupted their hushed words and halted their conversation. Everyone was returning now.

"The trees here are no good," Nika announced. "The ground isn't a safe place from the wildlife, but it will have to do."

Ever and Tekla watched very uneasily as everyone began to set up their own bed rolls. The two girls themselves sat frozen on the ground, their own rolls remaining unpacked. They watched Venea very carefully, but she did not unpack anything from the bag in which Teava had placed the item. Ever suddenly felt a panic, as if someone was watching them. Carefully, she scanned the surroundings. Then she locked eyes with Teava, who was watching the girls again. With a start, she moved to unpack her bed roll. Tekla followed her lead without seeing Teava.

The company fell asleep one by one. Ever had hoped to stay awake long enough to look into the bag, but she never felt Teava's eyes leave her. It would be a battle of who could remain awake longer. Ever began to weigh her options. She knew that

Teava was used to long hours keeping watch. The dragon seemed to need less sleep than most beings, certainly those in this group. If Ever did manage to stay awake longer than the dragon, surely the next day would be hard on her. She needed to rest, she knew that. But she also knew that she needed to find out what Teava had done. She weighed the pros and cons of the situation until, finally, her own thoughts had lulled her to sleep.

* * *

The morning came quickly, though the sun did not. As the company began to rise, each shivering from the still falling rain, they followed through with their morning routines wordlessly until they were ready to set off. The dark elves took the lead, with Venea's arms wrapped around Jesper's bicep. Tekla remained at Ever's side, but this time Teava did as well. Not a word was said between the three, nor did they look at each other. Ever was only growing more anxious with every step they took. She was well aware that Teava suspected the girls knew something. She was well aware that was the reason she was walking with them, despite how easily she could keep up with the leaders. Tekla, too, was aware of that. She stayed close for a while, but finally gave up and left Ever alone with the schemer, claiming that she saw the need for assistance with Cassio. She left to walk by Merenda's side and offered help, which Merenda politely declined. Still, she stayed at her side.

Ever refused to look at Teava, searching for a more believable excuse to leave her side as well. There never came such an opportunity. So she continued by Teava's side, sloshing through the mud. Occasionally, she slipped, and when she did, Teava made sure to catch her. Once again, Ever was confused about the dragon's behavior. It seemed that she was simultaneously helping and scheming. Finally, the fourth time Teava caught the falling dwarf, Ever made eye contact.

Teava's expression was her normal cold and distant one,

but her eyes were softer than usual.

"Do not question my loyalty," she said quietly. Her statement seemed like it should have been defensive, but her tone had told Ever that she was only trying to remind her of all the good that she had done for the group. "Certain things I cannot tell you, only because your mind is not as protected as mine. Your trust must remain in me."

They were the first words that either girl had spoken directly to her since Ever had yelled at her for telling her that she suspected dragon blood in her veins. Ever felt apprehensive, as if she should still be mad. But even still, so much had already happened that neither of the girls felt the full extent of the tension between them that they should have. And, if Ever was being honest, the trust she put in Teava might be wavering on the point of a knife, but it had never gone completely. At least, she didn't think it had.

Ever looked away as she righted herself and began to walk again.

"You cannot keep us all in the dark," she told Teava, her voice equally as soft. That surprised her. She felt as though anger should be in there somewhere, but she was simply too exhausted for emotion.

"I wish I did not have to," Teava answered her. "But we have a problem that I must fix. None of us will be hurt for it," she promised gravely, putting a new sense of fear in Ever's mind. The way she had spoken the words had implied that someone would be hurt. Ever's eyes wandered to the dark elf sisters. She knew instantly they were the problem that Teava was going to fix.

Unease settled into Ever as she came to the realization. She understood then why Teava had been sneaking around. The dark elves would easily know if they were being threatened by the whole group. But Ever also knew that they were exceptionally capable and evil beings. It may come as a surprise, but when Teava's plan came into action, they would quickly adapt. But she knew that there was nothing to do now except prepare to fight.

The mud beneath their feet continued to hinder them as the rain began to fall once more. Merenda had surrendered her cloak to Cassio's ever shivering body, causing her to shiver as well. Ever had to wonder if it might be best to let him die before they reached the dragon heart. It would be a shame to see the struggle of the group to keep him alive go to waste, but it would also be a shame to watch him fall into trap after trap. He did not seem like a pertinent part of the journey and she did not want to see him waste any more of their time.

She quickly cleared the thought from her mind. Never mind the fact that they might lose Merenda if Cassio died, she was wishing ill on another living being. She had been from the moment he had joined the group. There were moments when she had wished ill on Tekla as well, and the girl had only proven herself to be strong and capable in many situations. It was unfair and made her no better than the dark elves. She was on the side of the good hearted people, with the most well-meaning intentions; therefore, she needed to stop wishing ill on those who were on her side.

But when she saw Venea's hand around Jesper's lower back, she could not make herself wish well on the dark elf. She could not figure out why Venea specifically angered her, more than Tekla or Cassio or even Nika. It wasn't as if Venea had tricked the group – or Jesper – at all. She made her intentions very clear. And Jesper had willingly agreed to her terms. And yet, Ever found to herself seething at the thought of her friend spending an immortal life with the vixen.

She once again shook her head to clear her thoughts as they walked through the enchanted looking willow trees. She decided that, despite the rain that made the mud impossible to travel through, she liked the forest. The willow trees seemed happy and content, even if they were just trees. They gratefully accepted the water from the clouds and stretched far and wide. They all had something that sparkled in their foliage. At first, Ever though that they were lavender lights, placed there by the dark elves to provide light in the darkness, but she realized now that was not the case. They were lavender in color, and shined in a way that appeared less than natural. However, they were growing out of the trees. It certainly could have been a spell cast by the elves, but it was very becoming on the forest. Ever let herself relax in the serenity of the forest and forget about her negativity. She breathed in the scent of the rain as she listened to it fall to the ground. She let herself feel at peace and comfortable in the fact that they were nearing their destination.

Until Celeano's cries interrupted her tranquility. Everyone froze in their tracks, including Phantom, who still had a leg hovering over the soft ground. The sound of the beast was desperate, the howl of absolute anxiety. Ever imagined that she could hear a sob in it. And, most terrifying of all, it sounded closer than it had ever been.

"You said you could keep her away," Jesper said, looking at Nika with accusation in his eyes.

Nika and Venea both looked just as stricken with shock as the rest of the group.

"We never said that," Venea argued fearfully. "We are able to keep her tame because we took something of hers."

"What did you take?" Merenda demanded.

"Her child," Venea answered. "Her un-hatched egg. She searches for it, she can sense it, and she stays close to it. She only goes where we put the egg."

The egg. Realization struck Ever like lightening. Teava must have known how the dark elves were controlling the beast and used it against them. The egg must have been the item that Seg had given her.

"She shouldn't be on this side," Nika responded – a hint of fearful apology in her tone. "She should never have gotten this close."

"How close is she?" Ever asked softly to Teava without

taking her eyes and ears off of the conversation held by the elven creatures.

"Close," Teava responded with no emotion. Ever let herself peek at the unperturbed creature only for a moment.

"How far are we to the end of the forest?" Jesper asked, his muscles twitching as if they wanted to run.

"We won't make it in this weather and with…" Nika began, but left the statement unfinished. Ever knew what she meant, though. The elven races and the dragon would stand a chance out running the beast. But Nika honored her word over her life and proposed another plan. "The only thing to do is fight her. We will lose the legend and our forest will no longer be a place that we can live alone, but she will kill us all. She is not as tame as we might have let you believe. The humans need to lead Phantom away. The rest of us will stay and fight." Another cry sounded from the forest. Ever could begin to hear the faint noises of her footsteps, growing louder with each step as she quickly approached. "If things begin to look as if we might lose, keep her away as long as possible to give the humans a chance. The dwarf will follow behind them while the rest of us continue to distract her." Another cry. "After that, decide for yourselves. Go!" she commanded as everyone continued to stare, frozen in place.

The commandment broke them. Tekla took Phantom by the main – the steed seemed to recognize the danger and didn't even shake her. Merenda instead dismissed the girl and took her place. They would lose a strong fighter in Merenda, but no one said anything as the girls began to lead Cassio and Phantom away. They understood that Merenda's first priority was Cassio. As they disappeared in the trees, everyone else drew their weapons and held their stances, searching the trees and following the noise of Celeano with their eyes.

Ever ventured a glance at Teava. The dragon had taken a protective stance in front of her so she could not see her face. Ever now understood that Teava was behind this attack and meant for blood to be spilled. The dragon was not scared at all, it seemed, as the rest of the group was. Instead, she seemed rather prepared, as she had had time to expect it.

Ever refocused herself. Her breathing was staggered and she couldn't seem to keep her footing even while standing still. She knew she would have no chance of fleeing with the humans in the group, yet she also felt as though her fighting skills would only hinder the rest of the group.

In the distance, a tree snapped in half. The fall could be felt beneath the feet of each warrior. Ever had to stifle a scream as she realized the size of the beast before it emerged. When she did emerge, Ever realized that she had been underestimating the legendary Celeano.

Celeano stood in the trees just before the group, seeming to size them up just as they were sizing her up. She stood almost as tall as the tallest willow tree and was far thicker than their trunks. She was on all fours, with the body of a giant cat. Or, rather, Ever corrected, with the skeleton of a giant cat. She had a mane like a lion and her legs from the knees down still had orange fur and flesh in-tact. But beyond that, she looked like something from a cemetery. Behind her rib cage, all of her organs were exposed. Her massive sharp teeth looked even more threatening connected to the bone of her jaw and straight into her skull. Her eyes were a menacing black pit, and although she had no eye balls, she was looking straight at the group.

Until her gaze fixed on Venea.

A chill ran down Ever's spine.

An arrow from Jesper's quiver shot out and lodged itself in between Celeano's ribs. He had aimed for her heart, but his shot was obstructed. The beast let out a long, angered howl and shifted her gaze to Jesper.

The arrows began to fly from several directions as the elven races all shot. Celeano stood on her hind legs and let out a war cry. She launched herself forward, heading straight into the mess of arrows. Ever looked to Teava, begging her for a battle plan. Teava pulled her bow and began launching arrows from behind the beast.

Ever noticed, with dismay, that her shots all missed by a hair. Teava's battle plan, then, was to let the beast kill.

The beast ignored Teava and continued to charge at the elven creatures. The three dispersed. Celeano chose to focus on Venea.

Ever finally drew her axe and charged at Celeano from behind. Rather than begin to chop at her thick ankles, she latched on to the fur that was there and held on tight as the beast stampeded. Celeano did not seem even to notice the dwarf.

Arrows continued to fly in every direction. Ever was forced to sway in order to miss getting hit, causing her to nearly fall twice. She had no idea why she had chosen to cling on to the beast, but now that utter chaos had begun, she feared to let go. Her companions were constantly moving, both to keep the beast contained in the area, and to get better aim. She was moving so much that Ever only struggled to keep her hold.

Do something, she told herself. The time to make a move was not after tragedy struck. She took a breath and reached a hand higher, gripping more fur. She moved her other hand that held the axe to match and shimmied her body up with it. Celeano made a sharp turn to the left, following Venea with a seething hiss. Ever gripped hard to keep herself put. The beast crouched, readying a pounce. Ever seized the opportunity and thrust herself up the beast's leg once more. Twice more. She was nearing the end of the fleshy part of her body. Then Celeano charged at the dark elf, forcing Ever's legs to fly out. She clenched the fur in her hands.

Venea was notching arrow after arrow and waiting a dangerous amount of time before she shot it. She was aiming for the heart, but never could get past the rib cage. She threw herself into a roll and dodged to the right just before the beast launched at her.

Celeano's enormous paw stood on the ground that Venea

had occupied just seconds before. She snarled as she recognized her lost prey. Ever used the distraction once again to climb up higher. She could now smell the rotting puss of the exposed flesh. She could not help but wretch. She had no choice but to stick her hands right on the edge of the oozing skin as the beast collected itself and relocated Venea.

Venea had once again begun to launch numerous arrows at the beast as she came running towards her. This time, she aimed for the sockets of her eyes, praying for a different result. The beast seemed to notice none of it, even the arrows that hit her from two other directions. Once again, Venea dodged the beast at the last possible second.

Ever quickly climbed passed the stench of the flesh. Holding on to the bone was a much harder task, especially with hands slippery from sweat and puss, but she managed to find holds sturdy enough to get to a point where she was riding atop the skeletal beast. She found a place where she could grip the beast as she charged at the dark elf once more. When she was sure of her grip, she began to scoot up the spine, slowly and carefully avoiding the arrows as they shot around her. The beast continued to take no notice of her.

Venea ducked away once again. The beast took less time this time to recover, and took off after the dark elf quickly. Ever made her way to the rib cage as Venea turned to begin launching arrows. She reached into an empty quiver. Without a moment of hesitation, she dropped the bow and drew her sword. She held her ground and the beast came closer. Ever worked her way to the place above the exposed heart.

It was a big, ugly, pulsing, purple organ. The veins and arteries connecting to it were dried up at the end, having no proper system to pump the blood through. Ever was stricken by the smell, which was worse than the rotting flesh of her ankles. It was sour and sickening to her stomach. She opened her mouth to inhale in order to alleviate the putrid fumes.

Venea screamed from below. She had not gotten more than a single strike to the beast's huge face before it got her. Ever clung on tight as the beast whipped its head back with a screaming Venea between its teeth. The beast was wagging its head back and forth so ferociously that its spit was flying in every direction. A big glob landed on Ever's face and arm.

Not just spit, Ever noticed. Blood.

Ever trembled, her breathing growing unsteady as the reality finally set in. She was not playing a game, none of them were here to have fun. As the screams grew more and more frantic, Ever realized that Venea was about to pay the ultimate price, and perhaps the others would, too. She had little time to make her move. She raised her axe high in one hand, careful to hold on with the other, and took her aim at the big ugly organ. Just as she was about to throw the axe into the rib cage, the beast threw aside Venea, who had stopped screaming. The sudden movement caused Ever to lose her form and the axe lodged itself instead in the beast's lung. It would be a fatal hit, she knew, but not in time. They could not afford to wait for the blood to drown her. The beast roared in pain. The noise shook the forest.

Celeano ran to the body of Venea, yards away from where she had picked her up, lifeless now on the ground. She ignored the group as she nudged Venea's body about until something rolled out of the pack around Venea's back.

The egg.

She gingerly placed it under her tongue. Then she turned to face the rest of the group with anger in her fathomless eye sockets. Ever was not facing her, but she could feel the anger of the dying beast. Panic ran through her veins as she realized that this battle was coming to an end.

"Ever!" Teava called from below. She tossed her the dragon sword and, a bit clumsily, Ever caught it. She spared a single second to lock eyes with the dragon. Perhaps the reality of the situation set in her mind as well.

Ever gripped the sword tightly and watched as it glowed. She knew that whatever instinct she would have now was the right one. She recalled the Sarpa and knew that she should let the sword decide her actions. Allowing instinct to take over, she lifted the sword and plunged it straight into Celeano's heart. It was barely long enough to reach all the way through the skeleton and to the heart. But barely enough was enough, and the sword pierced the organ.

The big ugly heart let out a hiss the moment the sword touched it, causing the beast to stop in her tracks just before getting to Jesper. He froze where he stood, swords in hand, as Celeano stiffened on her back legs. The heart turned pale blue as she teetered back and forth. Ever quickly jumped off, fearing that if she waited too long, she would end up smashed under the monster. She landed on her rump, mouth agape, as she scrambled to get out of the danger zone. The heart jiggled and struggled to pulse. It was dying. Black spots began to appear. Eventually, the whole heart was eclipsed in black. Celeano fell backwards, shaking the ground as she hit it.

The air stood silent as moments passed. Beads of sweat trickled down everyone's face. The silence was broken by Nika.

"Venea!" she shrieked, rushing to the lifeless body. Venea had several deep teeth marks on her body, most of which had been painfully stretched out as the beast had shaken her about. Fresh dark blood was still gushing from her body, but that did not dissuade Nika from gathering her into an embrace as she sobbed. No one spoke for quite some time.

Teava was the first to move. She quietly went to the beast to collect her sword. Ever followed her lead. As she moved past Teava, she felt a friendly hand on her shoulder. She turned to meet Teava's approving eyes with an empty expression of her own. Silently, Teava nodded her approval,, seeming unable to read Ever's expression correctly, and walked away to speak to Jesper.

But Jesper would have none of it. He went over to console

the dark elf that was now screaming her denial. For that, Ever was both surprisingly glad and jealous at the same time. She was glad because only one dark elf had died. Although the dark elves had tricked them into an odd sort of alliance in which they stole Jesper, Ever knew very well that Teava had planned the death of both of them that day, and she did not want to continue the journey with unnecessary deaths. And she was jealous because…

No, she would not allow herself that type of feeling. She was surprisingly glad and that was it.

"Nika" Ever finally spoke, breaking the silence. The broken girl looked up at her, her violet eyes were rimmed with red already. Ever was reminded of her own breakdown at the Isola Ruins. She felt the same pain that Nika had felt; the pain of losing one's entire family. Her voice softened. "We can no longer hold up our end of the bargain. You are free to go, if you wish, so that you might…" She trailed off, unsure if it was best to so bluntly tell Nika to go cry over her dead sister alone, or if that was what the girl even wanted. Ever may not have been all too eager to join forces with a dark elf pair, but they had proven their worth.

In response, Nika simply began to weep again.

* * *

Tekla and Merenda made it out of the forest safely. They waited on the outskirts, neither making a sound. They had anxiously waited through the loud roars and cries of Celeano until suddenly they ceased. It seemed like neither of the girls could breathe at all as they waited to learn the meaning of the sudden quiet. Had their company succeeded? Or had they died? And then they heard the loudest, most dreadful shriek they had ever imagined. It sounded neither human nor animal.

"Vehsi?" Tekla whispered as if it might hear her. But the shrieking was followed by the faint sound of mournful wails. Tekla grew more anxious than before. She wanted desperately to run away, but she didn't know where to go, nor did she want Merenda to think her a coward. So she forced herself to stay put, waiting for what seemed like an eternity, for whatever might come next.

Finally, her breathing became steadier as, one by one, the company began to emerge from the trees. Teava, barely sweating, hair in disarray, was first. Next was Ever, who was filthy with mud, sweat, and something else that Tekla could not identify, but it smelled rancid. Jesper followed her, is elven perfection rather unchanged. Behind him was Nika. She was full of mud and blood, but underneath her dark elven beauty was unmarred. Nearly unmarred, Tekla realized. She had obviously been distraught. Her eyes were red and swollen, and it seemed as though tears were still threatening to come down. Tekla realized why before too long; Venea did not follow behind the group. Tekla went to Ever's side.

"What now?" she hissed in a whisper.

Ever turned to address the group as a whole.

"We will continue on to the dragon kingdom as planned. Venea is no longer with us. Obviously, the perils of this journey are very real. I will ask you all again," she said, looking at everyone in turn, with the exception of Nika who had already voiced her decision, "if you would like to continue on with us. It may be too late to return home now, but I will not deny you the opportunity to try. If you keep going forward, know that you are risking your very life. I do not hold it against you to have second thoughts. This is a serious decision and I ask you to think carefully."

Ever had hoped that Teava would turn around, but she only held Ever's gaze with a steady resolve. No one else made a move to leave, either.

"Then we will go," Ever continued, "but we will go together. We must use the strengths of everyone on the team," she said, emphasizing the team mentality. "We cannot forge on if any of us is against another. Teava, I do not know the way."

"I think," Jesper spoke before Teava could, "that it would

be wise to make camp now. We could use the rest… And perhaps the time to grieve."

Ever relented. She understood that Nika was not yet ready to move on. They decided to stay right where they were. The forest no longer threatened danger, but instead provided some protection from the elements under the trees. There was also a small creek that forked from the river close to the site. Before setting up camp, they all decided to wash up.

Ever was grateful for the oddly warm water. It was no elven bath, to be sure, but she felt so filthy that any water was a welcome change. The outer layer of filth came from the mud in which she, Jesper, and Nika had buried Venea. It had been the hardest thing Ever had done yet. The sorrow she felt did not compare to that of Nika's, yet she did feel it.

Venea was a vixen who had bound and kidnapped Ever before finding a way to steal Jesper away from her. She had never said a kind word, and barely any other words besides that. She had systematically killed most of her own race with the help of her sister. And yet, now that she was gone, Ever felt a new respect for the dark elves. When Celeano had begun to stir, they could have abandoned the group to their deaths. But they did not. They fought just as hard as they could, following direction and working with the group to save as many lives as they could. Even when Venea had been selected as the main target, neither elf acted selfishly, right up to the end. Nika did not even lose control when her sister lost the fight.

When most of the group had finished washing up, they left to set up camp. The only two remaining were Ever and Nika. Ever watched the girl with sadness in her eyes. She could not decide if she should say something or let the silence continue. Nika was the one to break it.

"Do not pity her," she said, speaking of her sister. "Nor should you pity me. We have not lived wholesome lives, as you have. Her sacrifice has been the only good we have done for this world."

"If you believe that," Ever began, "why have you chosen to stay with us?"

There was a pause before she answered.

"I have nothing left to live for any longer," she said. "My death should go to a greater cause, then. It will not make up for all the evil that I have caused in this world, but perhaps it will give me some favor in the eyes of the gods and they will take even a little pity on me."

"You're not an evil being," Ever said sympathetically. "Perhaps you have believed that for so long that you have acted it out, but your race does not define who you are. I believe that both you and your sister found reason in our journey to help us in the beginning. I do not believe that you truly sought after your gain from the bargain, but that you only needed a reason to make it seem like you agreed for selfish reason."

"I have always known that your journey is a valiant one. But I never wanted to come so that I might be a hero. I never came to put good into the world. Truthfully, you are right, I never wanted the information that I claimed in our bargain. It was a poor excuse that hid my motive surprisingly well."

"Your motive… Jesper and Venea?"

Nika gave a dry laugh.

"No. That was always Venea's motive. I do not care for such trivial affairs. I once told you that the dark elves did not survive because they were constantly at war with each other."

Ever nodded, recalling the conversation at the tree house.

"There is another dark elf whose destruction I seek."

"Why do you not leave us, then, to carry out your mission?" Ever asked, unsure why she was condoning a quest of death, but also struggling to understand Nika.

"Our quests are one and the same."

"We have set out to ensure the freedom of the world," Ever argued. "We have set out to make sure the races are free to live without fear of becoming like the dwarves. We have set out to give peace of mind to families like Tekla's."

"You think highly of yourself," Nika told her softly with a wry smile. "But do not fool yourself into thinking such heroic thoughts. Do not forget that yours is a quest of vengeance."

Her words pierced Ever's heart. Had she been lying to herself? She knew very well that her cause was a good one. Even if it was a vengeful one. The world did need to be rid of Terrisino.

"He's a dark elf," Ever gasped as realization suddenly struck her.

"He is more than that," Nika replied. "He is my father."

Ever did not know how to respond. Several thoughts ran through her mind, including, once again, mistrust. If Terrisino was her father, could she have any decency at all? Ever had to remind herself, once again, to be less judgmental.

"Please do not think differently of me," Nika said softly. "He is my father by blood only. I do not wish to be like him. I do not swear what he has sworn."

"I don't understand," Ever admitted. "You tell me that you are evil. If he is your father, should you not want what he wants?"

"Ever," Nika smiled, "I am not a good being, it's true. I have lived an evil life. But that does not mean I long to own the world. Actually, I'd prefer to be alone. Well," she corrected, "with Venea, that is. But that is of no matter right now. I had a mission so long ago. I had sworn that I would end the race of dark elves."

"Why would you end your own race?"

"Because they took away everything I loved. They betrayed me."

Ever looked at her in confusion.

"When I was young, war broke out among my race. I do not recall what it was about, as I was only a child. I did not understand. But I knew that it was my father who started it, and I knew that it lasted for a decade. It was a ruthless decade, and each death was more brutal than the last. I was sixteen when I fled. I had met someone just before. His name was Ruvik. He was tall and handsome. He asked me to marry him, and we were supposed to flee together. But I was forced to leave before him. My father had begun to kill close to home. I had to run, but Ruvik swore to meet me as soon as he could. I hid out in the spot we had agreed upon…"

"How long did you wait?"

Nika laughed bitterly.

"An eternity, so far, it seems. We agreed to meet in the forest. At first, I had taken my sister and merely camped out under the trees and waited. Day after day, I waited for the one I loved. But he never came. I suppose I never stopped hoping. I was the one who insisted on staying, on creating our home in the trees. I was the one who held Venea back. I was the reason that she never found another dark elf to be with. She chose to stay with me when I would not leave."

"But… The spirits?" Ever asked. "There were many more dark elves with you."

"It was a vengeful trap, Ever," Nika told her. "We became enraged by our race and killed them all as they took shelter in our trees. That is why you see no more of our kind in the world – my family is responsible for that, beginning with my father and ending with me."

"And Ruvik?"

"I never saw him again," she said longingly. "I assume that my father killed him before he was able to leave our land."

"And now you want to kill your father for taking him away?"

"Among many other reasons," she said, "but yes. I saw how much Venea loved Jesper. I know that was hard for you to watch," Nika said as she eyes Ever knowingly. "But it was equally hard for me to watch. You had nothing to worry about, and perhaps I should have told you that. Venea was distracted by her loneliness and did not see what I saw. Jesper is my half-brother."

Ever's jaw dropped. She had no words, and seemed unable at all to process this new information. Nika continued her explanation.

"Anyway, I miss my Ruvik very much. It is the reason I use to come with you. Can you accept me into your company, knowing that I very much seek my own vengeance?"

Ever forced her mouth closed and thought about everything she had been told. Could she really accept Nika, even though she had done such evil things? But Ever knew that Nika had never truly meant her or her group any harm. Or, if she had, and Jesper truly was the only reason the dark elves had kept the group alive, she knew that it was nothing personal. She knew that Nika had only wanted to keep her home sacred.

Ever also saw the dark elf differently at that moment. She was vulnerable. She was like Ever herself. She seemed more personable than Ever had ever seen her before. She truly felt sympathy for the dark elf now.

So she nodded, knowing full well that she truly could accept the dark elf into their group.

She only wished that she could know what to do with the new information about Jesper. She did not think that he would respond well to it.

VII.

Ever did not dream about the strange and dark man who shot an arrow into her heart. She could not sleep at all that night. Instead, memory haunted her. One scene in particular had played over and over the minute that she let her head rest on her pillow. The scene, she now realized, must have bothered her on some deep level, else it would not cause her to lose sleep. So she decided to let her mind play out the scene one last time and really think about what had bothered her.

The memory began earlier that day, in the moments of Venea's passing. Well, to be more exact, it was several minutes after the dark elf had died. Jesper had gone to Nika and rested a hand on her shoulder. Ever had expected the dark elf to shake him off and to scream terrible things at the group. But she did neither. In fact, she had leaned in to him as she held her dead sister and cried. They had waited for a long time. Everyone was silent, save for Nika. Everyone else felt as if she needed time to herself, time without meaningless words of comfort. No one would even know where to begin to comfort her anyway. So they simply waited until she was ready to speak. It was quite some time before that moment came.

Ever had still been waiting for an answer to her question, and it was supplied through sobbing breaths at the end of Nika's long mourning.

"Before we go," she had told Ever, "I need to bury her properly."

Ever had nodded, understanding that the girl was asking for help.

"Where do you wish to lay her to rest?" Jesper had asked her, understanding the same thing that Ever had.

"We cannot take much time," Nika had said with sorrow. "I would like to bury her close to my home. But I also do not think this can be my home any longer anyway. I will bury her where she died."

Ever and Jesper had nodded to each other and both of them moved to the soft dirt next to where Venea's body had been laying. They had no real tools, and their weapons would not have been enough of a substitution. Thus, with nothing else available to them and without even thinking about it for a moment, Ever and Jesper both began to claw their way through the ground. Nika put down Venea's body and began to help them dig.

Together, the three strange creatures would sit for a great deal of time, digging a grave for Venea with their hands. Ever had had plenty of time to think while she was digging, and she thought about the irony of the situation. She thought about how strange it had been that she was digging a grave for a creature that she had never liked. She had never wanted to be friends with Venea. She did not want to fight by her side or to finish the quest with her. And yet, as she was digging the grave with her ally and a dark elf, she felt nothing but sorrow and regret for what she was doing at that moment. Although she had even let the thought of killing both of the dark elves cross her mind, she was glad that she had played no part in the death of that one.

Once the trio had dug far enough into the ground, Nika allowed Jesper to lower her sister's body into the hole. She allowed that, but then they had to stop the burial. It was hard for her to see her sister lying lifeless in the ground. She had broken down into a fresh wave of sobs. She turned into Jesper's chest and he held her. He and Ever had looked at each other with a look that read pity. They both knew that time was being wasted, and that half of their group was on the other side of the forest waiting for them, but that did not matter in that moment. The only thing that mattered was seeing Nika through the burial of her sister.

Ever thought for a moment how it might have felt to bury one of her own clan. She had lived with them her whole life, just as Nika had been with Venea her whole life. And yet, for Ever that was only twenty-three years, and there would always be the knowledge of mortality. In the immortal life of the elven races, it is never expected to have to bury your family. Ever understood that it was hitting Nika pretty hard, just as it would have hit her pretty hard if she had stayed around to bury Otak.

So she waited patiently with a look of sympathy on her face until Nika was ready to move forward. Nika sniffled a bit more, but pulled away from Jesper's chest. She looked at the body in the hole as if she was unsure how to continue. Jesper saw the look on her face and decided he had to move the burial forward. He bent down and picked up a handful of dirt to show Nika. She looked in his hand, and, knowing precisely what he meant to do with that dirt, the sobs began again.

For a few more minutes, Jesper was left standing with one arm holding Nika while the other was holding a handful of dirt. Ever decided then that she was the one who had to move things forward. She put a hand on Nika, causing Nika to look up at her.

"Let her rest," she had told the dark elf.

Nika nodded gravely. Although she knew she was not, nor would she ever be, ready to let her sister go, it certainly was time. She picked up a handful of dirt and looked at Jesper. But Jesper made no movement. Instead, he nodded to Nika, prompting her to toss her dirt into the whole first. She looked at him with wild eyes.

But Jesper did not fold. He had begun to understand that Nika had to get over the fear of her sister's death. She needed to know that Venea was truly gone, and that no amount of waiting would bring her back. Because, certainly, Nika was afraid to bury her sister only to discover that she had merely been sleeping. It was not a practical fear, and even Nika herself knew that. Yet she could not shake it, and when she finally did toss that first handful onto Venea's body, she fell to her knees in sobs. The sight of the dirt on her sister's face was crushing to her. Jesper and Ever both threw a handful of dirt onto the body as well, and Nika screamed every time they did, begging them to stop. It was a slow process with breaks for comfort and even one break in which Nika dug through the dirt, convinced she had seen her sister take a breath. But finally, they had laid Venea to rest.

 Ever had seen such a deep side to Nika in that moment. Not once had she grown tired of the sobbing dark creature. Not once had she tried to rush through the process. She had understood that Nika needed to grieve, and that she had been forced to do it in an awful situation. She had also understood that, now left without any family at all, Nika needed someone to lean on while she grieved. Ever was happy to be there for her, and she was glad to see that Jesper was there, too.

 And then she realized the piece of the memory that had been bothering her. When they had emerged from the forest, everyone was covered in the blood and mud of Venea's small, humble funeral service. Everyone, that is, except for Teava. She had left herself out of it. Ever did not even notice what the dragon had chosen to do with her time rather than helping the funeral. All she knew was that Teava had been there to lead the way as soon as they were done.

 That was the single thing that had bothered Ever about that memory. She had begun to see Teava in a different light. She had begun to see a small bit of distrust in her own heart for the dragon. She decided that it was more important at that moment to rid herself of that trust so that she might be able to continue the quest with Teava on her side rather than on her list of worries. She sat up and looked around the campsite.

As usual, Teava had decided to take the first watch. Ever was glad for it that night. She knew that a serious conversation with the dragon was past due, and it needed to happen when no one could hear. Lucky for Ever, most of the company was as exhausted as she was and had already fallen asleep. She made sure that she could recognize the soft snoring that meant Tekla was asleep – she certainly would have put herself in the conversation that Ever needed to have alone. She slowly sat up and checked the faces of the company before she was satisfied that they were all asleep and went to Teava. Teava was a few feet away, with her back to them as she kept a diligent watch. If she heard Ever coming, she made no sign of it. Ever sat next to her on one of the fallen tree trunks. They sat in silence for a few moments.

"I will protect Nika," Ever finally said. "She is valuable to our cause, and has as much right to life as you and I do." She wasn't sure if she believed the words as they came out of her mouth, but she said them with conviction anyway. Surely murder in the group, no matter how justified, should not be tolerated. And especially when it put everyone else in danger as well.

"I do not regret playing a part in the death of the dark elf," Teava told her in a low, muted voice. "However, I will not harm the other one. I know when to act and when to stop."

"I understand," Ever admitted. "I thought several times of doing something like that, something to end them. But that is not our place, deciding who deserves to live and who should die, and deciding based on little more than attitude and race. They were our captors once, but I realize now that they never intended on hurting us. It was their plan all along to be part of us. They fought hard to save our lives, and Nika did not stop when Venea fell. They could have deserted us."

"If they had, Celeano would have followed them and left us in peace."

"Because you planted the egg on Venea," Ever accused.

"But that was unknown to her. They had a choice and chose to fight with us. So we must fight with them."

"It's a little ironic," Teava said, "that you have come to me to ask – nay, to order me – not to harm your little dark elf *friend* as if you have finally taken the roll of leader. Yet, at every turn so far you have looked to me to make the decisions."

"I am not here to be criticized," Ever argued, "nor did I claim to be her friend. I came simply to state that I will not tolerate any more conspiracies within the group. Tekla knows, too, what you have done. I only hope she keeps it quiet, so that we can move on completely. But I know she will not forget. She does not trust you."

"She never trusted me," Teava said apathetically. "That is because I am a dragon. Do not forget that you are, too," she said with a sudden sly grin. "Or is that why you suddenly cannot harm the dark one? You are trying to convince yourself that your race does not play a part in who you are. Unfortunately, my dragon half breed friend, that will always be a part of you."

Ever's temper flared.

"You need not worry," Teava continued. "I have no interest in trouble. I will not bring harm to the girl, you have my word. Is that enough? Or do you not trust the word of your own kind?"

Sufficiently angered, Ever rose from the tree and returned to her bed roll. But she could not sleep right away. She knew that Teava's word was enough – she no longer worried about Nika's life. But Teava did make her question her own motived. Had she been softer on Nika now simply because she discovered the possibility of an evil race's blood running in her veins? Had that possibility suddenly changed her world view? Why should it? Dragon half breed or not, she was still Ever. She was still a proud dwarf. Truly, she believed that race could not define a being, one must chose who they are for themselves. And Ever chose to be good, just as she believed that both Nika and Teava had.

Still, the thought of being a dragon half breed would not

leave her mind. She slept ill at ease that night.

Teava did not sleep, either, even when her watch shift had ended and Jesper rose to take her place. She, too, was plagued with thoughts of who she was becoming. She realized that she had put the whole group at risk – even the dwarfling that she fought to protect – in order to be rid of the dark elves. And for what? She was only able to get rid of one of them, and now she had turned half of the company against her. She tried not to care, but she knew in her heart that she had begun to feel a part of something again. She had left Abrya on a whim, and hadn't meant to stay away for so long. But she had seen something in Ever that made her stay. She had seen family in Ever. She was sure that Ever was a dragon mix, but even if she was wrong, there was still some sort of connection that she had felt. She had realized now that Ever's acceptance was important to her. Which meant that she would have to start acting less like a dragon and more like any other being in the Earth of Eald.

Although, she struggled even to know what that meant. All her life, she had felt the disagreement and war of the races. She had been alive when the dark elves fell to themselves. She had seen the elves of Sedona viciously turn away refugees when Terrisino first rose to power. She had seen the dragons kill for little more reason than that they could.

And she knew that she had been a part of the evil in the world. She may not have had anything to do with the way the dwarves fell, but certainly she did not do anything to help them. They had sent word to the dragon kingdom, begging for their help and offering their treasures in return. Teava had seen the letter, as many of the Emperik clan of dragons had, and no one offered more than a chuckle. They knew that if they wanted that treasure, they would take it. It did not matter if the dwarves gave it as a reward or as a plea for their lives. But the dragons did not have an interest in it, and so they turned their backs to the plea of the dwarves. Teava had remembered it so well, even though she thought nothing of it at the time. The dwarves were not of even the smallest importance to her.

If Ever had known that Teava had the opportunity to do something to save her people and turned her back instead, surely then Ever would have nothing to do with her. Truly, she was eager for acceptance, and had been ever since she was exiled. She was not upset that Venea had died because of her, and she still believed that Nika needed to die as well. But for the sake of Ever's acceptance, she would have to put aside her distrust of the dark elves and learn to work with them until she could reasonably see to Nika's death in a way that Ever would believe she was not part of.

She didn't scheme that night, despite Tekla's claim that the dragons' minds were constantly scheming. She wallowed in self-pity instead, which only angered her in the end. She had thought herself to be stronger than that, but she clearly relied on the emotions of other people far too much. When she rose from her bedroll the next morning, she was anything but rested.

Breakfast the next morning was a quiet event. It was as if no one had slept that night, each lost in their own thoughts. Or maybe the snoring that Ever had heard was not a sign of peaceful slumber, but of disruptive nightmares. Whatever the case was, everyone woke with dark circles under their eyes. They seemed to eat without tasting. They were growing tired of the repetitive taste of the waybread. Or perhaps they had grown tired of the journey altogether.

"The next landmark we will see is Zagnoula itself," Teava announced as she wrapped her food in the cloth once again, having barely touched it. "We have but one more night in the open before we get there. I do not doubt that the queen's scouts will alert her to our presence before we get there. Hopefully that will play to our favor."

She sounded nervous and unsure. It put everyone in a matching mindset. As she looked around, she saw the fear in the eyes of her companions.

"Take courage," she told them. "We should not see any other dangers between here and the mountain. The scouts will do nothing to us, if we should see any at all. And no one else would come this close to the forest or to the kingdom."

No one said a word, though, as Teava began to lead the way forward. As Nika walked forward, she felt no courage, despite her words to Ever. That is not to say that she felt cowardice, however. She felt raw and absent. The refreshing water of the creek did nothing for her dried lips or her puffy eyes. She could not walk more than a few minutes without shedding a tear – partly because of the gentle breeze which so easily bothered her already tired eyes, and partly because she was still hurting in ways she never expected to hurt. Although she had fallen asleep quickly, worn out from crying over her sister, it did not seem to make a difference in the way she felt when she woke. Her head was pounding and her heart felt empty with the loss of Venea. She eyed Teava with a blank, washed out expression. Although she knew that the dragon could not control Celeano, something spoke to her senses about the situation. She knew that somehow Teava had been involved. She knew it, but she could not bring herself to be angry about it. Any emotion at all was really well beyond her capacity to perform just then. She couldn't even say that she felt sad anymore.

She questioned for a moment why, indeed, she hadn't taken Ever's offer of desertion. What use was an empty dark elf to anyone, including herself? She might as well be as dead as Venea.

But she still had her senses, whereas Venea's corpse did not. She could still prove to be vital, not that she cared about proving herself in any way. She had a mission of her own. She would make sure her sister did not die in vain, and then if she was still alive after that, she would avenge her sister as well.

Her eyes shifted away from Teava and to Ever. Nika knew that Ever herself was unaware of just how far the mystery of the legendary dwarf went. If Nika was honest with herself, even she could not figure it out. Not with all the information and knowledgeable senses she had. She was sure the girl was important, but just how important she was, Nika was not certain. She knew that Teava sensed it, too.

The others, however, chose to blindly follow the tale of the legendary dwarf. They believed, and never once doubted, that Ever was that very dwarf from the minute she revealed her secret. Ever, although at times struggled under the pressure and doubted herself, felt somewhere inside that the legend was true and thus she must be that dwarf. Merenda did not know what to believe, save for that the fate of the world was carried by Ever, as her vision told her. And did that not make her the dwarf of legend?

But alas, legends did not matter wholly to Nika. She was concerned only with what might end her father. If Ever might be this dwarf that should be the one to kill the most powerful creature of any race, then so be it. Nika would lead her to him, whether she would kill or be killed.

VIII.

    The land became empty as they walked further away from the forest. The ground wasn't dry, but it seemed as though life of any sort was afraid to live so close to the dragon kingdom. Teava was right when she said that there would be no trouble. There was no orc camp anywhere, nor any noises from other strange and evil creatures. But there was no cover for them, either. No trees to hide under or boulder to duck behind in case a dragon flew over their heads. Ever tried to imagine that was a good thing – perhaps this queen that Teava spoke of would better receive them if she had a warning beforehand. Even so, she was glad that they had walked for half the day without a dragon sighting.

    There was something else, however, that was still bothering Ever. As she got closer, she felt pulled to go even closer. Her body seemed now to know the way to the kingdom, even though she had never been anywhere near it. She grew more and more anxious to enter the kingdom – which also made her feel more and more anxious to run away. She could feel her body tingle with anticipation, as if something inside of her was awakening. She tried to convince herself that she was only anxious about being in the presence of the dragon clans, that it was both fear of the beasts and excitement that they were nearing the next mark of their journey. But she knew in her core that it was more than that.

Ever was about to face herself. She was about to discover who she truly was. All of her non dwarven features were about to be recognized for what they were. She knew that she could never go back to her own clan after this discovery. She knew that, no matter how much her own body wanted to find the dragon heart, she should fight it so that she would be welcome still among the dwarves. But she also knew that she had to face her destiny.

The gentle breeze played with Ever's hair as she walked. She had not changed out of the elven garb borrowed from Merenda, she only placed her dwarven armor over it. Her hair had also been left in the elven braids, though far more messy than they had been before. What would the dragons think of her, she wondered? Surely, dressed as many different races and yet belonging to none, she would not be accepted into their kingdom. If they could be heartless enough to throw their princess out simply for loving who she chose, surely they could not care as much for a half breed such as herself.

A half breed? Had she really just thought the words?

She sighed in defeat. If she was going to start referring to herself as a halfbreed, she must have truly accepted, then, that her blood was not purely dwarven.

What is to become of me, she thought to herself, *if indeed I survive this quest? Who will accept me when this is over?*

Her anxiety grew.

Tekla removed her outer layer of clothing, leaving her in the barest fabric to shield her from the elements. As Ever noted that, she suddenly realized that, indeed, it was becoming hotter seemingly with every step. She wiped the sweat off of her own brow. Surely that could not be right. If they had been heading north, should it not be growing colder? But Teava knew where they were going, and Ever thought she seemed unperturbed by the strange rise in temperature. Actually, no one seemed unnerved by it at all. Ever supposed that the dragons must like it hotter, and perhaps they generated their own heat with their breath.

Once again, her anxiety grew as she now wondered what kind of place they were going to. This time, is was not a bad anxiety, but it was simply one of eager wonder. Perhaps it would be even more spectacular and fantastical then the elven kingdom. Perhaps, supposing they let her in, she could love it there and could find a home for herself in their presence. Supposing, of course, they did not banish her for her mixed heritage.

She sighed again, her hoped deflating. She did not even know what was to come of her, or what she truly was, and already felt without a home or a clan. She looked at Nika, who was still raw from emotion. Nika had lost her whole race and her entire family, save for her father who she knew had to die for his evil. She looked at Merenda and Cassio, who still had each other – if Cassio did actually survive – but had lost their city and families to the orcs. She looked at Jesper, who had lost his family and lived out his life as false royalty, an outcast in the palace, for which he was reminded every day. She looked at Teava, who had been exiled from the throne and her kingdom. Indeed, it seemed that Tekla was the only one who had a true home after all was said and done – if the small village of Ioka still stood, that is.

Suddenly, a wave of heavy nausea came over Ever. She stopped abruptly as it washed over her. The world around her seemed to spin uncontrollably. She felt unsteady on her feet, even without moving. She took a few deep breaths and tried to concentrate on the air going through her lungs. The nausea subsided enough that she was satisfied and took a few shaky running steps to catch up to the group.

And just as she reached them, she wretched loudly, doubling over as she let loose the contents of her stomach.

The company halted, to Ever's great embarrassment, as she wretched a second time. Jesper came to her side and gently tucked her hair behind her ears. He coaxed her into a sitting position.

Wordlessly, Merenda offered her some water. She took a swig to rinse out her mouth and spit before letting some trickle down her throat. To her relief, it stayed there and her stomach seemed to settle.

There was a small argument that ensued. Half of them thought it would be best to cut the day short so that Ever could rest. Merenda argued that both Ever and Cassio now needed healing while Teava and Nika argued for loss of time. Ever stayed quiet whilst they fought, feeling out her own state. The nausea was gone now, and she felt oddly strong. She was sure that it must have been the anxiety that she was feeling, for she certainly did not feel ill. When she did speak up, she sided with Teava and Nika, unwilling to waste any time. Defeated, Jesper, who fought harder than the rest, relented and they began to walk again. But Jesper did not leave her side, even though she gave no signs of being sick again.

So the walk through the empty land began once more after the short break. Ever did decide to take off her armor. The sweat had clammed around her face as the heat slowly rose, and it became increasingly uncomfortable. She let Phantom carry the heavy armor and silently hoped that Teava would prove right about the lack of trouble as they approached the kingdom, for now she was unprotected.

Annoyance shot through her veins, though, when she realized that the group collectively seemed to decide to slow their pace for her. She wanted to run ahead and force them to speed up, but the heat was beginning to become too much for fast travel anyway. She settled her pace and decided instead to concentrate on the walk.

Up ahead, the mountain had become bigger as they got closer. Mount Zagnoula, she assumed. It was massive, and it stood alone. It was a deep purple in color, and at that distance, she could now see streams of orange and red running downward. She had never imagined such a sight could be possible. It looked like no mountain she had seen yet. The orange and red streams flowed downward like thick porridge, and the royal purples of the rock seemed to glitter in the sunlight.

"Is that where the dragon heart is?" Ever asked Teava quietly.

"Indeed. Deep inside the mountain, behind the lava falls that hide the entrances, always guarded by a member of each of the five clans. Can you feel its power?"

Ever almost choked on a breath. She knew that she could, but she did not want to admit it yet. She looked at Cassio, who was in much the same state as he had been. Clearly he did not yet feel its power. She chose to divert the conversation.

"There are only five clans?"

Teava nodded, looking away from Ever. The diversion was enough of an answer for her.

"Why?"

"The five clans are as ancient as the race of dragons themselves. We are not an argumentative race. By no means are we peaceful, but amongst ourselves there has never been a reason to divide into any more clans. Our system has worked flawlessly since the dawn of time."

"Because you throw out anything that does not fit perfectly into that system."

To that, Teava did not have a response.

"Have you truly thought about this? If you are right about me, then my very existence does not fit into the dragon's ancient system," Ever pointed out, finally voicing a fear that she had been having. "We will never be granted entry."

"Have faith, little dragon," Teava said softly. Ever rolled her eyes at the nickname, but understood that it was meant to acknowledge the protective connection Teava had over her, to let her know that Teava considered her family. Ever tried to consider it no more than a nickname, though she had allowed the thoughts of dragon blood into her mind anyway. "It is like I said, we are not an argumentative race. Even a dragon can see when certain exceptions are to be made. Tomorrow, we will be at the base of the mountain where I shall explain to the guards who we are… Who *you* are. That will be enough to spare out lives and grant us time with the queen. Then the decision is up to her."

"How do you know she will not execute us right away? Even if you are right about me, perhaps it will not matter to her. Perhaps she will still choose the dragon ways. Do not forget, you were told never to go back."

"You must not forget, either, that she is my sister. Familial ties are strong bonds. I played with her as a child, and fought by her side as a warrior. That is not forgotten to her."

"I hope you are right," Ever said quietly.

Teava hoped that she was right, too. But she did not show her doubt.

"It was not her choice to take the throne from me."

The breeze began to pick up, turning into a strong wind. The air was clear, however, of any debris. The wet dirt stayed on the ground where it belonged, instead of in their eyes, and no plants were around to be blown about. It was only their own hair and clothes that got in the way of the company. The sky was beginning to darken as the sun set behind them. The stars began to speckle the dark purple sky. The mountain looked even more brilliant as the night grew closer. The orange and red streams glowed, lighting up the mountain in the dark. Ever now realized that these were streams of lava because Teava had mentioned it, and they were the reason for the heat. As the sun fell completely behind the earth and the moon rose to take its place high in the sky, Teava announced that it was time to make camp. There was no cover before the mountain, and she wanted to be far enough away from them that they could have a peaceful night of sleep without alerting the entire kingdom to their presence yet.

Anxiety kept Ever from sleeping much, however. She almost wished that the company would just arrive that very night.

Surely, if that was the case and the queen still felt a bond deep enough to keep Teava and the rest of them alive, she would offer them a place to rest that would have been better than the ground. Or she would spare them the rest of the journey and end them promptly. Either way, Ever was sick of sleeping on the ground. But it was nice not to need a fire. The cold wind actually turned out to be a nice break from the heat that emanated from the lava streams. Ever was excited to see what wonders lay beyond the mountain. She tried to ease her anxiety by imagining what it might be like. It was still a few hours before she was able to sleep.

* * *

The next morning, everyone had risen before the sun. Teava decided that would be a good thing, as it would mean an earlier departure as well as an earlier arrival. It seemed as though everyone was eager to get to the dragon kingdom. Or, perhaps, eager to get *out* of it. Either way, breakfast was a quick and quiet event.

"It is so silent in this part of the world," Tekla commented as they began to pack their bed rolls for hopefully the last time for a few nights.

Teava absently nodded her agreement.

"It is eerie, really," she added, looking blankly into the distance. "I have not seen a dragon nor any of the goblins that were behind us. I cannot hear the flames of the mountain, nor can I see the smoke. I wonder precisely what we will arrive to."

"Do you think…" Jesper began quietly, alarm in his voice. He cleared his throat and tried again, trying to sound less concerned. "Do you think Terrisino has already been here? Perhaps we might go another way."

"No," Teava answered. "Terrisino would not be able to penetrate the dragon defenses just yet. The dragons are still free, perhaps just weakened. All the more reason for the queen to listen to us."

Panic did, however, shoot through Ever despite Teava's words. Her vision with Merenda was not forgotten. She was not as sure as Teava was about the freedom of the dragons. Still, she said nothing as they walked forward, restraining even from looking at Merenda. If her fear was mirrored in the sorceress' eyes, she did not wish to know.

Once again, as they set out, anxiety wove its way through Ever's body. They hadn't walked long, either, before nausea set in and she was forced to double over and be sick once again. Worry passed over more than just Jesper's face as the sickness came a second day. In fact, Ever was beginning to wonder what was wrong as well. She wondered if perhaps this was what happened when a dragon came into contact with the dragon heart for the first time. Or perhaps, she assured herself, she was simply ill and coming closer to the relic would ease that. Still, she assured the group that it was no more than anxiety and that they should continue forward. It would be best to end the nerves as quickly as possible. Luckily, everyone was feeling pretty anxious to get on with the pit stop, so no one argued a word.

The mountain was close enough now that Ever could watch the lava as it flowed downward in streams along the surface. She could also now see where the lava falls were. They were tall and powerful, yet somehow peaceful and magnificent. They reminded Ever of the streams of water cascading down the elven palace. Except, whereas the elves portrayed the beauty in the natural world, the dragons seemed to use the falls to portray their power. And, indeed, Ever felt warned. It was obvious that the lava had not been formed naturally. The dragon clans had formed it as their message to those who dared approach; they were not interested in hosting strangers.

And yet, the company was quickly approaching, and without showing any sign of heeding the warning. On the contrary, they fully expected the dragons to host them.

When at last the company reached the base of the

mountain, Ever was shocked to see no gate. Unlike the Baia Village, whose heavy defensive system was a response to living on the dangerous side of the river, the dragons seemed almost callous in their defensive measures. There was but one guard by the fall, standing tall and sniffing the air like he thought nothing of the approaching company. Ever thought of him as disdainfully egotistical. The tall, black beast eyed them lazily with one solid black eyeball. Or, at least, Ever assumed he was looking at them. The color of his eye made it hard to tell. Actually, she had almost mistaken him for a statue. It was only his breathing that told her he was alive. With Teava in the lead, the entire company came to a halt in front of the mighty beast. Then Ever was positive that he was sizing them up, looking at each of them in turn before giving a final snort and transforming back down to a human form, a magic trick that she had seen Teava perform already, but it still amazed and horrified her.

The human form that now stood before them was incredibly attractive, drawing the attention of Nika right away. He was dark skinned, making the tattoo around his eye that marked him as a dragon almost invisible against his flesh. His muscles still rippled, as if to tell the company that, though his size was smaller now, he was still a threat. His black eyes sparkled with delight, and when he cracked a crooked, cocky grin, his white teeth sparkled with them. Ever got the sense that, though he was a threat and took his job very seriously, he was also young and far too cocky for his own good.

"Well, well, well," he chimed, almost excited at the guests in front of him. "If it isn't the long lost Queen Teava – oh, wait, my apologies, I meant *peasant* Teava." The guard chuckled, amused at himself. Ever tried not to glare. The dragons would prove to treat Teava worse than the elves treated Jesper, it seemed. Could there be no peace among kin?

But Teava seemed not to take notice of his cruel words.

"Sorventh," she greeted him gruffly. "As you have not yet

killed us, I assume you know why we are here."

"Kill you?" Sorventh said, taking a few graceful steps forward, closing the gap between them. Teava stiffly stood her ground. "Why, m'lady, I could never do such a thing. It would simply… devastate me… to lose you like that." His hand went to stroke her chin. She seemed paralyzed and seething at the same time. "I could have been your king," he said wistfully.

"That would not have been right," Teava told him coldly. "There is no point in having a king that I do not love. I would choose Salora all over again if I had to."

Sorventh shook his head.

"You fool. What does love matter when you are given the most powerful kingdom there ever has been? You could have taken anything you wanted, if you had just chosen me."

"I wanted Salora," she answered sternly.

Sorventh's lip curled in a disgusted and angry snarl.

"I do know why you are here," he said, changing the subject. "Or, at least, the entire kingdom has been instructed not to kill the small creatures," he said, turning his attention to Ever, "punishable by law. Something to do with the dwarven legend and all that. Pray tell, then, are you the dwarf we've been expecting?"

"You have been expecting me, then?" Ever responded with a cold tone that surprised even her. Sorventh laughed, his sinister attitude dissolving for a minute.

"Your dwarven friend here, then, saved your life. Although," he put a finger to his chin in thought, "I suppose the queen said only to spare the life of the dwarf. I could do away with the rest of you." His tongue darted out of his mouth like a snake, eliciting a squeal from Tekla.

"Sorventh, do not play," Teava commanded. "I know very well that my sister has heard news of us making our way here, and I expect fully that all of us are granted entrance."

"You are not my queen," he spat.

"Then kill us all now," Teava said without any emotion,

"and face the wrath of Queen Kylon and Terrisino both."

He snarled once more. Reluctantly, he turned to the lava fall behind him. Once again, the transformation took place as Sorventh changed into the giant black beast. He spread out one large, sparkling black wing under the fall, and the lava spread to either side, creating an umbrella effect for the company to enter. Allowing Teava to take the lead, everyone followed and entered the cave of Mount Zagnoula, with Sorventh coming behind in his human form.

IX.

The mountain glittered on the inside. The light of the lava played with the natural sparkle of the rock, making enough light that no torches were lit. It was still only a dim orange light, but it was glorious. Ever stood with her mouth agape as she took in the splendor of the simple beauty.

"We need to go to the dragon heart," Teava announced to Sorventh. "Our friend here is in dire need."

"You will go nowhere until her highness has approved it," he responded uncaringly.

"No," Merenda spoke up to the dragon, "you will save him." Her eyes seemed to burn up with the lava. She glared at Sorventh with hatred in them. Ever could see something else happening. Her hair began to fly in several directions as her fists clenched tightly at her side. The air around them all seemed to charge as something magical, Ever presumed, was about to happen. Jesper was suddenly at her side, attempting to calm her as Teava spoke again.

"Look," she told him, "we have all been on the road for weeks. We're all exhausted and beaten down at best. Every one of us could use a touch of its atmosphere. Please, let us do what we can for Cassio."

Sorventh was no longer nonchalant, but he did not seem shaken by Merenda, either. In fact, he seemed almost amused at this point.

"Please," Nika spoke up, catching his eye. She smiled a soft, sad smile that Ever had never seen from her before. Perhaps it was a trick of manipulation? "We've already lost a friend. My sister." She let a tear escape from her eye. "Do not let us lose another without trying all that we can first."

Sorventh lost his smile as he watched her. Ever could not even begin to guess what he was thinking. Everyone seemed to hold their breath then, waiting for him.

"Very well, then," he finally allowed. "I suppose, if the world has already lost such a lovely creature, as I'm sure any sister of yours must have been, then it should not yet be ready to lose another soul. Even one as weak as a human," he added callously as he turned and led them down a tunnel.

The temperature of the cave was a lot more comfortable than it was outside the mountain, despite being surrounded by the lava. It wasn't cold and moist like the mountain in which Ever grew up, but instead seemed like a nice living condition. Ever wondered if that would be where they slept that night. It would at least seem like home to her.

The tunnel twisted and turned in several directions, but Sorventh seemed to know exactly where he was going. Ever knew why. It was the calling of the dragon heart. Even without Sorventh as a guide, Ever was sure that she could have found her way down the winding paths by herself. She felt its presence somehow. When she looked over at Cassio, she knew that he, too, felt it. He was growing restless and sweaty in his slumber. Teava, too, knew the way well, despite not having been in the mountain for decades. The rest of the group seemed to stumble around in the dim light for a while longer till, one by one, they felt the pull of the relic.

Sorventh halted, finally, before a wall. The tunnel came to a dead end. Everyone in the company formed a line in front of the wide wall. The dragon heart lay just behind it, they all knew. Teava and Ever both took a step forward. Teava halted in order to watch Ever as she moved forward.

Ever reached out a tentative hand. The rock felt cool to the touch. Its texture was uneven and grainy, just like the rest of the cave. She ran both of her hands along the wall. There seemed to be no seem, no crack where a door might be located. And yet, there was also no tunnel to go around the wall. She put her ear up to it. Her skin was met with the cool dampness of rock. She selected a few places along the wall to knock. Nowhere did it seem as though the rock was a hallow trick. But she knew, she could feel, that the relic was just beyond it. She dropped her hands and stepped back to examine the dead end wall as a whole.

In her mind, she knew that there should not be a way to get beyond the rock. Not without the tools forged by her ancestors, least wise. She knew that they would go no further without help from the dragons, both of which were too busy eyeing her intently to offer a hand. She knew all of this, and yet, the calling of the dragon heart was too strong. It had become all that she was really aware of anymore, totally mesmerizing her. It was as if no one else was in the cave with her. Only her and the relic even existed. And space between them was something that neither she nor the relic seemed to desire. She could not explain why she did what she did next, but she did it like it was the most natural thing in the world.

She walked forward, without any sign of hesitation or fear. She took one step after another, as if the rock was not even there, and she lipped right through it. The company, save for Teava and Sorventh, stood flabbergasted. Teava explained.

"It is the finest magic known to the dragons. The wall does not exist, it is merely a perfect illusion. You can see it, you can feel it… But it is not there. It is a strong enough deterrent because, as long as you are expecting to be met by it, you will feel it. But if you walk through with confidence, knowing it is not there, it will give way."

"I suppose that means she is the foretold," Sorventh stated in a way that sounded like a question to Teava. She did not respond, but instead walked through the illusive wall. Sorventh looked impatiently at the rest of the company. "After you, then," he said with mock politeness.

Merenda immediately took Cassio in her arms and slipped through the wall, choosing not to think about it, and Jesper, Nika, and Tekla quickly followed suit with Sorventh just behind.

Behind the wall, no one could decide what to focus on. The orange crystal of the dragon heart was glowing, calling to everyone in the room as it sat on a pedestal in the center of the circular cave like room. Even Teava and Sorventh, who had already seen its beauty, had a hard time looking away. But alas, there was something else in the room that was fighting to hold everyone's attention. Ever was no longer there, but something else stood in her place, staring into the depths of the dragon heart.

In front of them was a small dragon. She was green, like a forest, but her outstretched wings were lined with yellow. She had no threatening horns, but her teeth were sharp enough to pierce rock. She had a scaly green mane that flowed from the crown of her head all the way down to the tip of her tail. Around her eyes was not the usual fiery and fierce lining of a dragon, but instead a delicate brown floral vine was there to decorate her.

This was Ever, everyone knew. She seemed to be the only one who was unaware of the fact that she was no longer in her dwarven form, as she was lost in the calling of the dragon heart.

And then Cassio began vying for everyone's attention, as he stopped his relentless slumber and woke from his long spell induced sleep. With a hypnotic look, much like Ever's own, he struggled away from Merenda's hold and walked forward to stare into the dragon heart. He and Ever of them were not seeing anything per say. It was not like having a vision or seeing inside the heart. Rather, they were both healing, each in their own way.

The stood like that for over an hour. Ever the dragon and

Cassio eventually became the only two who were entranced by the relic, as the others did not require its powers nearly as much. Finally, Ever began to look around the room, stunned at the way everyone was staring at her.

    Somehow, although she did not realize that she had ever made the transformation, she realized that she was in dragon form. She shrank back into a mist of clouds. They swirled around her, glowing green, until they began to dissipate. She felt the sensation of the transformation in her skin. It was even more amazing to be on the dragon's side of the magic, and Ever was unsure if it horrified her or not. When the transformation was done, she was looking at everyone from her proper dwarven height once more, unchanged, save for the pattern around her eyes.

    Jesper noticed that pattern right away, and wished that Ever could see it, too. It was very small, unlike Teava's pattern, or even Sorventh's. It sat just aboce the outer corner of her eyes. It was just a few small, brown flowers, Jesper believed he counted five or six from that distance, with a small vine twisting from the inner part of her eyes all the way to the end of the flowers. It was stunning, and, though Jesper knew that Ever might not appreciate it, he felt it added beauty and power to her already significant presence.

    Teava recognized the pattern around Ever's eyes right away. She knew it meant that Ever belonged to the Teras Erde clan. Her pattern was not as boldly defined as that of a pure dragon's, but that was only because Ever had the blood of a dwarf in her veins as well. She knew that she would have to tell Ever all about her new clan as soon as she got the chance.

    "Bravo," came a voice from behind them, clapping slowly as she broke the silence. Everyone turned, startled and disoriented.

    "Your highness," Sorventh said, taking a bow. Ever took in the queen. She was shorter than Teava, but built in much the same way. Her long black hair was braided down to her thigh, where her tight pants showed many sheathed weapons. Her tall crown was decorated in gems and scales. "They insisted I bring them here to heal their friend. Forgive me for my misjudgment."

"Do not fret," she waved aside his apology. "I would have had to bring the dwarfling down here myself anyway. Do tell, pet," she said, "what is your name?" she asked, approaching Ever and stroking her cheek. Ever gasped and jumped back at the touch.

Teava stepped forward.

"Leave her alone, Kylon," she snapped.

"Oh, sister," the queen said in a sing song-y way that Ever did not trust at all. "I knew it was you when I saw your pet at the base of the mountain." Se waved to Seg, who stood behind her legs. He peeked around her and spotted Teava. He quickly scurried to hide behind her legs instead. "I have been expecting your unapproved return. What would mother and father have to say if they saw the exiled princess set foot in their borders? I should have you put to death, you know."

"You would have already killed me if you did not need me."

"Oh? Now I need you? What of these others, then? Shall I have them killed for trespassing?"

"You and I both know that you would not do that. It is not your way."

"Oh?" she said, reaching out to Jesper and placing one sharpened nail under his chin. "Do we now? Perhaps I will start with your... *elven* friend, here. What an interesting mix of friends you have chosen for yourself, sister. It seems as though you could never choose right."

"I chose love," Teava defended herself once more with anger. "And I have continued to do so. These people are pure and seek the best for the land we share. Recognize the real enemy, as they have, as I have, and choose your side. You can kill us all, if you'd like. Or you can aid us, aid Ever, aid the dwarf of legend."

Ever did not like how nonchalantly Teava kept telling the dragons to kill them all, even though she seemed so sure that they would not do so. It was unnerving. But finally, Kylon dropped all pretenses of the villain and regarded Teava with seriousness.

"I think it best we discuss this with the council."

The queen's sudden personality change nearly winded Ever. She could not keep up with these dragon's pretenses of sinister behavior, it seemed, and she wondered if they were all like that.

"Make your choice," Ever demanded of the queen incredulously. The queen turned to her, offering her a gentle smile.

"My dear, I have long ago made my choice," she said gently. "I have seen the uprisings, the burning villages, the orcish conquests. Many of my people have already fled, in search of much safer lands. I do not hold much faith in a simple dwarfling, of course," she said, cocking her head at Ever, "but you are not just a dwarfling, are you? We have much to talk about, but this is neither the time nor the place. Sorventh and I shall escort you back to the castle, where you all shall rest while I call for the council."

"What do you mean they have fled? Who is gone?" Teava asked worriedly.

"These are dark times, sister, and darker times are yet to come. But let us save this conversation for now."

Queen Kylon left it at that and walked through the wall again. She was followed without hesitation by Teava, and the others were quickly moved along by Sorventh, with Cassio using his own legs once more and Merenda smiling wide at the fact.

Phantom had waited outside the illusive wall and began trotting behind them as they walked off. It should have been harder for Ever to leave the dragon heart and make her way forward through the confusing and poorly lit tunnels, but she found that her sight had improved. Even her dwarven eyes that were used to dark caves could not see as well as well as she could now. There was no more room to deny her dragon blood, and she was terrified of what that meant. But there wasn't much time to worry about that at the moment. She tried instead to listen to the conversation being held up ahead by the dragon sisters, but it was of no use. They were so hushed, she wondered how they could even hear themselves.

"What do you think will happen now?" she whispered to Jesper instead.

He looked at her for a moment as he struggled through the tunnels. Ever found it odd to be more sure footed than the elf.

"What, indeed, will happen?" he repeated her question with amusement. "It seems you, my little hunter, are full of surprises."

"Jesper, please," she begged, exasperated. "I do not wish to think about that right now. I mean, what's to happen with this council? Where are we to go next? When are we to leave?"

"Even that, I cannot say," he said somberly. "I suppose we shan't leave for a few days at least. The queen must send for the missing dragons, and in the mean time we can rest."

"Can we not just leave now and let her say what she must? I don't think we are welcome here."

"Ever," he said, reaching out to grab her hand for a moment. "Have faith and have strength. We have all been in a place in which we are not welcome. As long as we have the queen's protection, we will be okay. Don't forget," he added, "that this was the plan of action. We need the dragons to fight with us."

"But she has already said that she is with us," Ever argued.

"She might be the queen, but that does not mean she can choose to evade the council in her decisions. Her kingdom would not follow her then. No, we must make our request in front of the entire council and show them what is right. Then we will have the dragon kingdom behind us."

"Will they listen to us?"

Jesper sighed. He was out of cheerful answers to give her hope. This time, his doubt showed through.

"Teava should not be here, she knows that very well. Yet, she is part of our company, and vital to our survival… In my eyes, at least. Even so, having her involved will upset most of the dragons. Thus, it harms out chances of being heard. Then, there is you. You have dragon blood in your veins, but that will most likely upset them more than it will sway them to our side. Even those that believe the legend are only angered that the blood of the mighty dragon has been tainted. To make matters worse, we have brought a dark elf with us. They do not like my kind, either, nor do they have any respect for man. We are taking a gamble at best."

"And what is the risk, should we lose the game?"

Jesper took a moment to respond. They were nearing the lava fall which led to the exit of the mountain, facing toward Shodalea, their final destination for the moment.

"Ever, do you believe in our mission? Do you believe, the way Nika does, that Terrisino needs to die at any cost?"

"Of course," she answered with conviction.

"And would you give your life, if necessary, to see the end of him?"

She nodded fiercely.

"Then," he told her, "you should not concern yourself with the price of the gamble. Perhaps we shall proceed with our quest, or perhaps our quest will be met with an early end," he said as Sorventh, now in dragon form, held the lava back with an outstretched wing. "We will have to see what fate has planned for us."

That was of no comfort to Ever, but Jesper turned and left her with that. She let the subject drop as she followed him under the lava fall.

Queen Kylon had a carriage waiting outside for them. She, too, had thought of the risk brought by Teava and her companions and wished to get them to the palace seen by as few people as possible. The carriage was solid black with black curtains drawn on the inside. It was pulled by a black mare with a gray main and tail. As pure black horses were hard to come by, they ran a risk that Phantom might be recognized, but had very little choice. The inside of the carriage was quite roomy and luxurious, as it was fit for the queen. However, Ever found herself longing to pull back the curtain and peek outside at the dragon kingdom that lay just behind it. She restrained from the temptation.

Everyone sat quietly for several minutes as Merenda and Cassio finally had a minute to reunite. Ever, Jesper, and Tekla had stayed quiet out of respect and looked away, while the dragons stayed quiet simply because they felt uncomfortable in the situation. Indeed, it was a situation that was out of the normal for any of them.

"Oh, Cassio," Merenda said in a hushed voice, clinging on to him with her entire body as he sat frozen and a little shocked. "Cassio, Cassio, Cassio." She seemed to get some bit of comfort just in saying his name. "I thought I would never see your eyes open again. Oh, Cassio. Why'd you do that to me, you fool?" she suddenly snapped, her voice changing to an aggressive tone. And, to match her tone, she finally let go of him and slapped him right across the face. His cheek reddened in response.

"I didn't mean to!" he said, semi-apologetically as a part of the shock seemed to wear off. "It isn't my fault."

"Oh, it's never your fault," Merenda snapped sarcastically. "It wasn't your fault when the stage wasn't right, it wasn't your fault when no one paid for the play, it wasn't your fault when you forgot the medicine for your mother. Who can you blame this one on? You were the one who listened to the song when everyone else held their heads high and walked away. You were the one with the ego big enough to fall prey to creatures that were less than cunning. No, Cassio, this is your fault. Do you not remember any of it?"

"Of course I remember it," he snapped at her. "They wanted me." He seemed proud of that last bit. It only angered Merenda even more.

"You foolish, foolish man," she hissed. "Because of you, we all nearly died several times. It was terribly hard to keep you alive when you were under a spell. You'd best not make it as hard when you have your wits about you."

Try as she might, Ever could not help but over hear them in

the small carriage. She also could not help the small bit of satisfaction that came when she realized that Merenda had struggled with her thoughts of Cassio as much as she had.

"Oh, but Cassio," Merenda said once more, her tone taking a soft turn. "I did miss you." As she said it, she began to wrap herself around him again. He welcomed the embrace, as if he did not know that she had just yelled at him, and took her in an embrace of his own.

Ever felt uncomfortable in that moment. As she looked around the carriage, she saw that everyone else seemed just as confused as she was. Perhaps none of them had really questioned the relationship between the strange pair when they had picked them up outside of their burning city, but it seemed that there was something odd about it. Ever had never pictured them to be lovers. She had assumed that Merenda was Cassio's apprentice. But now she wondered if there might have been something more.

But she did not want to think about that. It was not her place to make judgments on whatever bond the two of them might have. And, certainly, her mind was already judging. She turned her attention to something else.

The ride to the castle was, for the most part, a smooth ride. It was smooth enough that Seg was not jostled in his spot on the floor of the carriage by Teava's feet. Ever imagined that to mean that the dragons had paved the roads within their kingdom. Perhaps a more civilized people than she had imagined. Though, she was not sure what she had expected at all.

Merenda was filling Cassio in on all the details of the journey, to most of which he responded in a way that made it clear he was glad to have been unconscious. Eventually, Merenda had said all that she felt needed saying, and Cassio muttered about wishing he had chosen to stay behind when Jesper had given him the chance. Soon enough, they both fell silent. The entire company sat quietly for a long while, each member lost in their own thoughts. Although fear and anxiety showed on many faces, most of them were fairly relaxed, save for Ever. Despite the smooth ride, she had begun to feel queasy and wished very much that the small jostling that did occur would cease. She did not ask for a break, though, nor did she ask for a bit of fresh air. She knew that she would be denied both, and anyway, she was very much annoyed with how sick she had been lately. Especially having just left the dragon heart.

"Are you throwing us in the dungeons, then?" Nika finally broke the silence, demanding of Kylon something that had hard pressed the dark elf's mind for some time.

The queen looked at her with a coy smile.

"And show you what I have down there?" she asked. "No, of course not. No sister of mine will sleep in the dragon dungeons. They would not contain her."

Nika glared in confusion as Tekla paled, neither understanding whether Kylon's plans for them were going to be comfortable or not. Teava rolled her eyes at everyone.

"It would be moot for her to do so," she assured them, "as Ever and I could break out and release the rest of you. The dragon dungeons are made for those not of our race. Although, we shall still be hiding from most of those that dwell in the castle, we will be given rooms and beds."

"So we will be little more than privileged prisoners," Nika said. "Is that it?"

Teava let out a sigh.

"If you do not approve, I'm sure the other dragons will find a comfortable space for you within the confines of their bellies."

"Dragons do not eat other races," Nika argued.

"Do they?" Tekla asked as she turned a few shades whiter.

"I might be sick," Cassio added, his own skin matching Tekla's. Ever stopped herself from rolling her eyes at his returned cowardice just in time to see Merenda roll hers.

"What kind of company have you brought to my kingdom?" Queen Kylon asked incredulously. "Where is the courageous one you spoke of?"

"You'll have to excuse them their flaws," Teava said with another roll of her eyes. It seemed, now that Cassio was back, there would be a lot of that going on.

"I must admit, sister, I am beginning to have doubts."

Teava grinned wickedly, and for a moment, Ever saw both of the dragons for the sinister race they were.

"Let those who cannot fight by our side die for our cause."

Ever realized that Teava truly did live by those words. A shiver ran through her body. Her stomach churned over and over. She was sure that part of her illness had something to do with the fact that she now knew beyond doubt that she was part of this sinister, callous race.

"We have all been brought here for a purpose," she announced, attempting to clear the air – and her own stomach. "We will all live out that purpose with bravery."

Kylon smiled coyly, but did not add anymore. Instead, she looked away from everyone and got lost in her own thoughts once again. Sorventh was not so kind. He looked over at Cassio and began to lick his lips once the man locked eyes with him. Cassio shrank back in his seat. Ever let it go that time. There was no way she could defend Cassio credibly.

The rest of the ride to the castle carried out in silence. Ever had questions, but realized it was best for them all to keep quiet. There were too many different personalities in the carriage, and the more negative personalities did not seem to want to be serious at the moment. The ride lasted for hours still, as they traveled across the small villages between Mount Zagnoula and Shodalea. It was becoming hard for the group to sit still, as they grew restless with anticipation. Queen Kylon seemed to be the only one who didn't mind the long ride. It was one she made fairly often, and it gave her time to think away from everyone else. Ever found that she did not even know what to think about. She was so unsure of what the future held for them that it troubled her to think about anything at all. She chose instead to concentrate on the clippety-clop of the horses outside.

When the carriage finally stopped, the company was instructed by Kylon to remain inside while she and Sorventh cleared the staff outside. When they were given the okay to come out, there was only Kylon, Sorventh, and the carriage driver, whose name Ever supposed must not have been important, waiting outside for them.

It was nightfall already. Although Ever wished there had still been a few hours in the day, she supposed that it was to their advantage that they arrived in the dark. It would make it easier to stay hidden, and, surely, most of the staff would have gone to bed by that time.

Queen Kylon ordered the group to stay close to her and to keep quiet. She led them past the door to the stables to a place in the wall that looked no different than the rest of the walls. Ever expected her to walk through it as they had the illusive wall in front of the dragon heart, but instead Kylon pushed it backwards with her hands, and several of the panels opened up like a door. Ever could not help it as a small smile spread on her face. The dragons seemed to have several tricks in their trick bags. She followed the group through the secret passageway that led into the castle. Her smile faded as she realized that she would not see the outside of the castle at all. At least not that night.

The tunnel was dark, and it wasn't lined with torches at all. Ever imagined that one must bring their own candle of sort when traveling through. Else, she supposed since it was made by dragons, some sort of fire breath. But since she had neither, nor did she think Kylon would permit it, she instead kept her hands on either side of the wall to help guide her. That was an easy endeavor, as the tunnel was very narrow. The company was forced to walk through single file. That, too, seemed to help guide them all, as each member had only to concentrate on the breath of the person in front of them to avoid turning down the wrong way.

The passage stretched for quite some time, occasionally winding upwards with strange turns. It seemed only to grow darker, so much that Ever had to blink to know that her eyes were even open. She wondered if the queen could see anything at all with her dragon eyes, or if she had simply traveled the tunnel often enough that she knew the way. Or perhaps they were lost. No matter the reason, Ever only kept putting one foot in front of the other, and tried to keep faith in the queen. She found herself growing a bit claustrophobic, though, in the small pitch black corridors. She longed to know what was beyond the walls that touched her hands. Still, she kept to the pattern of her walk.

After what must have been an hour of traveling though the dark, Queen Kylon finally stopped at a false wall and pushed it open. Eager to see the light, the company nearly stumbled over each other to get through. It took a beat for their eyes to adjust even just to the dim light of the torches that lined the walls.

The room that they had entered was clearly a study of sorts. Along the brick walls were several bookshelves, all full with books that had strange lettering along their spines. There was a desk on the left side of the room which had been crafted in beautiful mahogany. On the desk there were several stacks of books and papers strewn about recklessly. The queen walked past all of it and went straight to the door on the other side of the room. The company followed her lead.

She led them down a quiet hall. Beneath their feet was a deep red carpet. Ever thought its beauty was marred by the color of it – it looked as if it was stained by blood on every fiber. They walked down the hall at a brisk pace until they reached a door that the queen approved. She ushered them each in.

Inside the room there was a giant bed that Ever imagined could fit most of her clan. The wood was made of the same mahogany of the desk in the study. The canopy that draped from the four tall bed posts was a thin, red fabric that matched the comforter set. There were two couches in the corner opposite the bed, both of the same blood red color that seemed to be the décor of the castle. The vanity set had no mirror but was stocked with bottles of various colors.

The queen had a quiet word with the carriage driver before sending him off and turning to address the company.

"I cannot give you more than this for the time being, for the sake of secrecy. My personal servant will bring up some food for you – what he can without bringing questions up from the kitchen staff. Sorventh will stay with you until you are set, but I will not post guards. I think you understand what happens to trespassers here, so I assume you will not be thick enough to leave this room without my say so. I will return when I can."

With that, she left them. Sorventh took his place against the door and watched the company as they looked around the room. Ever watched Teava as she looked around with melancholy in her eyes. Ever imagined that she must miss walking freely about the castle. She couldn't help but feel bad for her.

"Does anyone want to explain to me," Sorventh began condescendingly, "what this dwarf-dragon half breed could possibly do to save the free world?"

"You can leave now, Sorventh," Teava hissed.

"You are not my queen," he retorted with a cold smile.

"Legends may be no more than stories," Nika answered softly, as Teava got ready to lunge in attack. "Stories passed down from generations, and may hold very little truth. But there is something they achieve, when told across the world, among every race, that is perhaps more powerful than the lies they might tell. And that is that they unite the most unlikely of allies with hope. Separately, we would surely fall one by one. But standing as a united front, surely one enemy cannot keep up from success."

Sorventh seemed mesmerized by Nika's voice. Ever thought that he didn't hear her words, simply listened to her sound.

"Those are wise words," he said, "from such a pretty face."

Teava could not help the giant eye roll that escaped in

response. Again, Ever felt bad for her. Luckily, the carriage driver then returned with some food, and both of the dragon men took their leave.

The food was little, but it was tasty. He had snuck them a simple meal of bread, freshly baked that morning, and fruit, fresh and juicy and quite exotic to Ever's taste buds. It was sweet and a good compliment to the bread. After they had eaten the last morsel, everyone became eager to clean themselves up. They quietly fought over who would be first in the tub room. It was decided by Teava and Jesper that Ever would go first. She didn't question their decision and went straight to the warm water of the bath.

She scrubbed herself as quickly as she could, being as considerate as possible to the rest of her company. She was enjoying the warmth of the water, and did not wish to leave it so soon, but she also knew that it was late and everyone was tired. They were all eager to be in bed and rested, and so she hurried through her bath.

But when she stepped out of the bath, wrapped herself in a cloth, and went to the glass, she realized why Teava and Jesper had insisted that she were to go first. They wanted to give her a moment to see the new addition to her face. She could not help the time she took to stare at her eyes in front of the glass, prolonging everyone else's wait to wash up.

Ever had never even considered having any additions to her dwarven form, even after she had begun to realize that she was a dragon. She had seen Teava's royal, fierce, and beautiful markings around her eyes, and understood that they were the markings of a dragon. Even so, she had never considered that she would ever see them around her own eyes. And yet, as she looked in the mirror, she saw the delicate floral pattern that branded her as a dragon.

Without even thinking about it, she lifted her hand to her eyelid and began rubbing fiercely. But, of course, it was of no use. The light brown markings would not even fade. A tear escaped her eye, and she quickly rubbed that away, glad to see that at least that was easy to be rid of.

She hated the look of it. She hated that it branded her as a dragon. She hated that even if she survived this quest, she truly never could go back home. If she did, what would her dwarven clan say of her? Surely they would cast her out. They did not look fondly on the dragon race. And now, her dragon heritage was not something that she could hide. It was not something that she could keep a secret by remaining in her dwarven form, because even in that form, she would always bare the marks that betrayed who she was. And surely the rest of the world would no longer look kindly on her, as she was no longer one of the gentle races. She now clearly belonged to the race of the schemers.

She wanted to punch the glass. She wanted to shatter the patterns that she could not rub off of her eyes. But instead, she turned her back to them. She took a few moments to gather her emotions and then decided that she was done washing up. She quickly dressed herself without looking back at the glass and left the tub room so that someone else could take their turn.

In the bedroom, everyone was busy in their own individual conversations. Jesper and Teava stopped theirs when Ever emerged from the other room and looked at her. She held their gazes for just a moment before she turned away from them, all too aware of the markings on her eyes. She wondered why no one had told her of them before. Surely they had noticed them. She went to the bed as Tekla rushed in to the tub room.

Teava watched Ever carefully. The conversation she knew she needed to have with the half breed was burning in her mind. But she recognized that it was not the time to have it. Ever needed the night to be to herself. Teava relented to that and decided to wait until morning.

Once everyone had washed up, they awkwardly eyed the bed. It was quickly decided that Ever, Tekla, Merenda, and Nika would take the bed while Jesper and Cassio would take the couches. Of course, Seg had found himself a place on the floor, curled up like a dog without so much as a cloth to keep him warm. When Jesper tried to insist that Teava sleep on his couch and he on the floor, she stubbornly insisted that she was not yet ready for sleep. He gave up before too long and quickly everyone fell asleep. Even Teava, who started the night standing at the window, eventually shrunk down to the floor in slumber.

* * *

When the morning came around, Ever was awake before anyone else. She did not feel exceptionally rested, but she did feel better about her situation than she had the day before. She had only a few minutes to herself before Teava was awake, and Teava was ready to finally fill Ever in a little more. She beckoned the half breed girl to cross the room so that they might talk in hushed tones without disturbing the other sleepers.

"You have asked me about the dragon clans before," Teava stated. Ever nodded her head. "There are five clans. The first is the clan of the royal family. They are called the Emperik clan. That is the clan that I am a part of, and the clan that Kylon is a part of. Then there is the Weiss Aritha clan, the Gohldun Sunne clan, the Teras Erde clan, and the Selver Eis clan. You asked me why there are only five clans and I told you simply that that has always been the way of the dragons. Do you remember that?"

Ever nodded her head again.

"It is not just a system that we have in place," Teava explained. "Each clan has certain abilities, so to speak, that are passed down through blood. The Emperik's have the capability to perform all of those abilities, which is what makes them the royal clan. They are the most powerful. Those of the Weiss Aritha clan are able to control the wind to an extent. The Gohldun Sunnes have a certain talent with fire. Although it is true that we all have the fire breath, there is much more to be done with fire that not all dragons can perform. Those of the Teras Erde clan possess a certain power over the land and stone. And those of the Selver Eis are capable of bending water. Do you understand this?"

"Not completely," Ever admitted.

"You have seen the mountain," Teava offered, "and you know very well that it was not formed naturally, don't you?"

"I assumed as much. I thought the dragons made it to show their power."

Teava chuckled.

"I'm sure that was one of their reasons," she allowed. "But the reasons do not matter altogether. At least not in ths conversation. Do you think it would be possible for the dwarves to create such a mountain? Or the elves or anyone else?"

"No," Ever admitted. "I suppose I don't even know how the dragons could have done it."

"Through the work of a team," Teava answered. "Each clan working together and bringing their own special powers do the project, each of them able to manipulate the world around them in a specific way. Do you understand that?"

Ever thought for a moment.

"I suppose I do," she said. "It is not that the clans have divided in the way that they have based on family or location, but based on the physical powers they possess."

"Precisely. And the patterns you see around the eyes of a dragon tell you which clan they belong to. Although each pattern is unique to the dragon, the elements of the clan can be seen in the marks. You will learn to tell the difference as you meet more dragons."

"So what does my mark say?" Ever asked tentatively.

"The color and the vines tell me that you belong to the clan of Teras Erde. That gives you the natural ability to bend the earth. The dwarves already have a knack for things involving the stone, which makes you perhaps the greatest dwarf, and also the greatest dragon of Teras Elde, in the Earth of Eald."

"I do not know of any abilities like that," Ever argued. "I am good at being a dwarf, but no better than my clan."

"That is because you do not know your dragon half yet. You will learn, and I will teach you."

Ever felt a string being tugged at her heart. Teava had been so gentle with her, even after she had shown her rough front to the company. Now she was welcoming Ever into the dragon world by taking her personally under her own wing. Although Ever certainly did not feel like she could be a part of any clan, dwarven or dragon, she felt peace knowing that she might not be completely alone.

As the day went on and the company began to wake, food was brought to them by Sorventh. They enjoyed their meal and then they were left wondering when they might be summoned. Everyone was left to their own anxious thoughts, but eventually, Jesper began to think his aloud.

"Do you remember the riddles?" he seemed to ask no one in particular.

"The riddles?" Nika asked when no one else spoke up.

"Yes, the riddles," he said. "The ones from the spirits."

"I remember them," Merenda said. "Why?"

"I have been thinking," he answered her, "trying to piece them together."

"What riddles?" Nika asked again.

"The fate of one seals the fate of many. The destiny of all not clearly written, but death reveals the path of any," Merenda began, reciting the riddle word for word.

"That was said to you by the spirits in my tree house?" Nika was baffled.

"Yes," Jesper answered. "Well, they were said to Ever specifically. But what do they mean?"

"I think," Merenda said, "that in that riddle, they were telling Ever that they knew what was to come. Through death, they had seen what would become of the Earth of Eald."

"I think that makes sense," Teava said tentatively. "That was probably why they wanted to communicate with her. Perhaps

Terrisino has messed with the dead in some way that it has begun to concern them as well."

"He has done quite a bit with the dead already," Ever put in wryly. "Perhaps that is the right way of thinking."

"The second riddle," Jesper began.

"You are two bred into one, and together with him, the fight will be won," Merenda finished for him.

"That is easy," Jesper said. "Two bred into one, the dragon and the dwarf blood."

"But who is the other one?" Ever asked. "Who is the 'him' in the riddle?"

To that, no one really had an answer. Everyone looked around the room, asking someone else to propose something.

"Okay," Jesper said, "we don't know the whole riddle yet. What was the third one?"

"You must experience the journey to experience the destination, but understand that the importance is carried within," Merenda once again answered.

No one had any more theories to propose about the riddles, though. Instead, questions were asked by Nika and Tekla about the spirits and their communications. The conversation had done little more than give the group something else to think about as they waited for the dragons to come back with news from the council.

Still, days passed before Kylon returned. Food was brought to them regularly, either by Sorventh or the carriage driver, but neither ever brought news of what was going on outside the walls. Ever ws itching more and more to get a peek of the dragon kingdom, but even the window remained covered by the curtains. No one, not even Teava, dared to move them to see what was beyond the glass. Even without Kylon's words of warning, everyone seemed to understand the risk that was involved when someone else in the kingdom might recognize a stranger in their midst.

The company was growing restless and more anxious with

each passing minute. After spending so much time in the wilderness as they made their way to the kingdom, they felt almost trapped by the four walls that now surrounded them. Even though it truly was a nice living space, as Teava had known would be provided, they all felt that Nika was right in calling them privileged prisoners. They were all eager to leave the small space and begin their travels again. But, when on the evening of the fourth day, around the time that they were usually brought food, Sorventh ordered them to follow him closely and quietly, no one seemed to want to leave anymore as the fear of the council was upon them.

End Book I

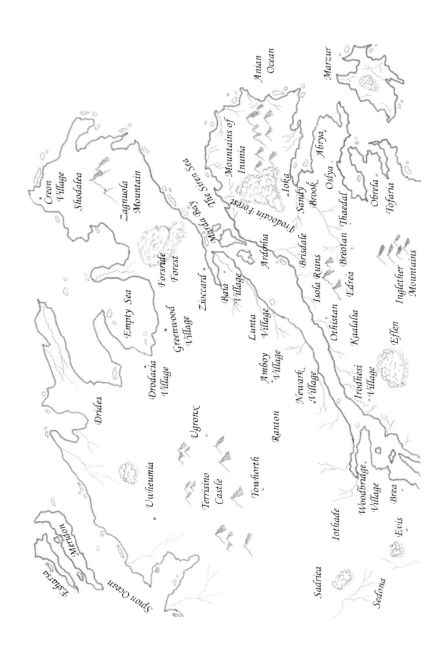

THE EARTH OF EALD

COMING 2017

ABOUT THE AUTHOR

Kate Bloom is a tenacious and edgy millennial with a BS in English and history, giving her a knack for story-telling. As a fantasy writer, her mind is constantly running wild in fictional worlds, such as that of her first project, *Alice in Dreamland* (kindle2016). Born in Albuquerque, New Mexico in 1994, and where she has lived her entire life, Kate found the dry dessert scenery to grow tiresome to look at. She found her escape in the fantastical worlds that played out in her head. She has fallen in love with the idea of putting those worlds in print so that everyone else might see those worlds as well.

Made in the USA
Charleston, SC
23 December 2016